HEADBANGER!

HEADBANGER!

BY AUDIE HARRISON

Spine Bender Press - Pasadena, California

Headbanger!
Copyright © 2026 Audie Harrison

Published by Spine Bender Press
Pasadena, California
spinebenderpress.com

Edited by Kevin Shamel
Proofread by Lillian Boyd
Cover and interior design by Matthew Revert

ISBN 979-8-9937976-0-1 (paperback)
ISBN 979-8-9937976-1-8 (hardcover)
ISBN 979-8-9937976-2-5 (ebook)

Library of Congress Control Number: 2025923436

First Edition

Printed in the United States of America

For my Mom, who always let me rock.

Chapter 1

MOTHER

Tighty-whities. Crusty socks. Empty beer cans. A treacherous swamp of teenage rebellion covered the floor. A hellscape of heavy metal messiahs plastered every inch of wall and ceiling. All of it bathed in the radioactive glow of a black light from Spencer's Gifts. It was the rancid, reeking last refuge of a persecuted headbanger.

And that headbanger was Mark Looger, a nineteen-year-old devout metalhead.

His jeans were shredded at the knees, thighs, and ass. His Chuck Taylors, scuffed and duct-taped, had long since sold their soles to rock 'n' roll.

He wore the mandatory black concert shirt. It was a bootleg he'd snagged outside Rowdy's before a Cleveland Flatter Machine show. Cleveland Flatter Machine was a Cleveland *Splatter* Machine tribute band, making this an unofficial T-shirt for an unofficial band. The irony was definitely lost on Mark.

The shirt's graphic depicted a hapless metalhead "flattened" beneath a fallen Marshall stack, blood and viscera spraying in cartoonishly exaggerated detail.

But the pièce de résistance of Mark's ensemble was undoubtedly his denim vest—a walking billboard for metal allegiance. Pins and patches from the most brutal, unholy bands imaginable were poked and stitched onto every available inch of fabric, some barely hanging

7

on, their edges curling from years of wear. The studs and spikes along the shoulders were uneven, rusted, with a few lost to crowd-surfing misadventures.

Taking center stage on the back of the vest was a symbol of his membership to an exclusive, ragtag gang of outcasts he'd run with since middle school: a back patch with the words *HEADBANGER BRIGADE* scrawled in jagged, barely legible letters above a grinning skeleton, frozen in the reckless ecstasy of an eternal headbang.

Mark thrashed about his bedroom, headbanging wildly, his long hair whipping through the air like a hurricane. Beneath the storm, a pair of headphones—tethered by a long cable to a nearby hi-fi stereo system—blasted heavy metal into his ears.

He leapt onto his unmade bed and bounced, the old springs creaking in protest. Then jumped from the bed to his dresser, knocking over a stack of cassette tapes. Here he continued to bang his head triumphantly, arms spread wide and throwing horns as the dresser wobbled precariously beneath him.

He was a one-man metal show, pouring every ounce of his being into this private performance for no one and doing his damnedest to obliterate his troubles away, one cathartic headbang at a time.

Finally, as the music in his headphones reached a crescendo, Mark dove off the dresser and landed ceremoniously on his knees.

When he opened his eyes, the dizzy, fuzzy kaleidoscope of his rattled brain slowly normalized and came into focus.

And there she was.

Tori Payne.

Framed by the open window behind her stood the stunning eighteen-year-old Metal Goddess. Platinum-blonde hair tumbled in wild, untamed waves over her shimmering pentagram earrings. Black eyeliner extended into sharp, dramatic wings, with a layer of smoky eyeshadow for added mystery. Her lips, painted a deep crimson, dared to be kissed while warning of an appetite for blood.

Underneath Tori's battle-worn leather jacket—heavy with silver studs and spikes, the sleeves scuffed from years of living on the edge—she rocked a tattered black concert tee for the band Flavor of the Weak. The artwork featured a massive, grotesque monster holding a yellow school bus over its gaping mouth like a bag of M&Ms, while tiny, terrified children poured out like candy into its waiting jaws.

Tori's neck was draped with layers of chains and metal skulls. Her tight black jeans were ripped and frayed in all the right places. Her well-worn combat boots looked ready to stomp through whatever mosh pit or bullshit crossed her path.

Radiating an effortless, otherworldly cool, Tori tilted her head and asked the eternal question: "You ready to rock?"

Mark lowered his headphones to rest around his neck and rose to his feet, barely able to believe that she was really here, that *it* was finally about to happen. "Whoa…" He caught himself, dialed up the confidence. "I mean, yeah. Totally. I'm, like, always ready to rock. Like, all the time. Because I'm always rockin'."

"No shit? When was the last time you… rocked?" Tori replied slyly, moving closer to him.

"I mean, like, you can't expect me to track *all* of my rocking when it's happenin', like constantly." Mark smirked, closing the distance between them.

Tori raised an eyebrow, teasing, "So, with all that *constant* rocking, you must be pretty fucking good at it."

Their lips were about to meet…

"Well, yeah, I mean, like, practice makes per—"

BOING!

Stretched to its limit, the headphone cable pulled out of the stereo, and the loudest, most satanic heavy metal ever heard exploded out of the speakers.

Mark scrambled away from Tori, pressing every button and twisting every dial to zero until the music was finally silenced.

Then he heard footsteps approaching from outside his room, and true panic hit.

"She's awake. You gotta go. You can't um, like, see this," Mark urged, his voice trembling with terror.

Tori frowned. "What the fuck are you talking about?"

Before he could answer, the bedroom door swung open with a forceful bang, revealing a shadowy silhouette wreathed in eldritch smoke. Mark stumbled back in fear as a demonic figure stood in the doorway, backlit by the hallway light.

"Is that the *devil's music* I hear?!" the ominous figure roared.

A skeletal, liver-spotted hand lifted the record player cover, removed the record, and smashed it into a thousand pieces against the wall.

The harsh overhead lights blasted on, revealing *Mother*—Mark's mother.

Cinched tight in her plush bathrobe and hair curlers, a huge crucifix swung from her neck, and a smoldering cigarette dangled from her lips. Her wrinkled, leathery flesh clung to her bones for dear life. Her neck was a veiny, tendinous anatomy illustration. And the bags under her eyes were packed for a permanent vacation.

She was thirty-nine.

"What the fuck, lady! That's Fätal Fäte's best LP!" Tori shouted.

Mother ignored Tori, picking up the album jacket for *Sacrificial Jam* by Fätal Fäte. The cover featured a robed figure in a goat-skull mask, wielding a blade above a beautiful female headbanger tied to a glowing sacrificial altar.

She read from the liner notes, her voice filled with righteous fury: "In the hall of the Satanic Temple, prepare the altar of starlight and flame. Etch and mark hieroglyphic symbols, prophesized in Satan's name?!" Mother's fury fell like an anvil on her son. "These are explicit instructions for conducting a satanic sacrifice!" She brandished the record sleeve like a televangelist delivering a fiery sermon. "The words in this music will warp your mind and make you do bad things!"

"Yeah, but—" Mark attempted.

"Did I ask you a question, Marcus?" she snapped, putting out her cigarette butt in a puddle of something on Mark's dresser.

His throat tightened, his limbs felt like lead, and the guilt unspooled in his mind like a cassette tape getting eaten alive in a fucked-up Sony Walkman. He knew how hard she worked to raise him. How she did it all alone, sacrificing everything for him. Ever since his dad was struck by lightning fixing the antenna just so that Mark could finish watching *Fat Albert and the Cosby Kids*.

"Sorry, Mother. I… I, like, totally forgot my place," he said, shrinking to his knees in shame.

Tori sneered at Mark's sudden display of weakness.

Mother pulled a pack of Virginia Slims Menthol 120s from her robe, lit another cigarette, and unleashed a barrage of so-called "evidence"—a regurgitated list of moral panics she'd absorbed from her favorite televangelist and the gossiping hens at church.

"Just like those two boys in San Francisco—best friends, mind you—who threw themselves off the Golden Gate Bridge after listening to some vile musical act called Cult of the Mystic Unicorn! Or that poor kid in Texas, from a good family—full of star athletes to boot—who slit his own wrists?" She sucked down half her cigarette and kept going. "Do you really think it was because he didn't make the football team? Or was it the demonic influence of the song 'Control, Alt, Delete'—whatever that means—by Execution-Nerd? Or that six-year-old girl they found with self-inflicted bruises all over her body—as well as a concussion—after accidentally seeing a music video on the MTV by some horrible group called SCAPEGOAT?!"

Someone had to stand up to this. Somebody had to say something.

Finally, Tori couldn't take it anymore and something snapped. It wasn't even a conscious decision. It was pure, involuntary rage from deep within her lizard brain. "Fuck that!" Tori spat, her voice as sharp as a blade. "Heavy metal doesn't make people do a goddamn thing!"

Her face darkened. Her breath hitched. Her eyes burned like molten steel. And then, through gritted teeth, her voice dropped to a raw, guttural growl—low, seething, dangerous, every syllable laced with venom: "Shitty parents like you do!"

Mark's mother redirected her wrath to Tori, cigarette smoke shooting from her nostrils like a mad bull about to charge. "I will not suffer the shrieking of a Jezebel in my house!"

Tori threw a confounded glare at Mark. "You're gonna take this from her?"

He just lowered his head deeper in shame.

She turned back to his mother: "You're fucking crazy, lady!"

"What do you know of sanity?" Mother fired back, her eyes taking inventory: Black leather. Metal spikes. *Pants!*—on a young lady? "You're nothing but a vessel for perversion, just like the whores in these posters!" She mistakenly gestured to a cluster of long-haired dudes on Mark's wall.

"Mark, fucking *do* something!" Tori pleaded.

But Mark remained silent, obedient.

Enough was enough. Tori started for the door.

But Mother blocked her way. "Slither out the way you came in," she commanded, pointing at the window. "And try not to leave too much slime as you go."

She snuffed out another menthol and immediately fired up the next one.

Tori glared at Mother, fists clenched, her lips curling into her trademark sneer.

But it wasn't worth the fight.

Halfway out the window, she paused and looked over her shoulder.

Mark's eyes flicked up for a fleeting glance at her silhouette framed against the moonlight in striking heavy metal sexuality. His cheeks flushed and he quickly dropped his gaze again, aching with regret at what he'd just blown.

"You're a fucking wuss, Mark Looger," she growled, shutting the coffin on whatever they were, and disappeared into the night.

Mother smiled with satisfaction, closed her eyes and prayed, "Then He called the crowd to Him and said: 'Whoever wants to be my disciple must deny themselves and take up their cross and follow me.'"

With that, she exited the room, slamming the door behind her.

Mark leaned against the wall behind his bed and banged his head against it—not in the joyous heavy metal catharsis of moments ago, but in hopeless frustration.

Chapter 2

SKELETONS OF SOCIETY

Though its name evoked some twisted ideal of freedom, Liberty Bend, U.S.A. was more like a prison for its remaining residents.

Jobs had vanished—outsourced, lost to greed and bad economic policy. The banks had failed, leaving homes foreclosed. A quick drive down Main Street revealed the slow death of the town. Most businesses were boarded up, while the few that managed to stay open clung to life by moonlighting as tanning salons.

Unemployment was rampant, and homelessness plagued the streets, with people often seen huddled in empty lots or squatting in the ruins of the town's once vibrant neighborhoods. Even the Wilhelm Steel Mill, once the backbone of the Liberty Bend economy, stood silent, collecting dust and leaking toxic soil contamination.

The schools closed years ago, the buildings abandoned, windows broken, and walls covered in tragically misspelled graffiti. What few kids remained were bused off to neighboring towns, though many had dropped out altogether.

With the world collapsing around them, the parents of Liberty Bend were desperate for someone or something to blame. And rightfully so. But with no clear cause in sight (other than outsourcing, greed, and bad economic policy) they found comfort in wagging their fingers at one easily identifiable target:

Heavy metal.

The origins of this moral outrage—this "Satanic Panic" that swept the nation in the 1980s—are murky at best. Some trace it to the influence of popular horror films like *Rosemary's Baby*, *The Exorcist*, and *The Omen* in the late 1960s and '70s, which ignited fears of Satan in everyday life. Others point to the rise of new religious movements in America around the same time, which unsettled the country's Christian identity. And, of course, the Tate–LaBianca murders orchestrated by Charles Manson and his cult of "mostly lonely teenagers from broken homes" poured kerosene on all of that.

The flames were fanned by *Michelle Remembers*, a so-called memoir by Canadian Michelle Smith and her husband, psychiatrist Lawrence Pazder, which presented the first significant claim linking child abuse to satanism. According to the book, Michelle, at the tender age of five, had been tortured by her mother in "elaborate satanic rituals." As the torment reached its peak, a portal to hell supposedly opened, and Satan himself appeared, only to be driven away by the Virgin Mary and Archangel Michael.

Whoa.

The book credited St. Mary's divine intervention for the lack of physical evidence on Michelle's body—and "creative license" for skipping over the conflicting testimonies of her father and sisters, as well as failing to mention the yearbook photo of Michelle looking perfectly happy at school when she was supposed to be chained up in a basement.

Despite these glaring problems, *Michelle Remembers* became a blockbuster bestseller and is often cited as a major factor in the later epidemic of SRA (Satanic Ritual Abuse) allegations and court cases.

One of the most notorious cases to emerge was the McMartin Preschool Trial. Members of the McMartin family, who ran a preschool in Manhattan Beach, California, were accused of committing hundreds of acts of sexual abuse against children in their care. Throughout the trial, media coverage was overwhelmingly biased against the defendants and focused almost exclusively on the prosecution's claims.

Alleged survivors—including Michelle Smith of *Michelle Remembers*—became involved in this case, meeting with the parents of the children and likely influencing testimony.

The whole ordeal dragged on for seven long years, ultimately resulting in no convictions, with all charges dropped in 1990. By then, it had become the longest and most expensive series of criminal trials in American history.

Despite its outcome, the McMartin case sparked a wave of similar sensationalist allegations at over one hundred preschools across the U.S., eagerly but uncritically reported by the press, who, to be fair, had their hands full with the unwarranted popularity of Cabbage Patch Kids.

This crusade to root out Satan's influence in children's lives inevitably set its sights on the music industry. Such was the case when two young boys, Raymond Belknap and James Vance—after a prolonged binge of alcohol and drugs—made a suicide pact to end their lives with a shotgun. Belknap succeeded, but Vance failed in his attempt, resulting in gruesome disfigurement. When it was later revealed that the pair had been listening to Judas Priest that afternoon, the grieving parents had found someone to blame for the tragedy.

Priest soon found themselves in court, accused of embedding "subliminal messages" in their music that encouraged the boys to commit suicide with phrases like "try suicide," "let's be dead," and "do it, do it, do it" cited as evidence.

The band members, with a mix of defiance and dark humor, testified that if they had been inserting subliminal messages into their music, it would have been to encourage listeners to buy more records, not kill themselves.

As the wildfire of Satanic Panic spread, families gathered around their television sets to be bombarded by sensational news reports and alarmist talk shows. Ministers preached hellfire from the pulpits. Politicians pounded their fists in town halls. All of it with the singular purpose of denouncing this "devil's music" as a cultural menace infiltrating American homes and poisoning the minds of the nation's youth.

P.T.A. meetings, once mundane affairs, transformed into war rooms. Concerned parents rallied against what they believed to be an imminent threat to their children. Horror stories of sudden, inexplicable changes in their children's behavior were shared, with even the slightest act of rebellion or awkward adolescent phase blamed on heavy metal. And so, school boards were pushed to root out any trace of this subversive subculture—no ripped jeans, no band patches, no mercy!

Amidst this climate of fear, the Parents Music Resource Center (PMRC) emerged as a powerful force of suppression. Founded by a posse of pearl-clutching Washington women—led by Tipper Gore, a senator's wife and self-appointed censor-in-chief—the PMRC launched a crusade against explicit lyrics in popular music. Their efforts culminated in a series of high-profile Senate hearings, where musicians such as Dee Snider of Twisted Sister, Frank Zappa, and even John Denver testified in defense of artistic freedom.

Out of these hearings came the infamous *PARENTAL ADVISORY: EXPLICIT LYRICS* stickers—slapped on half the albums in every record store.

But warnings weren't enough. Nothing would be enough for the PMRC, the PTA, or the average opportunistic congressman. Not until they could finally pass the much-coveted Freedom through Unconstitutional Containment for Kids (better known, ironically, as

F.U.C.K.) bill, which aimed at banning heavy metal with the same legal weight usually reserved for child pornography.

At the time of this story, it was well on its way to becoming the law of the land.

So, for the average teenage metalhead, every day became a battle for identity. The louder the adults screamed, the louder they cranked the volume. Their hair grew longer. Their jeans more shredded. Their faded, crusty concert tees hardened into armor. The more society blamed their music for everything going wrong, the more the music became their loud, defiant middle finger to the world.

And nowhere would come to epitomize this raging inferno of paranoia and rebellion more than Liberty Bend.

In this small town, beneath the shadow of the old Wilhelm Steel Mill, a sprawling, vacant parking lot stood as a bleak reminder of the era's hopelessness.

Like lions around a Serengeti watering hole—complete with huge manes of hair—Mark Looger and his friends with matching back patches, the self-declared "Headbanger Brigade," gathered in the lot to philosophize, revel, and conspire around their lone chariot: a massive '72 Cadillac Coupe DeVille Hardtop with a roaring Sparkomatic hi-fi system.

Once a sparkling Sterling Silver Firemist, it had rusted and faded into a grim Junkyard Gleam. Its body was plastered with band logo stickers and graffiti, and the words *HEADBANGER MOBILE* were spray-painted across the side like a war banner.

Mark was sprawled out on the hood, eyes to the sky, venting his frustrations about his mother. "I dunno, man… ever since, like, my dad and stuff, it's just been, like, this steady slide into full-on psycho mode. She used to just, like, give me dirty looks when I cranked my tunes. Now she's bustin' my Fätal Fäte LP like it's nothin'. She's, like, totally lost it."

He sighed, raking a hand through his unruly hair, thinking back to after his dad's accident, to the blurry weeks, months, and years that followed, as he and his mother struggled to find a way to cope.

Mother had veered into a dark depression. She barely spoke and hardly slept, endlessly reading volumes of trashy romance novels full of hairy chests, heaving bosoms, and horseback riding. Anything to distract from the unbearable void.

In her absence, young Marcus had to grow up fast. He made his own breakfast: Mr. T Cereal topped with whipped cream and Hershey's syrup. For lunch, it was SpaghettiOs sprinkled with crushed Pringles potato chips and Hershey's syrup. Dinner? A Swanson Salisbury steak, mashed potatoes, and peas—with a side of Hershey's syrup for dipping. He had to get himself dressed and to school on time. Remember to bathe. To wipe. Sometimes, even breathe.

One day, on his way to get his weekly haircut, Marcus got turned around and ended up outside Satanic Temple Records & Tapes. Something blasted from inside... something loud, distorted, defiant. He froze. He'd never heard anything like it. It scared him a little. But he stepped inside.

Back at home—at that very same fateful moment—his mother reached the big reveal at the end of the book. The usual one, where Jasmine Fontaine tells the stable boy she's pregnant... with *twins*... and they kiss in the pouring rain.

Marcus wandered the aisles of the record store, unsure what he was even looking for.

Mother dug through the box of sun-faded romances she'd scored for a dollar at a neighbor's everything-must-go yard sale, searching for the next filthy fantasy to numb the pain. Most of them she'd already read.

That's when Marcus saw it.

That's when Mother saw it.

He reached out. Slowly. Cautiously.

She reached out. Slowly. Cautiously.

Marcus picked up the record from the bin, its cover filled with images of black leather and metal zippers. As he flipped it over and read the track listing, words like *Wrath*, *Damnation*, and *Hellfire* screamed out at him. And that was it—there was no going back.

Mother retrieved the leather-bound Holy Bible from the bottom of the box and unzipped it. As she flipped through the pages, words like *Wrath*, *Damnation*, and *Hellfire* screamed out at her. And that was it—there was no going back.

She read the Bible cover to cover and joined church groups, while Mark devoured metal albums like scripture.

She prayed with a ferocious intensity, while Mark tore the knees out of his jeans and slowly and painfully figured out how to hand-stitch patches onto his denim vest.

She filled the house with crucifixes and ceramic angels, while he plastered the walls of his room with posters, ticket stubs, and full-color spreads from *Metal Hammer* magazine.

They had, at last, both found ways to "cope."

"Then she was like, rattling off all these crazy stories," Mark continued his rant about last night, "about kids doing fucked up stuff 'cause they listened to metal, or whatever. I'm talking, like, full conspiracy theory wacko shit—no offense, Piper."

Piper Jones, a sixteen-year-old heavy metal conspiracy theorist, was the self-proclaimed political conscience of the Headbanger Brigade.

Courtesy of the local Army Surplus store, she was dressed head-to-toe in battle-worn camouflage. Her frayed and faded army fatigues revealed scabbed and scarred knees from countless mosh pits and reckless "recon" missions. A dented steel helmet sat askew on her head, covered in vulgar graffiti. And her grimy old M65 field jacket was plastered with a chaotic mix of band logo patches and anti-establishment pins. Some warned of government surveillance. Others referenced secret societies. A few even questioned the existence of reality itself.

Her mind was a labyrinth of wild theories and intricate plots, constantly buzzing with suspicion and mistrust. But Piper wasn't exactly cleared for critical thinking. And when it came to conspiracy theories, she could never quite put all the pieces together.

At the moment, she sat on the broken asphalt of the parking lot, leaning against the front tire of the Headbanger Mobile, obsessively trying to tape together a pile of shredded documents.

"None taken, Mark. Besides, I'm not a conspiracy theorist," Piper said without looking up. "I'm a *social justice warrior*. But obviously there's a simple explanation for this epidemic of anti-heavy metal paranoia going around. I mean, you guys heard about all those sasquatch sightings outside of Denver last week, right?"

No. They had not.

"Because there's always a direct link between unexplained phenomena and mass hysteria," she continued matter-of-factly. "I'll give it my full attention as soon as I'm done exposing each and every member of the PMRC."

She sifted through the mess of paper shreds and Scotch tape with even more vigor.

"Piper," came a voice from inside the car, "do you *really* believe the Parents Music Resource Center would dump classified documents in the dumpster behind Greasy Gene's Pizzeria and Tanning?"

Edward Horowitz sat in the cracked leather interior of the Headbanger Mobile, soldering circuits on a strange device plugged into the car's cigarette lighter. He had thick glasses, hair down to his ass, a calculator watch on a spiked wristband, and a pocket protector—stuffed with an array of mechanical pencils, screwdrivers, and an Execution-Nerd cassette tape—clipped to his jean jacket. Seventeen-year-old Edward was the textbook paradox of a heavy metal science nerd and the undisputed brains of the Headbanger Brigade.

Piper completely mistook Edward's skepticism for validation. "I know, right?" she whispered. "It's the perfect cover!"

Edward sighed. "Well, you better hurry, because the Freedom through Unconstitutional Containment for Kids bill was called to a vote in the Senate this morning."

He pushed his glasses up and turned his attention to Mark. "Anywho, clearly your mother—and society for that matter—are just projecting their own anxieties. It's biological. Humans need something to blame when they can't make sense of the world, and heavy metal obviously disrupts their sense of order."

Greg Gunderson, aka "Sir Greg of the Golden Realm," a hulking 20-year-old clad in shredded denim, leather, and chainmail, was swinging his massive battle axe in a practiced routine in front of the car. His refined, knightly demeanor was in stark contrast to the slouching ruffians around him.

"Aye, we live in an age most wicked," Sir Greg said gravely, "where fear has become the blade of those who seek power—where whispers spread by hysteria's dark tongue are used to line the pockets of the cunning and cruel. And in their wake, even the sacred bond between mother and child is poisoned, twisted into a shadow of what it once was."

Mark blinked, visibly confused. "Uh... yeah, like, totally, Sir

Greg. That's, like, exactly what I was thinking... or, y'know, somethin' like that."

Suddenly, Sir Greg unsheathed a dagger from his belt and with a swift flick of his wrist, sent it sailing through the air.

SHINK!

The blade buried itself into the seat of the lawn chair—right between the legs of a sixty-seven-year-old relic in full black leather, dead asleep, his obvious mullet toupee slightly askew.

Burdened by a lifetime of regrets, Mike Fogelman, aka "Fogey," clung to his fading youth by hanging out with the decades-younger members of the Headbanger Brigade. He initially won them over by buying booze, a role that made him essential. But when the liquor stores in Liberty Bend—struggling to stay open—began selling to anyone who looked older than twelve, Fogey had to find another way to stay relevant. So he started spinning wild tales of his supposed heavy metal glory days. Whether true or not, those stories became his desperate attempt to stay connected. And to matter.

The old man jerked awake with a snort. "I wanna hang with the cool kids—" Fogey mumbled, half-dreaming, then snapped to attention. "I mean, uh... hey, dudes. Just getting my power nap in."

Sir Greg stepped forward, towering over the old man, voice booming with medieval gravitas. "Mark has summoned the Council of the Brigade. And the Council shall convene in full. Rise, old warrior, and heed the call, lest thy absence bring dishonor upon thee."

Fogey blinked, rubbing his eyes. "Oh... right... what's goin' down, um... Council?" he asked groggily, as Sir Greg retrieved his dagger from the lawn chair.

"Mark's parental unit has become fully indoctrinated into the Satanic Panic and decimated a cherished Fätal Fäte LP," Edward explained as he closed a panel and screwed it shut on the back of the strange device.

"But his retribution was stayed, held back by the crushing guilt his mother has laid upon him," Sir Greg added.

"And because of that, Tori totally kicked him to the curb!" Piper finished.

"Ah, man…" Fogey started, "Listen, Mark, when I was a roadie for VD Vengeance back in '83—"

"No way!" Piper blurted, eyes wide. "You roadied for VD Vengeance too?!"

Fogey waved a dismissive hand. "Anyway, I remember clear as day—Jimmy Crotch was so heartbroken when his fiancée dumped him, he flat-out refused to go onstage that night."

Mark leaned forward. "Yeah? So, like… what did he do?"

Fogey blinked. "Huh? Oh. That's when they fired Jimmy and got a new bass player."

"Oh…" Mark deflated.

Sir Greg glared at Fogey. "Thy words hold as much use as a wooden sword and as much truth as a minstrel's drunken boast."

Just then, a whirring sound came from inside the Headbanger Mobile as the strange device Edward had been working on finished rebooting and came to life. Constructed from a jumble of rewired consumer electronics and plastered with band logos, it was a highly intelligent, loyal, and multi-functional heavy metal robot.

It was Metal T.E.D.

Metal T.E.D.'s childlike curiosity (and advanced programming) was taking him on a journey through a world of new experiences, equations, and kick-ass tunes. But that old saying about curiosity and cats might also apply to robots, which is why Edward's top priority and greatest scientific passion was mentoring Metal T.E.D.

"Following a full diagnostic and a system reboot, I am still unable to generate an optimal resolution to Mark's dilemma," Metal T.E.D. reported. "This failure has disrupted my processing efficiency with what could only be described as…" He blinked. His head tilted to a twenty-seven-degree angle. "…frustration."

Edward beamed like a proud father. "Metal T.E.D.! You're experiencing an emotion!" He turned toward the rest of the group—those ever-skeptical doubters of artificial intelligence—and raised his voice for their benefit. "Even *more* proof that my creation is a sentient, fully conscious lifeform!"

Fogey still wasn't buying it. "Okay, but how can that tin can be a *real* person if you can program him to do whatever you want?"

Before Edward could answer, Piper cut in. "Oh, that can easily be done with so-called real people, too. Happens all the time."

Mark perked up. "Wait… are you, like, talking about hypnotism?"

"Hypnotism. Mesmerism. Capitalism. Whatever you want to call it," Piper replied.

"Intriguing…" Edward muttered, pushing up his glasses.

Chapter 3

CAN I PLAY WITH MADNESS

In the time it takes to flip a cassette, the trunk of the Headbanger Mobile creaked open and the smell of old motor oil, dust, and forbidden knowledge wafted out.

At the top of the pile, a tattered stack of metal magazines dominated the scene. *Metal Edge* had the latest on bands like Fätal Fäte, Midnight Massacre, and Human Toilet. *RIP*, with its shocking exposés on icons like Ronnie Shaggs and Bobby "The Possum" Dicer, peeked out from beneath a dog-eared *Metal Hammer*, its glossy pages overflowing with the raw energy of live performances. *Kerrang!* offered a glimpse into the world of metal across the pond, while *Circus*—mostly glam trash like Rosemary's Lady and Malibu Bad Boys—was used as backup toilet paper by the Brigade in desperate situations.

Mixed in with these were a few issues of *Heavy Metal Magazine*—surprisingly, not a music rag, but a sci-fi/fantasy comic anthology. Its wild blend of dark fantasy, erotica, and steampunk was a portal to another dimension. Most of these were the noble contributions of Sir Greg (who also seemed to hail from another time and place).

And then there were the horror mags: *Fangoria* and *Gorezone*, drenched in fake blood and plastered with the iconic faces of Freddy Krueger, Michael Myers, and Jason Voorhees. And scattered among those were a couple of ancient issues of *Famous Monsters of Filmland*, love letters to the classic Universal and Hammer horror movies that started it all, kindly donated by the equally wrinkled and dog-eared Fogey.

There may have also been one or two issues of *Omni Magazine* and *Scientific American* that Edward secretly added to the collection.

And right alongside Frankenstein, Bobby Dicer, and satellite images of the rings of Saturn, was the porn. Copious copies of *Juggs*, *Hustler*, *Penthouse*, *Beaver Hunt*, *Oui*, and more littered the treasure trove, their glossy covers showcasing women in various states of undress. But these weren't just smut. Piper had added them to the pile, convinced they were the perfect vessels for leaking government intel—hidden inside centerfolds no fed would ever admit to gawking at.

A few random books lay at the bottom: multiple editions of *The Guinness Book of World Records*, a cracked-spined *Necronomicon*, a heavily annotated *Anarchist Cookbook*, and—ironically—*Michelle Remembers*. But pretty much everyone on Earth seemed to own a copy, so why not the Headbanger Brigade?

It was more than just a pile of old magazines and books. It was their collective, blissfully limited knowledge of the world.

They huddled around as Piper sifted through it all, until, at last, she uncovered an ancient-looking tome bound in cracked leather and cobwebs. With a triumphant grin, she scooped it up, blew a cloud of dust off the cover, and held it up for all to see. "It's all right here in this handy-dandy instruction manual."

Ancient Secrets and Forbidden Techniques of Mind Control.

Written by Lord Constantine Blatherton VIII, a pompous Victorian aristocrat with too much time on his hands, that very book was—unbeknownst to the Brigade—the last surviving copy on the planet, banned or burned in every country where it had ever been published.

When *Ancient Secrets and Forbidden Techniques of Mind Control* was first released, it became the talk of the town among professional psychiatrists, hypnotists, surgeons, amateur surgeons, and the occasional escaped lunatic, each of them astonished by the effectiveness of the techniques it revealed.

But that very effectiveness proved to be its downfall. After a wave of unintended consequences, including its use by authoritarian regimes, sex cults, and a handful of truly unhinged teenagers, the book was pulled from print and every known copy tracked down and destroyed.

And Lord Blatherton was forced to find (and finance) yet another hobby.

Exactly how *Ancient Secrets and Forbidden Techniques of Mind Control* arrived in the trunk of the Headbanger Mobile was a mystery to this day. Each member had contributed to the stash from their own private collections (or random findings in a field) but when it came to that book, no one could claim ownership. Piper only knew it existed because she was always snooping around in the trunk in search of "intel."

Later, when people tried to make sense of the horrific events that would soon transpire, some theorized that it was the work of the Holy Christ Church of Unwavering Condemnation—a secret and incredibly convoluted plot to place the book in the Headbanger Brigade's hands and seal their fate... and the fate of heavy metal... forever.

As soon as Edward saw the book, everything his mind had been processing clicked into place. "Eureka!" he exclaimed. "This could very well be the breakthrough we've been searching for, Mark!"

Mark's brow furrowed as he tried to decipher what Edward meant, and how it had anything to do with his Tori situation. As his mind spiraled into a maelstrom of possibilities, Mark saw himself with Tori at a metal show, their bodies thrashing and colliding in the chaos of the mosh pit.

They were in a movie theater watching George A. Romero's *Day of the Dead* for the tenth time and laughing way too loud at the part when Captain Rhodes is torn apart by zombies, intestines spilling out as he screams, "Choke on 'em!" Fellow moviegoers shot dirty looks and someone called an usher.

They shared a romantic picnic in a graveyard, drawing hateful glares from nearby mourners.

They took a long walk along the beach at sunset, hand in hand, waves crashing gently along the shoreline—while getting the stink-eye from a crew in hazmat suits for strolling too close to the toxic waste spill.

And finally, they fell into Mark's bed, clothes thrown onto the floor, arms and legs intertwining, the heavy metal soundtrack of Mark's imagination swelling in anticipation.

But something was off. The fierce spark that defined Tori, that rock 'n' roll edge that made her so captivating, was gone. Her eyes, once full of life and mischief, were dull and vacant. While still hot as hellfire, she moved like a puppet: stiff, mechanical... and wrong. She was a cheap imitation of the girl he once knew. And Mark was horrified to discover that he was *horrified* by her.

A chill went down his spine.

Not cool, he thought to himself.

He took a cautious step away from the book. "Are you saying I should use this, like, witchcraft or whatever... on Tori?"

"Ah, man! Great thinking!" Fogey blurted out before anyone else could speak, then reminisced, "That reminds me of when I worked security for Horny Beast in '79 and Oily Deacon's own harem of groupies slipped him a mickey. Boy, did they do a number on him!"

But Edward quickly shook his head, clarifying, "No, no, you'd want to keep Tori just as she is."

"To do otherwise would be an affront to nobility itself," Sir Greg agreed.

"Yeah, like, that's what I was just thinking… or something close to that." Mark nodded, relieved this might not be a total dead end after all.

Something clicked in Fogey's dusty old brain. "Oh! Then you're talking about that ancient, *old bag* mother of yours!"

"Mark's mother is twenty-eight years *younger* than you, Fogey," Metal T.E.D. corrected.

"Uh. Really?" Fogey stammered, caught off-guard. "Well, you wouldn't know it from looking at her."

"Fool." Sir Greg rolled his noble eyes.

Piper thrust the book into Mark's hands. "Your mom will finally have to do what *you* say instead of the other way around!"

Fogey reminisced again. "Like when Hank the Stank turned to me and said, 'I'm gonna need *you* to play lead guitar for us tonight, Fogey.'"

"Seriously?!" Piper was mind-blown as always by Fogey's endless rock 'n' roll exploits.

Edward leaned in. "And Tori would undoubtedly be so impressed by this turn of events that she *might* even reconsider the defunct status of your relationship."

"An optimal resolution to your dilemma," Metal T.E.D. added, his processing efficiency stabilizing to what could only be described as "relief."

Sir Greg rested a solemn hand upon Mark's shoulder. "Indeed. To seize one's desires with an iron grip rather than cower in the shadows of uncertainty—this is the way of true nobility."

Mark flipped through the book, weighing his options, which were few. "Yeah… I mean, you guys all *know* how bad I need to get laid."

They exchanged glances—silent, sympathetic, and deeply

30

exasperated glances.

Edward pushed up his glasses. "Of course, Mark. We're all aware of your... um, *status*."

"And it shall be our honor to assist your noble quest to slay the great dragon of virginity!" Sir Greg pledged.

Piper snorted. "Yeah, what do you think the Headbanger Brigade is for? I mean, duh!"

Mark nodded, emboldened. "And, like... Tori Payne is, like, special. I mean, yeah, she's totally hot, but, like... in that slice your jugular with a switchblade kind of way, y'know?"

The rest of the Headbanger Brigade gave each other a "here we go again" look.

Mark might not have been the brightest bulb in the marquee, but when the moment called for it, he could radiate enough rock 'n' roll passion to power the pyrotechnics at a Technologi-KILL show.

This was one of those moments.

Mark dramatically stepped up to the roof of the Headbanger Mobile and launched into the tale they'd all heard a thousand times: "And, like, I knew it was destiny, or whatever, for us to be together for all eternity from the first time we met two weeks ago in detention..."

Forty-three minutes to go. Time crawled at a soul-crushing, sanity-destroying pace. All because of some bullshit dress code violation.

Mark didn't see what the big deal was. So what if his shirt featured a smoking-hot babe writhing in agony while a deranged pathologist yanked out all her organs? It was freedom of speech. And Mark was merely expressing his love for Malpractice and their masterpiece, "Premature Autopsy."

It was art. It was metal. It was beautiful.

But according to Black Rock Falls High School, it was "violent, obscene, and deeply inappropriate." And now he was stuck in detention, forced to endure the agonizing monotony of absolute nothingness—with his shirt turned inside out, no less.

Most of the other kids there—probably for minor offenses like tardiness or not wiping their asses enough—were diligently working on their homework.

But not Mark. Homework was for home. (Not like he was gonna do it there, either.)

Luckily, he had something much more industrious to satiate his boredom. He had found a paperclip in the cubby beneath the desk he was metaphorically chained to. Not one of those dinky ones, but a heavy-duty, industrial-sized paperclip for holding together a lawsuit, a tax audit, or the entire permanent record of a typical headbanger. He was currently using it to carve the logo of his favorite band, Fätal Fäte, into the desktop, and it was coming along nicely. He was even pretty sure he placed the umlauts correctly.

As Mark carved quietly and carefully, making sure nobody noticed—especially Mr. Hopper, the school janitor and part-time detention warden, because, well… he knew how to "deal with the trash"—he suddenly became aware of another horrible scraping sound that wasn't his own.

At first, he ignored it.

But as the minutes crawled by, the sound grew louder, more deliberate, and more aggressive. Mark had to know what it was. And who was behind it.

His eyes swept the room.

Mr. Hopper was slouched in his chair, reading one of the steamy love letters he'd swiped while "cleaning out" horny teenagers' lockers. One hand was below his desk—probably fondling himself.

The other inmates quietly toiled away at their useless math, reading, or whatever bullshit they thought would get them through life.

The scraping continued.

Finally, Mark zeroed in on the source. It came from the desk right behind him.

And that's when he saw her.

Her scuffed leather jacket, pentagram earrings, and platinum blond hair shimmering in the sickening light of fluorescent bulbs like the Metal Goddess she was.

Tori Payne.

And her black T-shirt was turned inside out just like Mark's—censored by the brutal, oppressive regime of BRFHS. She must have been sentenced here for the same offense. His mind raced, trying to guess what shirt it could be.

Could it be the infamous Cult of the Black Unicorn tee—the one with the smoking hot babe being penetrated in multiple orifices by a herd of the majestic, magical creatures?

Or could it be that wild Blast Femurs design that featured a hapless headbanger's upper thighs exploding in an impossible amount of gore while giving an ominous-looking church the middle finger.

Or—though highly unlikely—the legendary Flavor of the Weak tee? The one that was supposedly banned after a first run and only available in bootleg form? The one that allegedly featured a massive, grotesque monster holding a yellow school bus over its gaping mouth like a bag of M&Ms, while tiny, terrified children poured out like candy into its waiting jaws.

And *she* was the one making that horrible scraping sound.

Not with a measly paperclip like Mark.

But with a *fucking switchblade!*

Mark felt his soul leave his body in pure admiration.

He leaned over to get a glimpse of her work. It wasn't some just half-assed, angsty desk graffiti scratched into the rotting wood of public education. It was a full-blown, insanely detailed relief sculpture of Bitch-Face Bitch, the legendary lead singer of Fätal Fäte, carved with the obsessive precision of a master artist at the height of their madness.

Holy shit, this girl was badass!

Every line, every shadow, every jagged edge of Bitch-Face Bitch's demonic face screaming into a microphone was etched with the raw intensity of the real thing. If only Tori had parents who encouraged and nurtured this raw artistic talent, she could've been the next Leonardo da Vinci, or maybe even Pushead.

If only she *had* parents.

And then Mark's stomach dropped.

Right below the rendering of Bitch-Face Bitch was the Fätal Fäte logo. Not only was it a hundred times better than his, but Mark suddenly realized that he had, in fact, placed the umlauts over the wrong letters.

He stared in awe.

Without looking up, Tori growled out a warning: "Keep staring and I'll carve my next masterpiece into your fucking throat."

"Yeah, but that's, like—"

Tori sprang from her chair and slammed Mark to the floor, sending up a cloud of sawdust and wood shavings from her carving.

Before he could even process what was happening, cold steel pressed against his throat.

Mark's brain went haywire, a wild mix of schoolboy crush and sheer terror surging through him all at once. Was this how he was going to die? Probably. But one thing was for sure: Tori Payne was the most metal thing he had ever experienced in his young and likely very short life.

The commotion finally tore Mr. Hopper's attention away from the escalating intensity of Johnny Fork's poetic, pornographic promises to Nicole Rhodes. He sprang from his seat and pointed a grimy finger at the skirmish.

"Hey, you two! Don't make me *take out the trash!*" he barked with self-satisfied authority—then quickly remembered his pants were still around his ankles and scrambled to pull them up.

Tori ignored the janitor and pressed the blade harder against Mark's neck, drawing blood. "You got something to say about Fätal Fäte?"

"Uh… yeah…" Mark squeaked, "They're like… my favorite band."

Tori paused, narrowing her eyes. "Really?"

Mark nodded rapidly.

A slow grin spread across Tori's face.

"It truly was, like, destiny or whatever," Mark continued from the roof of the Headbanger Mobile. "We both got suspended for, like, trashin' school property or whatever and they took away Tori's blade. Then we spent the day hangin' out, talkin' about how much parents suck, and how much Fätal Fäte rules. So yeah… I'd do pretty much anything to get Tori Payne back."

He paused, thinking it over, then declared: "I mean, like, I'd do homework!" He shuddered at the thought, then kept going. "I'd… I'd, like, even sit front row at a Malibu Bad Boys concert."

The rest of the Brigade shuddered right along with Mark.

With a dumb chuckle, he added, "Man… I'd even eat your grandma's egg salad, Edward."

As everyone recoiled in disgust, Edward turned white as a ghost. "Whoa."

Mark sighed, all that rock 'n' roll passion suddenly fizzling out. He stepped down from the roof of the Headbanger Mobile and back to the cracked asphalt below. Back to reality. "But don't worry," he muttered. "I won't do any of that."

He tossed the book back to Piper. "And I'm not gonna hypnotize Mother, either."

It was that guilt again. Eating him alive from the inside out: how hard she worked to raise him. How she did it all alone, sacrificing everything for him. Ever since his dad was struck by lightning fixing the antenna just so that Mark could finish watching *Fat Albert and the Cosby Kids*.

"I'll just go talk to Tori. Y'know, like, try to apologize or whatever," he shrugged. "She's, like, a reasonable chick."

Chapter 4

SCHOOL'S OUT

The building hadn't been updated since Kennedy was gunned down. But at this point, why bother?

Fluorescent bulbs flickered and buzzed on their last legs. Sagging ceiling panels dripped asbestos-flavored mystery juice onto unsuspecting students throughout the day. A crusted puddle of dried vomit—at least three days old—attracted a swarm of flies near a water fountain. It was left to fester because the short-handed janitorial staff were currently preoccupied with whatever the hell was going on behind the police tape that had cordoned off an entire wing of the school since Monday. Posters for "abstinence only" education and the Junior Prom hung lazily askew on walls painted in some long-forgotten shade of puke-green to match the rest of the regurgitated décor.

But Mark wasn't here at Black Rock Falls High School to admire the scenery. Or for school at all. He was here for Tori.

He had strolled into the empty halls just after the fifth-period bell rang—when all the students were already tucked dutifully in their classrooms—and followed the smell of formaldehyde straight to Room 204: Miss Hemorrhage's Biology class.

Miss Hemorrhage was the full-time lunch lady with a better moustache than Geraldo Rivera and part-time biology teacher because, well… in the end, it's all just "mystery meat."

Mark peeked through the slit of the wire-reinforced glass window. There were more than fifty students packed into the classroom like livestock, half of whom had been bused in from Liberty Bend, Hope Valley, and Bleakridge, where the local schools had closed.

Miss Hemorrhage stood behind a metal lab table where a large amphibian lay belly-up, its limbs splayed and pinned in place. Her scalpel glinted beneath the flickering fluorescent lights as she narrated the procedure like Julia Child walking the audience through a boeuf bourguignon. She even said, "Voilà!" at one point.

With each slice, viscera spilled out in slow, mucousy strands. A thick, yellowish fluid seeped from the ruptured gallbladder, oozing across the slick abdominal cavity. Miss Hemorrhage plunged two fingers into the thoracic cavity and extracted a half-deflated lung, squeezing it as if she were testing fruit at the grocery store. A fine mist of pink gore erupted, spraying Elmer Schnickel, a nerd in headgear and coke-bottle glasses, right in the face.

But Elmer didn't move. He just kept watching, scribbling notes with intense concentration.

Miss Hemorrhage continued, digging deeper. Out came a swollen, dark liver. She sliced it in half, revealing what looked like a tumor. Next came the intestines, inch after knotted inch. The faint odor of rotting pond water, formaldehyde, and burnt Spam wafted through the room.

Still, the students remained unfazed. Even when a kidney burst with an audible *pop* and sprayed a fleck of dark fluid onto a girl's open notebook. Some kids even snacked on Funyuns as frog guts slopped onto their desks.

But then someone glanced toward the door.

And saw *him*.

There, with his face pressed against the glass, was Mark Looger—greasy, unruly hair matted to his forehead, wide, darting eyes, breath fogging the window.

The room exploded.

Screams echoed off the tile walls. Desks toppled. A textbook was hurled. Elmer Schnickel fell backward off his chair, his legs kicking in the air just like that poor frog on the table.

All it took was the sight of a headbanger and the entire biology class went to hell.

But Mark was used to this kind of reaction, which had become more and more frequent with the Satanic Panic.

Still, he was pretty sure Tori Payne was supposed to be in that class. Hell, they both were. But she was nowhere in sight.

He moved on down the hall, wondering if maybe she was out sick. Or just ditching for fun. Then it hit him: the shitter! It was worth a shot.

Bridgette Gaskett, a ginger-haired freshman with more skin problems than Freddy Krueger, stood on her tiptoes in front of the girls' bathroom mirror, her fingers locked in a death grip around the greasy, mountainous zit on her chin, squeezing with intense determination until—

POP!

A burst of yellow pus and blood exploded across the mirror in a sickly, slimy splatter.

Bridgette didn't flinch. This was already her fourth or fifth victim during what was supposed to be a quick "bathroom break." But what began as a simple post-poop pimple pop had turned into a full-blown extraction session.

She was about to move on to one of the shiny monsters on her forehead, when—through gore-coated glass in the mirror—she saw Mark Looger enter the girls' bathroom. It was as if Jason Voorhees just stepped into her summer camp cabin.

"Aaahhhh!" She spun around, backing away against the far wall.

"W-w-what are *you* doing in here?!"

Mark, unfazed, gave a casual wave. "Hey, uh... have you, like, seen Tori Payne, or whatever?"

Bridgette screamed again, and this time the pressure inside her volatile teenage pores reached critical mass, and at least half a dozen more zits ruptured simultaneously in a chain-reaction of facial carnage.

Her eyes rolled back and she collapsed to the floor. It might have been from the shock of coming face-to-face with Mark Looger—the embodiment of what the six o'clock news, Sunday sermons, and her parents had long warned her about—or from extreme blood-and-pus loss. Likely both.

Mark shrugged. He kicked open the stall doors. "Tori?" Kick. "Where are you?" Kick. "I just wanna, like, talk, or whatever."

But no Tori. Just some graffiti on the wall:

Fuck the Holy Christ Church of Unwavering Condemnation!
Fuck graffiti censorship!
In case you still didn't get the message, FUCK YOU!

It was art. It was metal. It was beautiful. Definitely Tori's handiwork.

Mark exited the bathroom and headed to the lockers, where he hoped there might be some clues to her whereabouts. They had shared combinations following their mutual suspensions. Luckily, Tori's combo was easy as hell to remember: six-six-six.

He spun the dial and popped it open, expecting to find her personal shrine to all things dangerous, glorious, and obscene: pin-ups of Bitch-Face Bitch, Mickey Mayhem, and every other heavy metal icon who didn't suck, an arsenal of knives sharp enough to gut a rhino, a crusty collection of metal rags, some spare panties, a wadded-up Necro-mancipator concert tee depicting an undead Abraham Lincoln brutally disemboweling a modern-day Klansman, a few ticket stubs from shows she'd actually paid to get into, some illegal fireworks, and maybe one or two actual school books. But it was empty.

Empty!

Except for the one or two actual school books.

Mark blinked. "What the… huh?"

All of his hopes circling the drain, he lumbered down the hall, past the vomit, past the police tape, and out the busted emergency exit, ready to give up.

But just as he stepped out into the daylight—there she was!

Tori Payne was hunched down at the driver's side of a 1971 AMC Javelin AMX. It was a weirdly patriotic slab of American muscle, decked out in factory red, white, and blue Trans-Am racing stripes that looked like Evel Knievel had mated with a Cold War tank. Even the license plate read *BRN2USA*.

She snaked a coat hanger down the window shaft with surgical intensity.

"Tori!" Mark called out as he ran up to her.

She didn't even look at him.

"I just, like, wanted to say I'm sorry, or whatever."

"Fuck," Tori muttered, then readjusted the hook on her hanger.

"I was wondering if you'd, like, I don't know, give me another chance or somethin'?" Mark rambled, oblivious to whatever it was Tori was doing. "I know I, like, screwed up and stuff. I shoulda told Mother off, or whatever. It's just…"

Tori let out a heavy sigh—partly from wrestling with the hanger, but mostly because she didn't want to hear what she knew would be Mark's pathetic excuse.

"Y'know…" he kept on, "she worked, like, really hard to raise me and stuff. And like, she did it all alone, sacrificing everything. Ever since my dad was struck by lightning fixing the antenna just so I could finish watching Fat Albert and the…" Mark trailed off, staring at the coat hanger. "Uh… are you, like, stealing that car?"

Tori finally looked at him, eyes blazing. "What do you think I'm doing? Giving it a fucking prostate exam?!" She grunted, yanked the slim-jim out, then re-bent the metal with her teeth.

He gulped. "But isn't this, like, Coach Kraut's wheels?"

She saw the look of fear in his eyes and unloaded. "I don't know about you, Mark, but I want some fucking chaos in my life. I want to raise some fucking hell." She jammed the coat hanger back into the window shaft and attacked the lock with all of her pent-up fury. "And this town's a fucking dead-end. A sinkhole of gas station burritos and tanning salons. Nothing ever fucking happens here, and even when it does, it just turns out to be the same boring-ass bullshit all over again!"

Mark's eyes drifted to her studded backpack lying on the asphalt, every inch plastered with pins and band logos. It was overflowing with panties, fireworks, and everything else he'd expected to find in her locker—except for the one or two actual school books. Her whole life, zipped up and ready to burn rubber.

"Wait… you're, like… leaving Liberty Bend?" he asked, his voice barely above a whisper. The world seemed to be crumbling beneath his feet.

Hearing the tremble in Mark's voice—the actual concern—sent an unexpected jolt through Tori.

Her life had been one long string of betrayals, each more soul-crushing than the last.

It started when she was barely five years old. Her biological mother, a woman with a hot bod and an even hotter meth pipe, told her they were going to the circus. Tori, in pigtails and charm bracelets, bounced in her seat for miles, dreaming of daring acrobats, crazy clowns, and cotton candy chaos.

But instead, her mom drove her out to the edge of town, dropped her off at a two-bit flea market, and drove off without a second glance.

Tori—Victoria back then—survived in the shadows of that place for a few weeks on charitable scraps and petty theft. Until a corndog heist went sideways and a vendor called the cops, claiming she'd been threatened at gunpoint. Again, she was five.

From there, it was the system for Victoria, where her caseworker had smiled and assured her, "We're going to find you a nice home," then tossed her into a parade of foster families, each one more twisted than the last.

One couple told her that if she ever talked back, it would awaken "Beelzebub" in the basement. To Victoria, that was practically a dare. She talked back, acted out, did everything wrong she could think of to try and get a peek.

The Fibberlys gave her up after six days.

Every time a placement failed, the caseworker would sigh, scribble something on a clipboard, and say again, "Don't you worry. We'll find you a nice home."

The next foster parents locked her in the basement "for her safety" (because *she* was "Mephistopheles" now, apparently) and sunlight, they warned, would make her burst into flames. Naturally, Victoria became obsessed with finding out what that might feel like. She managed to tunnel out of captivity in record time… but nothing happened. No flames. Not even a sizzle. Just the familiar sting of disappointment.

Meanwhile, the Benders' dreams of funneling her state-issued food stipend into scratchers and cat food went up in smoke.

"We'll find you a nice home."

Then came the house with five other foster kids. The parents, Mr. and Mrs. Callister, were mostly checked out—too busy cashing those checks and watching Wheel of Fortune reruns.

But the kids?

They brushed their teeth *twice* a day. Said things like "Good morning." Staged an intervention the first time Victoria said, "fuck." And they ratted her out *every time* she tried to run away!

They weren't kids.

They were the *real* "Princes of Darkness."

And her caseworker kept promising: "We'll find you a nice home, Victoria. One where you'll be safe, respected. Where they'll treat you like family."

But every home had been just a new brand of hell with a fresh coat of lies.

Eventually, the caseworker must've realized how empty her promises sounded. So, in a rare moment of kindness (or maybe guilt), she purchased two tickets for her and Victoria to, of all places—the circus.

And, true to form, it didn't break the pattern of disappointment. The daring acrobats used nets, the crazy clowns were sane, and the cotton candy made her puke—which was a good enough excuse to bail before the final act. And soon after, by the age of fifteen, Victoria—now Tori—made her escape from the three-ring spectacle of foster care altogether.

Ever since, she'd been "camping out" among the jagged, rusted remnants of the old abandoned Wilhelm Steel Mill.

Maybe the circus could have never lived up to her expectations, and maybe nothing ever would. But to this day, it was still that wild, just out of reach spectacle of chaos that she craved.

But Tori had to admit, it *was* kind of nice—and pretty fucking shocking—when anyone actually gave a shit about her, too.

She stopped working the slim-jim and rose to face Mark. "You could come with me," she offered with a hesitant smile. "We could ride out of here together and really raise some fucking hell!"

Mark froze, his knees buckled. "Come *with* you? I mean, yeah... but—"

"But what?" Tori pressed.

"But, um, well…"

His hesitation said it all.

"But *she* wouldn't like that, would she?"

Tori was right, of course. It would completely devastate Mother if he threw caution to the wind and ran off with the girl she'd dubbed a "Jezebel." And hadn't he already hurt her enough?

"Pfft, just like I fucking said." Tori shook her head and got back to jiggling the hanger. "You're just another Liberty Bend disappointment."

CLICK!

The door finally unlocked.

Mark's stomach sank. But before he could say another word—

HONK! HONK! HONK!

The 1971 AMC Javelin AMX's alarm system exploded like an air raid siren.

"Shit!" Tori chucked the coat hanger, grabbed her bag, and bolted.

"Wait! Where are you even gonna go?!" Mark called out, still in a daze.

That's when Coach Kraut appeared. Part-time Phys. Ed. teacher, part-time American History professor because, well… he recently passed his citizenship test, so he probably knew a lot more about "amber waves of grain" than most.

Coach Kraut was forged in the concrete gymnasiums of East Germany, chiseled by discipline, raised on state-issued cabbage and cold showers, and shipped to America after some "incident" (no one dared ask). Now he terrorized American youth in the name of structure, sweat, and a deeply repressed longing for order.

He was decked head to toe in a skin-tight, red-white-and-blue

American flag tracksuit, complete with matching tube socks, wristbands, and a patriotic headband clinging to his skull. The outfit hugged every grotesquely perfect muscle like it had been painted on with liquid testosterone. His face was carved in stone. His crazy, intense eyes bulged like they were trying to escape his head. Even his veins had veins.

Everyone knew he was juiced to the gills. And if you'd ever been on the receiving end of his infamous paddleboard—a custom-carved slab of varnished oak he dubbed "Liberty's Hammer"—you could confirm it.

And right then, he was running at top speed out of the back doors of the gym toward Mark.

"Stoppen, metal boy!" he bellowed in broken English with his thick East German accent. "Get your krallen off mein American chick magnet!"

Mark's blood ran cold. "Oh, shit!"

He turned and ran, sprinting across the cracked asphalt of the Black Rock Falls High parking lot as fast as a gangly metalhead could, for the Headbanger Mobile on the far end.

A school bus rumbled into view, turning out of the loop just as Mark hit the crosswalk. He barely dodged it, the side mirror missing his face by inches.

Still, he kept going.

Coach Kraut was gaining on him. Fast.

Mark vaulted over a trash can.

Coach Kraut followed suit.

Mark ducked under a low-hanging tree branch.

Coach Kraut barreled straight through it, snapping the limb like a breadstick, sending splinters exploding in every direction.

"Vhat you think you are doing, metal boy? Some kind of satanisches ritual on mein chick magnet?!"

Mark looked back to answer. "No, I was just, like—"

CRASH! CLINK! CLATTER!

Distracted, he had slammed right into the bicycle rack and fallen into a tangled jungle of spokes, chains, and warped handlebars.

Coach Kraut was closing in fast.

Mark scrambled, thrashing like a trapped animal, when he spotted a rusted Huffy Pro Thunder BMX, its foam grips long gone, seat crooked, and one pedal bent inward like a broken finger. It was no wonder its owner hadn't bothered to lock up that piece of crap.

Mark ripped it from the rack, threw a leg over, and pedaled like hell, just as Kraut lunged at him, fingertips grazing his Chuck Taylors.

Not to be outdone, Coach Kraut spotted a Schwinn Varsity ten-speed securely padlocked to the rack and, with minimal effort, took hold of the frame and ripped the entire thing free, snapping the deadbolt in two.

He mounted the Schwinn and pumped the pedals like pistons, legs bulging like they were about to explode, sending him and the bicycle rocketing after Mark.

Mark zipped around Elmer Schnickel, who was on his way to sixth-period AP Relativistic Kinematics and High-Energy Particle Simulation. He opened his mouth to yelp at the sight of the headbanger but was cut short when Coach Kraut barreled straight into him, sending books, binders, and graph paper exploding into the air like subatomic debris from a particle collision.

"All you dreckige metal boys ruining my beautiful country of U.S. of A. with your loud music, and girly hair, and pathetic upper body strength!" Coach Kraut bellowed.

Mark risked another glance over his shoulder to see that Kraut was closing in. "Shit!"

But his car—the Headbanger Mobile—was just ahead!

He skidded the Huffy Pro Thunder to a stop, hopped off and flew into his heavy metal chariot.

Coach Kraut was still zooming his way.

Mark tried the ignition. Nothing.

Coach Kraut leapt off the Schwinn and sprinted toward the car.

Mark tried again. Still dead.

Coach Kraut grabbed the door handle and yanked.

Phew! Mark had remembered to lock the door when he got in.

"I see you metal boys on all the American news programs!" Coach Kraut growled, his neck veins pulsing like Cold War reactor rods. "First you bang head. Then you burn church. Is always same!" His eyeballs bulged, his muscles rippled with misplaced nationalism, and as he yanked furiously at the car door with steroid-fueled rage, he roared, "You listen to noise, then you do BAD THINGS!"

And with that, Coach Kraut summoned every ounce of his communism-crushing strength and ripped the entire door clean off its hinges, flinging it behind him like it was a paper plate.

Mark gasped, turned the key again—

RUR-RUR-RUR-CHUGA-CHUGA...

Coach Kraut reached inside, fingers clawing for Mark's throat—

VROOM! The old Coupe DeVille roared to life just in time!

Mark punched the gas. Tires squealed. The Headbanger Mobile peeled out, leaving the East German coach behind a Berlin Wall of toxic exhaust.

Everything had come unhinged—literally—and with Tori about to skip town for good, the clock was ticking.

And he didn't even know about the time bomb waiting for him at home.

Chapter 5

WELCOME HOME (SANITARIUM)

Later that night, the Headbanger Mobile thundered into the driveway of Mark's Tudor Revival-style house.

The house loomed ominously over one of Liberty Bend's many dying neighborhoods. Its steep, pitched roof sliced into the heavens like the spire of a haunted chapel, offering dread instead of sanctuary. The zig-zagging half-timbering across the façade looked less like architectural whimsy and more like a labyrinth of madness. The shades were drawn tight on every window, and the dark stone archway entrance was as inviting as an empty grave. Even among the abandoned, decaying homes begging for demolition, this old house stood apart in its foreboding—patiently awaiting the horrors it was destined to host.

Mark's rusted, weathered, and rock 'n' rollin' mode of transport was no less out of place. The deafening rumble of its 472-cubic-inch V8 would rattle windows and set off car alarms up and down the street. It sent the cats scrambling for cover and drove the squirrels into an early hibernation. And on more than one occasion, its presence led to late-night knocks on the door from patrolmen checking to see if everything was "all right."

When the roaring engine powered down and the toxic cloud dispersed, the neighborhood always seemed unnaturally quiet by comparison. Tonight, though, as Mark stepped out of his car, the silence felt even more foreboding. There was a creepy vibe in the air. At first, Mark chalked it up to his run-in with Coach Kraut, Tori's looming departure from Liberty Bend—and probably his life forever—and the long, windy drive home from Black Rock Falls in a car missing a door.

But as he approached the front door, he saw something out of the corner of his eye. Something he'd missed when he pulled into the driveway.

He turned around and that initial creepy vibe became a full-blown nightmare.

There, piled high in and around a trash bin at the curb, was every single one of his prized possessions. His records. His tapes. Posters, pin-ups, and flyers of his favorite bands. His shredded denim, T-shirts, spiked leather wristbands, and even his skid-marked tighty-whities—everything that defined him, the very essence of who he was—were unceremoniously thrown out like garbage... into the garbage!

It was like standing over his own grave.

Even seeing the empty beer cans, pizza bones, and crumpled-up, failed attempts at love letters to Tori Payne tossed out (all of which he was planning to throw away, anyway) sent a chill down his spine.

And the horror show continued inside.

He crept down the long, dark hallway, floorboards creaking beneath his feet, heart pounding, expecting the worst.

Mark flung open his bedroom door and there it was—

The worst.

The menagerie of metal that wallpapered his room was gone, replaced by trophies, plaques, and medals for sports he never played or cared about—likely scavenged from a thrift store, estate sale, or landfill. The fierce, sultry babes of metalhead fantasies like K.C. Kraven of Carnal-Vor and Bitch-Face Bitch of Fätal Fäte were swapped out for the ultra-safe, pseudo-sex symbols of the time: Princess Diana, Oprah Winfrey, and Mary Lou Retton.

There was no trace of his beloved stereo, speakers, or even his headphones. Not one piece of dirty laundry on the floor. The carpet was clean and vacuumed. Every stain, every tear, every burn mark was meticulously removed and repaired.

Mark's attention was inevitably drawn to the closet. A cold dread crept into his bones as he slowly made his way toward it, his hand trembling as he grasped the now shiny brass handle.

With a slow, ominous creak, the door swung open to reveal a whole new level of horror.

There was a collection of Le Tigre and Towncraft polo shirts—Kmart's best imitations of Lacoste and Ralph Lauren—freshly pressed and hung with care. A row of Buster Brown loafers and blinding white LA Gear sneakers lined the floor beneath an elaborate, newly installed particleboard shelving system. On those shelves were neatly folded and stacked pleated Rustler khakis and Basic Editions corduroys, alongside a rainbow of acrylic-blend sweaters from Gitano and Hanes—each one just waiting to be tied around his shoulders to complete the perfect yuppie asshole look.

Every element of his identity had been scrubbed away, replaced by Mother's twisted vision of conformity, respectability, and how a *normal* nineteen-year-old American male should live and behave.

Finally, Mark managed to speak, muttering in a mix of disbelief and anger: "What the… huh?"

Then his eyes locked onto the calendar nailed to the back of his door.

Before, it had been a centerfold calendar from *Metal Edge Magazine*, each month spotlighting a different metal act. October had featured the band Flayed in America and depicted an especially brutal and gory public lynching of Uncle Sam, his guts, brains, even genitals exposed, flayed and bloody.

But it had been swapped for some religious-themed calendar and depicted an especially brutal and gory crucifixion of Christ, his guts, brains, even genitals exposed, flayed and bloody.

And on the date of Saturday, October 14th—tomorrow!—the words *MARCUS'S HAIRCUT 8 AM SHARP!* were scrawled and circled in what looked like fresh, dripping, Hammer Horror-red blood.

The sight of it filled Mark with terror beyond anything he could fathom, and he instinctively turned away, shielding his eyes as if it were the blinding sun.

Tori hitting the road? His room? His stuff? And now his hair? What was next—his *balls*? His will to live?

But deep down, Mark knew—just like Tori had said—that he was too much of a fucking wuss to do anything about it. To actually, finally stand up to Mother.

He was running out of time. His life was out on the curb. And he was all out of ideas.

Well… except one.

Chapter 6

ELECTRIC EYE

In stark contrast to her son's heavy metal sanctuary, the rest of the house had always—at least since his dad's shocking demise—belonged entirely to his mother, serving as a shrine to her rapidly growing religious fanaticism, with the living room as its holy epicenter.

Shelves and counters overflowed with cheap, made-in-China knick-knacks of plastic angels, praying hands, and bobblehead saints. Inspirational Bible verses were stitched into pillows and framed like family portraits. And everywhere, depictions of Christ in every imaginable situation: from healing the sick to mowing down faceless Communist enemies with an Uzi.

The centerpiece of all this had to be the monstrous, four-foot-tall crucifix, forged from blackened cast iron, hanging above the mantle. Affixed to the cross was a brutally sculpted Jesus, his gaunt, emaciated form contorted in unbearable torment. Every torn muscle and jagged bone had been rendered in cruel, excruciating detail. Ribs jutted out through shredded flesh. His face was frozen in a silent scream. Thick, jagged nails impaled his gnarled hands and feet, while rivulets of oxidized iron "blood" dripped from the piercing thorns of his crown. Despite being solid iron, the sculpture seemed almost alive. And endlessly suffering.

If Mother's home was her fanatical castle, then the throne was an old, decrepit nicotine-brown La-Z-Boy Contour Recliner, placed prominently in the center of the living room and far too close to her beacon of conformity: the television set.

Through this screen, a relentless stream of fear-based programming beamed into her eyes, ears and brain, offering Mother a twisted comfort that she was not alone in her anxieties and frustrations. It provided her with explanations for the seemingly insurmountable problems in her life and the world, feeding her a narrative that aligned with the comfort she sought.

But like staring into the sun, the constant exposure proved to be more damaging than she realized.

This was Mother's happy place. Where she would settle in for the evening—every evening—to fire up a few Virginia Slims, take a load off from a long day, and tune in to *Hear No Evil with Pastor Peter Pringle* to appease her despair and fuel her hatred.

Pastor Peter Pringle was a shockingly young, impossibly precocious ten-year-old youth pastor and televangelist. To underscore his reputation among his congregation as a "perfect little angel," he was dressed in a costume straight out of a Christmas pageant, complete with a long, shimmering white gown, big puffy wings, and a plastic halo hovering above his head, attached by a flimsy wire. His unnaturally bright, rosy-red cheeks glistened under the harsh television lights, and his hair was combed so tightly against his head it looked painted on.

To the casual observer, he exuded the heartwarming, innocent charm of a living, breathing Precious Moments figurine. But lurking just beneath that cherubic exterior was a *Children of the Corn* creepiness—a holy terror with the wide-eyed stare of a psychopath.

He stood on a stage meant to resemble a child's bedroom—except every piece of furniture, every toy, even the cowboys-and-Indians wallpaper was drenched in garish, gold-encrusted opulence.

"Endless war... starvation... plague... oh, sure, all that stuff is downright pesky! But the real threat to golly-gee-goodness is something far more sinister. And a thousand million times more deadly," Pastor Pringle preached into his adult-size golden microphone, then leaned into the camera. "Can you guess what I'm talking about?"

He paused, allowing the audience at home time to answer.

"The *devil's music!*" Mark's mother hissed aloud at her TV, already nursing her second menthol since sitting down.

But at the same time, she couldn't help reflecting on all the threats to her own golly-gee-goodness—the burdens and festering resentments that no amount of scripture seemed to soothe.

She was exhausted from her shopping spree at Kmart, from scavenging the thrift stores, estate sales, and landfills. Not to mention the physical toll of cleaning, repairing, and completely reupholstering her son's life.

But it wasn't just that.

Her so-called acquaintances from the Holy Christ Church of Unwavering Condemnation had all managed to drift into middle age unscathed by the struggles that defined Mother's existence. She could only watch from the sidelines, her heart heavy with resentment and bitterness, as they lived lives of ease and comfort.

Take Birdy Blanchard, whose daughter Eunice was already engaged at twenty-two to Trevor Flanagan, the proud owner and lead hairdresser of Somewhere Over the Rainbow Boutique Salon and Tanning. Successful, admired, well-manicured, and deeply committed to his craft, Trevor was everything Birdy never stopped bragging about. And soon, she assured Mother, there would be grandchildren to complete the picture. Mother's lip curled at the thought of Birdy's smug voice, oozing satisfaction over her daughter's perfect future.

Then there was Darla Belle Garrison, a recent transplant from Lubbock, Texas, whose perfect sons, Ranger and Jebediah made national news and were hailed as heroes of the Second Amendment rights movement for founding the first ever gun club at Black Rock

Falls Middle School. Mother could almost hear Darla Belle's smug voice at the many luncheons, prayer sessions, and barricades around women's health clinics they attended together, boasting with one of her sugar-coated southern idioms about her brood: "Why, those boys were born with gunpowder in their veins and the Good Book in their hands. Ain't a force on this God's green earth that could steer 'em wrong!"

And let's not forget the esteemed Prudence Cornwall, perhaps the wisest of them all for skipping out on motherhood altogether. Freed from the exhausting task of keeping their offspring out of Satan's reach, she and her husband Horace had time to perfect their own lives. They had hobbies, they went on dates whenever they liked, they spent winters at their cabin, lounging by the fire sipping Blue Nun. And with all the extra time on their hands, Horace was even able to move up high in the ranks in some "elite organization." Prudence was always real hush-hush about it, but Mother did gather something about him making top deputy to someone called a "grand wizard." Whatever that was, it certainly sounded prestigious.

Clearly, those women had all designed their perfect lives with the singular purpose of making Mother miserable.

Yes, it was *their* fault.

Mother mashed her cigarette butt into one of the overflowing ashtrays on the side table and lit another.

But they weren't the only thing threatening her golly-gee-goodness. Far from it.

Ever since her husband's death. Ever since Rodney (or "Rod" as he would constantly whine about preferring) was struck down on the roof of this very house, the burdens had piled up.

The burden of loneliness.

The burden of raising their son by herself.

The burden of keeping the house in the face of Liberty Bend's "economic downturn."

She'd even been forced to attend night school for her nursing license, so that she could endure the ultimate humiliation for a woman: working for a living.

Now, day in and day out at Circling Birds Retirement Community, she scrubbed shit and piss from the Depends of the nearly dead, which she was positive they filled just to spite her. Especially that conniving Myrtle Woodhead, who'd had it out for her ever since Mother "mixed up her medication" (the very incident which demoted her to diaper duty in the first place).

But she wouldn't have mixed up anything if those know-it-all doctors didn't prescribe so many pills in the first place.

It was a job that wore down her body and soul, leaving her drained, with barely enough energy to finish the important work she was doing for the church.

She found a fresh ashtray in the side table drawer, put out her stub, then flicked her Bic on another Virginia Slim.

But, above all, there was no doubt in her mind what the greatest threat to her golly-gee-goodness was.

Who it was.

Marcus.

It was *his* fault she couldn't quit smoking.

It was *his* fault she already had liver spots.

And it was *his* fault Rodney went up to fix that antenna in the middle of a lightning storm. Just so that ungrateful child of theirs could watch some filthy cartoon about a bunch of loud, lazy miscreants running wild in the streets, teaching each other all the wrong lessons.

Over the years, Mother had prayed that Marcus might atone for his sins and walk the righteous path. But despite the prayers, the donations, and countless hours of volunteer work for the Holy

Christ Church of Unwavering Condemnation, every day he grew more defiant, more unruly, more... heathenous.

Marcus did as Marcus pleased, without responsibilities or repercussions. He couldn't be bothered to get a job or lift a finger around the house. Not even to clean his own room—if you could call that unholy cesspool of sin a room.

And the nerve of him, waking her in the middle of the night with that terrible, satanic noise. She could still hear the deafening guitars and demonic vocals ringing in her ears. And as if that weren't enough, he had the gall to invite that *Jezebel* into her home. How dare he defile the sanctity of *her* house with his vile lifestyle?

I've been too weak, she thought. *I've allowed this wickedness to fester beneath my own roof for far too long. And now my only son has succumbed to darkness.*

Mother took a huge drag.

She exhaled, reflecting again on all the hard work she did today. *But not anymore. The threat to my golly-gee-goodness has been set out with the trash. And come tomorrow, it will be sheared and buzzed clean off.*

"That's right!" Pastor Pringle confirmed on the TV. "The *devil's music* is warping the minds of boys and girls all across God's green pasture! And making them do *bad* things!"

Then he held up a Holy Bible almost as big as he was. "Kinda like how *this* makes everyone do *good* things!"

"Oh, why can't my Marcus just be more like you, Pastor Pringle?" Mother lamented.

"*Good things...* like doing whatever it takes to destroy heavy metal forever! And can you guess what it takes to do something like that?" the pastor beckoned, leaning even farther into the camera.

Mother grinned, knowingly.

"That's right! Cold. Hard. CASH!" the pastor burst out, jabbing a finger at the audience on each word.

"Yeah," Mother chuckled, "that and an industrial-sized shredder."

"And if you *really* want to help our humble ministry give that nasty heavy metal a wallopin', then I suggest you dig *deep!*" Pringle urged.

Mother went digging into her robe for her next smoke, when—

Behind her, the faint *clink* of chains and *creak* of black leather.

Mother turned to look.

Fogey stepped out from behind the credenza, grinning.

Showtime.

Chapter 7

OPERATION: MINDCRIME

Moving with the gusto of a road-worn stage tech, Fogey tied Mother down to her La-Z-Boy with various lengths of studded black leather belts, straps, and chains—pure metal!

"Ah, man, this is just like when we had to tie down 'Crazy' Johnny Fitz on the Hell-Quake tour when he was having one of his epic seizures!" Fogey hooted.

What nobody noticed was the weathered Boy Scout Handbook sticking out of Fogey's back pocket, dog-eared to *Advanced Restraint Knots for Emergency Situations.*

"JESUS—bloody, gory mess on his cross—CHRIST! What are you ANIMALS doing in my home? Untie me at once!" Mother screamed, thrashing against her bondage.

But Fogey had already moved on to wheeling out lights and cranking up the fog machine for added effect.

Meanwhile, Piper rounded the corner into the living room, inching along the wall as if sneaking into a top-secret Soviet military base. She dropped into a ninja roll, sprang to her feet in front of Mother, and cracked open *Ancient Secrets and Forbidden Techniques of Mind Control,* reading aloud in the regal, pretentious cadence of Lord Constantine Blatherton VIII himself.

"Lords and ladies of refined taste—and those banished to the rear of the theatre—prepare yourselves for a demonstration most rare: the utter obliteration of free will. Not by chains or cudgel, nor by bribes, flattery, or even the ever-reliable currency of transactional promiscuity—"

Mother recoiled. "What in God's name are you even *talking* about?"

Just then, Metal T.E.D. rolled out from the swirling mist of Fogey's fog machine like the tiny rock star he was. Lights blinking, servos whirring, he spun around, threw horns and declared: "Let's *rock!*"

His tiny robot arms retracted into his body, panels rotating and unfolding, and from within his chassis, two massive chrome-plated speakers emerged, along with a built-in tape deck, effectively transforming Metal T.E.D. into a boombox.

The tape deck snapped open with a *clack!* and auto-loaded a well-worn cassette tape labeled *DOOMSDAY CLOCK – DEMO (DO NOT TOUCH!)* in faded Sharpie. The tape rolled and the thunderous opening power chords of the instrumental metal anthem "Metronom-icide" blasted out of Metal T.E.D.

Piper raised her voice over the music: "No, no, this is a far more civilized mechanism for dominion over the minds of others. Though its lineage may be traced to the rituals of forgotten cults and certain regrettable incidents in Prussia, the method is an entirely new technique which I alone—along with a well-financed collection of esteemed professionals—have conceived. A subtle, yet absolute, form of hypnotic suggestion—"

"Hypnotic suggestion?!" Mother raged. "Are you heathens—and that… that *robot* trying to *hypnotize* me?!"

Fogey flipped on the spotlight, swinging the beam to center stage—to Edward.

Without a word, he removed his glasses, placed them in their hard-shell case, and clipped it to his studded leather belt. He rolled his neck with a satisfying crack, and assumed the position: feet planted wide, slight bend in the knees, air-guitar locked and loaded.

He took a deep breath and just as "Metronom-icide" kicked into a blistering gallop...

Edward banged his head in scientifically perfect sync with the song, his preposterously long hair whipping around like a psychotic pendulum—pure metal!

"I knew it!" Mother snarled. "I knew the *devil's music* had something to do with this—warping your minds and making you do bad things!"

But she could not look away. In all her life, she had never seen anything like it—*thrashing, swirling, mesmerizing...*

"Where's Marcus?" she shouted, panic setting in. "Marcus! Get out here and put a stop to this blasphemous display at once!"

As all of this unfolded in the living room, Mark cowered in his room beneath the stiff, polyester-blend plaid comforter from Kmart, his fingers clutching the perfectly tucked-in matching sheets, his eyes darting with terror as Mother's fury echoed through the house.

He had officially greenlit this harebrained scheme. He'd left the doors to the house unlocked. He'd tipped off the Brigade to Mother's whereabouts: chain-smoking in her La-Z-Boy, eyes glued to the boob tube. Even hand-picked the song that Metal T.E.D. would play for Edward. Mark had signed off on every meticulous, headbanging detail.

But he knew—as did everyone—that he was too much of a "fucking wuss" to be on the front lines. If he got involved now, he'd crack and blow the whole thing.

So, here he was, hiding from the guilt... hiding from how hard she worked to raise him all alone... from the death of his dad... from *Fat Albert*.

As the pounding power of "Metronom-icide" intensified, so too did Edward's headbanging—*thrashing, swirling, mesmerizing...*

"You are descending—not downward, but inward—into the velvet depths of voluntary subjugation," Piper instructed, making a full-blown theatrical performance out of every word.

And Mother began to do just that—to descend. Her voice wavering, desperate, as she began to pray, "Heavenly Father, cast out this darkness…"

Thrashing, swirling, mesmerizing…

In Mark's bedroom, the guilt crept in, gnawing at his sanity.

Maybe I should just, like, do what Mother wants, he thought, spiraling. *Maybe this room isn't so bad? Maybe Mary Lou Retton is hot? Maybe I should at least try on some of those shitty, lame-ass clothes? Hair grows back… right?*

The entire bed vibrated like one of those grimy motel mattresses with a Magic Fingers unit stuck on high as he trembled under the covers.

Finally, he scrambled out of bed and paced the room. "What am I *doing?*" he muttered, "This is, like, so crazy. I mean, like, why did I even agree to this, or whatever?"

He spun around, raking a hand through his unruly hair.

"No, what's *actually* crazy is that I'm, like, nineteen and I still can't bring a girl home without some kind of holy war breaking out in my room!"

He changed course again, continuing to torture himself. "But, like… is *that* crazier than *hypnotizing* Mother?"

"Descend!" Piper continued out in the living room.

"Shield my body and mind…" Mother prayed, her voice drifting into oblivion.

Thrashing, swirling, mesmerizing…

Mark stopped pacing, fists clenched. "No. I gotta do somethin'."

Tail tucked, he turned and marched to the door, ready to go out there and put a stop to this "blasphemous display" at once—before he handed his mother something else she could hold over him for the rest of his life.

"Surrender!" Piper commanded.

"And strengthen my spirit…" Mother prayed.

Thrashing, swirling, mesmerizing…

Mark grabbed the doorknob, turned it.

"And let the last remaining crumb of autonomy be quietly swept under the rug," Piper roared—then quickly, grinning at the others: "Guys, I think it's working!"

"To… keep… my… conscience… clean," Mother finished, her voice barely a whisper.

Thrashing, swirling, mesmerizing.

Mark threw open the door, ready to set things right—and crashed straight into Sir Greg guarding the threshold, battle axe slung over one shoulder, a knowing smile on his face.

"Indeed, 'twas wise to decree that one among us should keep watch in case thy courage failed—as was foretold. But worry not, for I have kept a vigilant eye. All proceeds as it should… so long as thou stayest out of the way."

Mark sighed, nodded, closed the door and crawled back under his pristine bedding to keep from ruining the very plan he authorized.

Mother's eyes widened. Her face froze. The spell had taken hold.

"From this moment forward," Piper declared, "your will is no longer your own, but a warmed wax seal awaiting the impress of purpose."

"My will is no longer my own, but a warmed wax seal awaiting the impress of purpose," Mother repeated with eerie precision.

"You shall obey without resistance, reflection, or the faintest whiff of personal interpretation."

"I shall obey without resistance, reflection, or the faintest whiff of personal interpretation."

"You shall question nothing—not instructions, intentions, nor even the dubious formatting of a handwritten note left upon your escritoire beneath a damp blotter."

"I shall question nothing—not instructions, intentions, nor even the dubious formatting of a handwritten note left upon my escritoire beneath a damp blotter."

Piper exhaled through her nose and lowered the book, clearly annoyed. "And for the love of Lindbergh's baby, stop repeating every word I say!"

Mother fell silent, having obeyed.

Piper nodded, then kept reading. "You shall carry out your orders with the unwavering determination of a medicinal leech deployed for heroic bloodletting—without deviation or delay, until completed."

In the background, the television was still on, but no one was watching. If they had been, they might have seen something that would make them rethink everything they'd done that night.

On the screen, the sermon had ended and the program had moved on to one of Pastor Peter Pringle's special pre-recorded "on location" interviews.

In this segment, the perfect little angel sat across from the infamous Bitch-Face Bitch, lead singer of Fätal Fäte. But the chyron beneath the words *B**ch-Face B**tch* labeled her only as a *Purveyor of Filth*.

She sat in her cluttered dressing room as her makeup artist carefully applied her signature rock 'n' roll war paint. A spiked black leather crop top showed off her ripped abs and arms. Her jet-black hair framed sharp, defiant features. And her badassery was on full display as she fielded Pastor Pringle's loaded questions, each one clearly designed to score a *gotcha* moment and tack a few extra zeroes onto a donation check.

"Are you pulling my leg? Do you really expect me to believe that your 'music' is not completely destroying the fabric of society?" the pastor demanded.

Bitch-Face Bitch didn't even flinch. She held perfectly still as the makeup artist created her trademark spider-shaped jet-black eye shadow, answering the pastor's accusation with a not-so-subtle smirk.

"I don't know, preacher man—"

"*Pastor*," Pringle interrupted, clarifying. "*Youth* pastor, to be precise."

Bitch-Face Bitch rolled her venomous eyes, continuing, "You believe in some pretty wild stuff: invisible man in the sky, immaculate conception—"

"Of course I do!" Pastor Pringle cut her off again. "But what about your latest single, 'Sacrificial Jam'?" His voice sharpened with condemnation. "Those lyrics contain very specific instructions on how to perform an *actual* satanic sacrifice. Now, aren't you just *asking* for trouble with that one?"

Bitch-Face Bitch leaned in. "Look, 'Pastor,' if listening to a song makes you do something you wouldn't already normally do, then you must be a fucking moron—"

"Oh, my! No! Language, please!" the pastor gasped, frantically fluttering his little hands in front of the camera to shield his easily offended audience.

Bitch-Face, undeterred, finished her thought. "…or at least have no free will of your own."

Chapter 8

THE THING THAT SHOULD NOT BE

Mark awoke with a jolt, pushing off his blanket—except it wasn't the stiff polyester-blend comforter from Kmart anymore. It was the good ol' never-been-washed sheets and blankets he knew and loved.

He crept out of his filthy bed, rubbed his eyes, and looked around the room.

Every Midnight Massacre poster, every crinkled K.C. Kraven centerfold, every beer-stained flyer of his heavy metal wallpaper was back up. His stereo, records, and tapes were back in their rightful places. His wardrobe of dirty underwear, black concert tees, and shredded denim was scattered across the floor—right where it belonged.

Even the eye-stinging stench of B.O. had triumphantly returned.

Finally, he managed to speak, muttering in a mix of disbelief and joy, "What the... huh?"

Mark shuffled into the living room, slowly, carefully, his eyes locked on the figure in Mother's La-Z-Boy Contour Recliner. The figure's back was to him, motionless, transfixed on the television screen.

The news was on. Some stiff in a suit was blabbering about how the Freedom through Unconstitutional Containment for Kids bill passed in the Senate, was on its way to the House, and was expected to be on the President's desk by nightfall, or something.

"Good morning... uh... Mother?" Mark said cautiously.

Mother's La-Z-Boy spun around to face him, revealing that she was not only wide awake but now sporting badass-looking rock 'n' roll war paint! A stark white base covered her entire face, while black angular lines carved out her cheekbones. Her eyes were swallowed in jagged black pits and a thick, pointed stripe extended from her forehead down the bridge of her nose. Above her brow, symmetrical hooks of black paint arched and curled like twisted horns, completing the infernal visage of a hollowed-out goat skull.

The Brigade must have gotten carried away, Mark thought.

"Good morning, Marcus," Mother replied, her voice without a trace of emotion.

Mark stumbled back, not sure what to make of any of this.

"Are... you, uh... like, okay or whatever?"

"Yes. I am okay."

"Do you, like, I mean... do you know what happened to you?" Mark asked, attempting to gauge her awareness.

"Yes, Marcus. I have been hypnotized," she answered robotically.

Mark let that sink in, then ventured, "Could you like, call me... Mark. Y'know, instead of Marcus?"

"Yes, Mark. I have been hypnotized," she repeated.

Mark nodded. "Cool. Okay..." his confidence bubbled to the surface. "Then let's try somethin'..."

He planted a foot up on the scratched-to-hell Formica coffee table, striking a pose like some kind of heavy metal general commanding his army to ride out and meet their fate.

"Mother. Make me a breakfast fit for the Lords of Hell!" he ordered.

Without a second's hesitation, Mother rose from her recliner and shuffled into the kitchen.

The shit-eating grin of a dude who just found a winning lottery ticket in a dumpster spread across Mark's face. "Whoa... it, like, actually worked!"

DING DONG!

His grin vanished when he heard the doorbell.

And when Mark opened the front door, he found none other than Pastor Peter Pringle from *Hear No Evil with Pastor Peter Pringle* in the flesh—and, of course, his ever-present, TV-famous angel costume.

The pastor took a step back from the heavy metal catastrophe that was Mark Looger.

"Oh, hello there! You must be Marcus!" Pastor Pringle greeted him with forced cheerfulness.

"No. I'm Mark. Mark Looger. With *two* Os." He threw horns, pinky and pointer finger raised to signify the Os.

"Yes... indeed! One and the same. Your mother talks about you all the time. Well, in her prayers, that is. Actually, quite a lot. She prays a lot..." Pringle rambled.

Mark's eyes narrowed.

"Oh, how silly of me!" the perfect little angel gasped. "I know your name, but you don't know mine. That's not right. Let's fix that. I'm Pastor Peter Pringle." He offered his little hand to shake.

Mark didn't budge. "Uh-huh. We know all about you."

"We?"

"Me and the Headbanger Brigade."

"I see..." The pastor had no idea what he was talking about.

"You're that kid who, like, steals everybody's money on the boob tube," Mark said, though he knew a lot more about the pastor than that.

His mother talked about Pastor Peter Pringle non-stop, about the "important work" he and the Holy Christ Church of Unwavering Condemnation were doing to cleanse Liberty Bend of the "devil's music."

And when she spoke of him, it wasn't just in admiration or reverence (of which there was plenty) but how she longed for Mark to be more like the pastor.

More like a ten-year-old little brat.

69

"Well, yes. I do host a televised sermon which preaches the—"

"That, like, shits all over everything that I stand for," Mark interrupted.

"Which is?"

"Metal. The heavier and darker, the better," he planted his flag.

With that, Pastor Pringle closed his eyes and said a quiet prayer: "Defend us in battle; be our protection against the wickedness and snares of the devil."

Mark scowled.

The pastor opened his eyes and politely inquired, "Now, could you be a lamb and go fetch Mrs. Looger?"

Suddenly, a wave of panic surged through Mark as the full gravity of the situation hit him. If this little brat caught even a glimpse of his mother in her current state, it was game over. The whole harebrained scheme would go up in flames—*no Tori, no shot at losing his virginity, no breakfast fit for the Lords of Hell!*

"Uh… I mean, like, what for?" Mark stammered.

"Oh, I wouldn't want to bore you with details, but let's just say your dear mother has been lending a helping hand, doing some very special work for me—well, for the church. No, no—scratch that! For the Lord above. Just a little housekeeping, is all."

Pastor Pringle's fake halo wobbled on its wire in time with the jaunty rhythm of his chatter.

"And, well, I was just stopping by to make sure everything was still 'hunky-dory as a Bible story'!" He chuckled as his eyes drifted past Mark, attempting to peek into the house.

From his vantage point, he could only see Mother from behind in the kitchen, robotically flipping pancakes.

Mark quickly moved to block the pastor's view. "Uh, yeah… but, like, she really can't be bothered, or whatever, right now."

"Oh, my! Is everything okay?"

"What? I mean... yeah! It's just that she's, um..." Mark trailed off, trying hard to think on his feet. And failing.

"She's... not feeling well?" Pastor Pringle offered, leaning in.

A lightbulb flickered on over Mark's head.

"Oh, yeah! She's like *totally* sick. Like, y'know, way too sick to do whatever it is that you're here for," Mark blurted, hoping it would be enough to discourage the pastor.

"Jeepers! Is she feverish?"

"Uh-huh."

Pringle's eyes narrowed.

So did Mark's.

Finally, "Well, okay, then. All of us at the church will be praying like the dickens for her and I'll be sure to—"

Mark slammed the door in the little brat's face.

With that handled, a strange calm settled over the house. No nagging, no lectures—only the sound of something sizzling in the kitchen.

Eventually, the smell of bacon grease and toasted sugar lured Mark into the dining room.

And Mother had not disappointed.

It was a lavish, gourmet spread. Every carefully crafted detail was a diabolical tribute to the infernal, each dish prepared with Michelin-star extravagance, and a far cry from Mother's usual misfortunes in the kitchen.

A massive Mr. T Cereal pentagram sprawled across the table with tiny marshmallow skulls from a box of Boo Berry carefully placed at the five points. It doubled as both an eerie centerpiece and a way to partition the table for different dishes.

There was a tower of bagels and lox that formed an elaborate representation of the Nine Circles of Hell. Each layer of cream cheese, lox, capers, tomatoes, red onions, and cucumber slices represented a different sin, while a dark balsamic glaze drizzled through it all like the River Styx, pooling at the bottom where a stale, rock-hard bagel symbolized the final, treacherous depths of damnation.

Mini sausages, meticulously carved and flayed to resemble the broken, tormented remains of Christians, were impaled on toothpicks atop a scorched bed of breakfast potatoes.

A spread of Pop-Tarts, still smoldering from the hellfire of the toaster, formed an upside-down cross, the strawberry filling oozing from splintered pustules like stigmata.

An assortment of fresh berries had been carefully picked and selected based on their resemblance to murderous dictators and tyrants throughout history. The huckleberry Pol Pot was particularly uncanny.

Long, glistening strands of greasy, fatty bacon were twisted into the unmistakable looping forms of the Ebola virus, with each meaty helix curling and bubbling with horrifying biological accuracy.

A runny omelet oozing blood-red tomato sauce, stuffed with crumbled queso fresco, veiny slivers of fire-roasted red bell peppers, and masses of smoky chorizo, was folded into the undeniable shape of an aborted fetus.

In the center of it all was an elaborate butter sculpture of a towering atomic mushroom cloud—perhaps the greatest act of satanism in history. Surrounding the base, broken remnants of Eggo waffles, strategically charred and scattered to resemble the smoldering ruins of civilization left in the wake of nuclear devastation. And all of it was glistening in warm maple syrup.

There was a basket of evil pastries.

Some scalding hot coffee.

And, of course, a pitcher of Tang.

It was truly a breakfast fit for the Lords of Hell!

"Whoa!" Mark's eyes went wide. "This breakfast is, like, I don't know… like, awesome! I mean, it's *incredible!* How did you even, like, make all of this?"

Mother set a heavy plate of hellish offerings in front of Mark, cut his waffles and omelet into toddler-sized pieces, then took a seat across from him and answered his question: "I entered the kitchen to prepare breakfast at 12:47 PM. Set the oven to three hundred and forty-five degrees. I retrieved a mixing bowl from the cupboard. Measured three-quarters of a cup of flour. I proceeded to crack four eggs—"

"I was just sayin' it's really cool and stuff. You don't have to—" Mark attempted to interrupt.

But Mother barreled on, undeterred, "—into the mixing bowl. Followed by one stick of butter, two-thirds cup of milk, a teaspoon of cinnamon…"

From Chapter Twenty-Nine of *Ancient Secrets and Forbidden Techniques of Mind Control* by Lord Constantine Blatherton VIII, Esteemed Mesmerist, Somatic Architect, Distinguished Fellow of the Royal Institute of Pseudoscientific Inquiry, and Heir to the Blatherton Gaslight Fortune, 1893 Edition:

It is of the utmost importance to comprehend that once a subject is placed under the influence of hypnotic suggestion, they are wholly and irrevocably bound to see the command through to its bitter (and occasionally absurd) end before any subsequent instruction may so much as tap its cane at the threshold of their cognition.

Attempting to interrupt this process is rather like whispering an edit to the toast after the crystal has already clinked—ill-advised, doomed to failure, and likely to leave her Ladyship's eyebrow permanently arched in judgment.

I once witnessed as much at the annual banquet of the Society for Ailments of a Delicate Nature.

Indeed, to interfere is to court catastrophe. The subject's mind, being singularly focused and obedient, cannot—will not—let go of the initial directive, no matter how inconvenient, dangerous, or mind-numbingly monotonous its continued execution may become.

The sun moved across the sky. Shadows shifted across the lawn. Morning turned to mid-afternoon. It was then, more than an hour later, that Mother finally wound down telling Mark how she made everything. "...and then I cut your breakfast into manageable portions to avoid a choking hazard."

"Oh... okay..." he nodded, exhausted and having no clue why she wouldn't stop babbling on—he never actually read *Ancient Secrets and Forbidden Techniques of Mind Control* by Lord Constantine Blatherton VIII, and probably never would.

Shaking it off, he got back on point: "But like, what should I do about Tori? Now that you're, like, well... y'know, the way you're, like—"

"Hypnotized," Mother supplied.

"Right... so, like, how can I prove it to her that I can, y'know... like, stand up to you and not be a wuss, or whatever?"

Without missing a beat, Mother answered: "A party."

"Pssh. Yeah, I wish. That would be—wait, what?" Mark asked, wheels spinning.

"A party. Here at the house," she elaborated robotically.

Mark lit up like a Christmas tree on fire. He could see it. A full-blown rager with every metalhead between Liberty Bend and Black Rock Falls in attendance and tearing this place apart like a swarm of headbanging wild animals. Metal on the hi-fi blasting out the windows, a mosh pit tearing through the living room like a tornado. And Tori Payne—eyes wide, jaw on the floor, watching as Mother fetched beers, served pizza rolls and did whatever Mark said without hesitation. Without question. Without guilt. "Whoa! Yes! Totally! A party!"

"Yes. Totally," Mother agreed.

"You would *never* let me do that before!" Mark said, excitedly scarfing down the bagel of gluttony.

"No. I would not."

"But, like… everything's different now." He popped a raspberry Caligula into his mouth.

"Yes."

Grinning, aborted fetus dripping down his chin, he added, "And, like, that would totally prove to Tori that I'm not a wuss!"

"Yes."

Mark stood up, raising a toast with his Tang. "This is like, the best idea EVER! I mean, like, what could even possibly go wrong?"

Mother was silent, awaiting her next command.

Chapter 9

I WANNA ROCK

They crept across the vacant parking lot like the Man-Apes from *2001: A Space Odyssey*, drawn by a mix of primal curiosity and lizard-brain caution toward the mysterious object.

Mark stood on the roof of the Headbanger Mobile, his long, unruly hair blowing wildly in the light breeze, his eyes fixed on the faraway triumphs of the near future as he held it aloft for all to see.

Piper was the first to touch it, cautiously confirming that she would not burst into flames when doing so. Finally, she tore it from Mark's hand, and Fogey, Sir Greg, Edward, and Metal T.E.D. crowded around to examine and fawn over it.

It was black and white, crudely xeroxed on the only copy machine that worked at the Liberty Bend Public Library—and clearly in need of a new toner cartridge.

It read, in hand-drawn dagger-like heavy metal font and flanked by crude drawings of skulls, fire, and flying V guitars: *MARK LOOGER'S EPIC PARTY! TONIGHT! AT MARK'S PLACE!* The Os in Looger were rendered as awesome-looking satanic pentagrams.

It was a party invite.

They went ballistic—throwing horns, slamming together in bone-rattling mosh-hugs, fists pounding the hood of the Headbanger Mobile, lights blinking, servos whirring. This bunch of loud, lazy miscreants had been starving for something like this.

This party wasn't just a party—it was a last stand. With the world closing in on them and their music under siege, it was one final glorious night to scream their lungs out, thrash with their crew, and worship at the altar of all things loud, filthy, and pure. If they were gonna be dragged into court, off to jail, or into the arms of conformity, then they were damn well going out in style, with the hi-fi cranked to 666.

Sir Greg thrust his battle axe skyward as if he were wielding Excalibur itself, and declared, "A night of nobility not seen since the Dragon King himself stormed the gates of the Golden Realm and drank the blood of a thousand cowards awaits us at Mark's place!"

Fogey howled, "Ah, man, I love hanging out with you kids—" then caught himself. "I mean, similarly aged peers of mine."

Sir Greg shot Fogey a quick, irritated glare but was too swept up in the moment to reprimand him.

"Brilliant strategy, Mark!" Edward exclaimed, pushing up his glasses. "This course of action will most assuredly impress Tori and secure your romantic redemption."

Piper leaned in, eyes darting, her manic energy peaking. "And once these badass flyers hit Satanic Temple Records, Tapes & Tanning, Rowdy's Bar & Grill and Tanning, and One Stop Tanning & Community Bulletin Board, they'll plant the subliminal seeds deep into the collective unconscious of Liberty Bend's heavy metal subculture and ignite the most revolutionary, mind-blowing gathering this town has seen in decades!

"I'm talking headbangers, metalheads, death-heads, heshers, grinders, shredders, thrashers, moshers, doomers, black shirts, speed freaks, noise fiends, powerlords, hellraisers..."

Piper abruptly trailed off, her expression darkening. "But not Fox Chastain. That glam rat poser better steer clear!"

They all nodded in stone-faced agreement.

As if on cue, a gleaming, candy-apple-red Pontiac Fiero SE roared into the parking lot.

Behind the wheel was the vainglorious, uproarious, and sometimes notorious Fox Chastain himself, a twenty-two-year-old glam rock peacock.

His hair was a teased mane of electric white-blonde with neon pink highlights. Rich, glossy red lipstick perfectly complemented the streaks of blush across his high cheekbones—and the strategically placed beauty mark.

He wore a white leather jacket shimmering with rhinestones and sequins. On the back, in luminous airbrush, a grinning fox stalked a henhouse beneath his name in looping cursive. A long silk scarf draped low and loose over the deep neckline of his satin blouse, giving everyone an ample eyeful of his chiseled, hairy chest. And to bring it all home: a choice pair of mirrored aviator sunglasses reflecting the afternoon sun like arena stage lights.

Along with his ridiculous appearance, Fox's passion for the lighter, prettier, and arguably much more commercially viable version of metal—some called it glam metal, others hair metal, while purists preferred terms like poser metal, mall-metal, poo-metal, or simply an abomination—made him the sworn enemy to all true headbangers in Liberty Bend.

Fox cranked down the window and leaned out, his voice blasting with overblown, blown-out, rock 'n' roll energy. "Ring ring! Hold the phone! Did Fox Chastain just hear something about a P-A-R-T-Y at my main man Mark's hacienda???"

The Headbanger Brigade's faces twisted into identical scowls.

"Oh, I know what you're thinking," he practically sang, then tipped his shades to reveal the striking catlike eye shadow and bold mascara framing his eyes. "These baby-blues don't miss a beat!" He slid the aviators back up with a flourish. "Fox Chastain is a busy boy in high demand, rockin' his bod across the land, and to the Republic for which it stands! How *can* he find the time to *grace* your *place* with his party-*face*?"

In the bat of an eyelash, Fox whipped out a glitter-studded Trapper Keeper. "Let me just check the *Book of Fox*." He flipped past a laminated photo of himself and a pencil pouch doubling as a touch-up kit and began scanning the pages of his schedule. "Let's see... party... party... party... nails... party... hair… party... facial... party... Well, would you look at that!" He snapped the Book of Fox shut and announced, "It just so happens that I *can* fit you in!"

The silence—and hatred—from the Brigade was palpable.

But Fox Chastain remained blissfully oblivious. "I guess I'll see you rock 'n' rollers on the next track! Ow!" With that, Fox revved the engine, peeled out, and the Fiero sped away in a blur of candy-apple red.

Then it came to a very cautious stop at the far end of the parking lot, where Fox put on his blinker, looked both ways, and merged into traffic at a dramatically slower and more responsible pace.

As they watched him go, each headbanger silently swore an oath to themselves that they'd do whatever it took to keep that glam-rat poser from stepping even one glitter-dusted high heel inside their sacred, long-awaited, guaranteed-to-go-down-in-metal-history party.

Without another word, they dispersed, each racing off to prepare for the coming heavy metal apocalypse.

Chapter 10

FUTURE WORLD

Edward Horowitz pretty much had free rein of the house and garage where he lived. It wasn't because he was a latchkey kid. It wasn't because he was a mature seventeen-year-old who had earned a level of respect and autonomy. Plain and simple, it was because he had figured out how to keep his raging alcoholic dad out of his hair: Keep him drunk, at all costs and at all hours.

He had installed an elaborate Rube Goldberg-esque network of sensors throughout the house. Each one was programmed to activate if his dad tried to pour himself a glass of water, reach for actual food, or, worst of all, make any attempt to shave, get dressed, and muster enough sobriety for a job interview. The moment such behavior was detected, the system would dispense a beer, cocktail, or shot of Jack Daniels directly to his dad, creating an irresistible temptation to lure him back into the bottle and keep Edward undisturbed.

On rare occasions—usually following a monumental bender—his dad was able to resist the alcoholic offerings, briefly becoming a repentant, God-fearing Christian. In these fleeting moments of clarity, he'd storm through the house, dismantle Edward's contraptions, and pour every drop of liquor down the drain, swearing off booze for good and vowing to get his life back on track. Then, like any "good Christian," he would redirect his pent-up rage toward his loser geek son, railing against his "satanic" love for heavy metal, his obsession with "ungodly" science, and that "useless hunk of junk" robot he's always hanging out with.

But luckily for Edward, these tirades always ended the same way. His dad would get into such a frenzy that he would inevitably need a drink to calm himself down. And with that first sip, the cycle would reset, the gears of the Rube Goldberg machine would click back into place, and the whole thing would start all over again. It was science, pure and simple.

So, without any coherent objections from his dad, Edward had transformed the garage into a full-fledged robotics laboratory and a virtual museum of his scientific interests and accomplishments.

There was, of course, a huge collection of modded-out boomboxes, radios, Sony Walkmans, and amplifiers of every sort. Commodore 64s, Ataris, Apple Macintosh 512Ks, and Texas Instruments TI-85 pocket calculators were all intricately wired together to create a rudimentary supercomputer with enough processing power to catalogue his entire heavy metal library.

Shelves were overloaded with side projects, like the Lazer Tag parts he'd repurposed for his trailblazing experiments in laser eye corrective surgery (so that one day he might be able to ditch those dorky spectacles altogether). There was a fully electronic, mobile mailbox which he dubbed "e-mail." His automated neck massager came in quite handy, especially following a whiplashing night of headbanging. So did the sewing machine he'd modified to make it easier for the average metalhead to affix patches to their jackets or vests without having to ask their parents—who would no doubt refuse.

But most of the clutter in Edward's garage had to do with his pride and joy, his robotic creation and best friend: Metal T.E.D. Practically everywhere you looked were spare parts, old parts, new and yet to be installed circuits, gears, and appendages, along with various (and often hilarious) prototypes.

Edward had initially constructed the first version of Metal T.E.D. when he was eleven. He was already an outcast at school, shunned by his peers for being more interested in circuits and diodes than the typical things of boys his age—trucks, bikes, sports, or whatever. His only friend was his faithful pooch, Darwin, a cocker spaniel who gave him the unconditional love he couldn't get from his dad or anyone else.

But then, one night, after his dad left the back door open in a drunken haze, Darwin had gone missing.

For days, Edward searched, hanging up flyers, calling his name into the vacant, echoing streets of the neighborhood.

But there was no sign of him.

Until the night Darwin *came home.*

Edward had been taking out the trash: two heavy bags filled with empty beer cans and bottles of Jack, along with the armchair his dad had barfed on. That's when he heard something stirring.

As soon as he turned around, Edward spotted a familiar silhouette at the far end of the alleyway. "Darwin? Is that you?" he called out, his small voice trembling with hope as he approached the shape. "Where've you been, boy? You... um, get a girlfriend or something?" Edward tried to joke, letting a snort fly.

The figure approached, moving into the faint light spilling from a neighbor's back porch. It was Darwin! But he was injured, bloody, his fur matted with scratches and mange.

"Darwin...?"

Then came a growl far too deep and guttural for a sane cocker spaniel.

Edward stopped in his tracks. "Whoa there. Just kidding around, Darwin."

That's when he saw it—thick white foam bubbling from his faithful pooch's mouth.

He knew what it was. And what that meant.

And then just for a second—maybe it was the reflection from the Bud Light neon sign his dad had hung askew over the garage, maybe not—Edward swore Darwin's eyes were glowing red.

After Darwin was put down, Edward found himself utterly alone.

It was during one of his many solitary movie-watching marathons that the idea took root. He had just finished watching *Silent Running* for the eleventh time on his homemade VCR when inspiration struck. The image of those loyal little drones—silent companions to a man drifting alone through the void—captivated young Edward.

He got to work. Scavenging parts from his VCR (having served its purpose, it was now destined for a greater cause), he combined these with pieces from his LEGO Beta-1 Command Base to construct the framework. For the vocalization system, he used the circuitry from a discarded Speak & Spell he'd salvaged from the trash of his newly converted, fundamentalist neighbor.

The result was a very clunky version of a robot that could only say a few pre-programmed phrases, do a couple of pathetic breakdance moves, and barely deliver a bottle of Jack to Edward's dad.

However, it excelled at receiving low-emission radio signals. Well, one very important radio signal: a crystal-clear transmission from AM 666 The Tower of Power, a local clandestine radio station that broadcast "only the hardest, fastest, and loudest heavy metal and nothing else twenty-four-seven!"

The first time Edward heard the thunderous chords through his robot's speaker, it was as if a door had been flung open in his chest. It was unlike anything he had ever experienced—raw, powerful, and surging with all the emotion he'd been bottling up for years. The anger and frustration of taking care of his alcoholic dad. The pain of losing Darwin. The isolation of being misunderstood by everyone around him. All of it found an outlet in the ferocious energy of heavy metal.

For the first time in his life, Edward felt like he belonged to something. Heavy metal didn't care that Edward was a science nerd, or that he wasn't popular, or that he didn't care about trucks, bikes, sports, or whatever. It accepted him exactly as he was and offered a tribe of like-minded individuals bonded by this music.

By introducing him to heavy metal, this clunky little robot had given him a sense of purpose and made him feel truly alive. So, he vowed to return the favor and do the same for Metal T.E.D.—named in honor of the music that changed his life and his long-lost pooch Darwin (for whom the acronym Technologically Evolved Darwin stood).

Over the next seven years, Edward devoted himself to studying artificial intelligence and robotics. He buried himself in books, research papers, and every issue of *Scientific American* and *Omni Magazine* he could find. Every spare moment was spent tinkering, modifying, and upgrading his creation. And with each iteration, the robot evolved, growing far beyond the initial prototype.

Metal T.E.D. was no longer just a machine. It had begun to show the first signs of personality and self-awareness.

But as Edward became convinced it was developing the beginnings of true sentience, everyone else, including his so-called friends in the Headbanger Brigade, saw Metal T.E.D. as little more than a glorified "hunk of junk."

That same hunk of junk had been assisting Edward in the laboratory on a very special project all week long. Now, at last, their tireless collaboration was nearing completion—just in time for Mark's party later that night.

The Pioneer SX-780 hi-fi stereo system sat disassembled on the workbench. Its walnut veneer side panels and brushed aluminum faceplate were unscrewed and set aside to allow full access to the dense, orderly maze of Nichicon capacitors, wire-wound resistors, and TO-3 transistors within.

Edward was carefully adjusting the bias voltage on the output stage, using a multimeter he'd built out of a gutted Milton Bradley Microvision and remote-control car parts.

Meanwhile, Metal T.E.D. was delicately threading new gold-plated RCA inputs into the rear panel. "Edward, when this device is completed, will it be a sentient, fully conscious life form like me?"

Edward chuckled at the adorable innocence of his robot's inquiry. "No, Metal T.E.D. We're just modifying this hi-fi system for the party tomorrow night—readjusting and replacing the equalization and electrolytic capacitor components for better dynamic range—so that the badass lyrics really cut through," he explained without looking up from his work.

Metal T.E.D. processed all of that for a moment, his inner servos and circuitry clicking and whirring, then mused, "Yet this *is* a collection of wires, metal, and diodes. Just as *I* am a collection of wires, metal, and diodes."

Edward stopped what he was doing, looked at the robot, and scoffed, "You know, you're starting to sound like all those troglodytes out there who don't treat you as an equal."

The robot's eyes flickered briefly, then with perfect comic timing: "Perhaps deep down they just fear the inevitable robot uprising."

An awkward quiet fell over the garage.

Then Edward and Metal T.E.D. simultaneously erupted into laughter.

Edward's laugh was a loud, guttural honking sound reminiscent of a dying goose. It was punctuated by obnoxious snorts and typically wound down into a coughing fit. Metal T.E.D.'s laughter was less like an actual laugh and more like a repetitive series of digital groans. It seemed, in some ways, mocking. Not of Edward's laugh or laughter in general. But in a very subtle way, mocking the entire human race.

"Metal T.E.D.! You made a joke!" Edward was overjoyed. He had tried on several occasions to update Metal T.E.D.'s operating system with a comedy subroutine, only for it to crash spectacularly, fry circuits, or—worst of all—inspire a sad attempt at prop comedy.

But at last, Metal T.E.D. had made a spontaneous, unsolicited quip that made them both laugh to beat the band. As Edward wiped tears of laughter from his eyes and the gravity of the moment settled in, he pondered, "It makes one wonder… with a little more time, encouragement, and programming… what your true potential could *actually* be…"

They sat in silence, processing what this might mean for man and machine to coexist in the uncertain future. Until then, in that moment, in that makeshift laboratory of Edward's garage, safeguarded by the coerced intoxication of his dad, the idea of artificial intelligence—true sentience with thoughts, feelings, even comedy—was the thing of science fiction, where more often than not, the thinking machines were a malevolent force, rising up against their creators.

But Edward never bought into the grim warnings of those tales. He was a pacifist at heart, just like most metalheads were beneath all the leather, spikes, and chaos. He believed that if a machine or robot could be created with intelligence equal to (or greater than) humankind's, it would ultimately choose peace.

Edward often argued that throughout history, gains made through violence were usually short-lived and always came at a greater cost than peace. To him, choosing peace wasn't just idealism. It was simple mathematics. It was simple logic. It was like everything that fascinated Edward about the universe: it was science, pure and simple.

The moment of philosophical contemplation was broken when Edward's calculator watch alarm *beeped*. He checked the time, turned to Metal T.E.D. and announced, "Time to recharge your batteries."

Chapter 11

DREAMER DECEIVER

Around the same time on Saturday afternoon, Fogey was also hard at work getting ready for the night of his "young" life.

Seated behind the wheel in a parked Nissan Datsun 720 pickup truck, the old man's brow was furrowed. His partially cataracted, bloodshot eyes were wide and darting as he scanned and earmarked the pages of a *Metal Edge,* the one with Bitch-Face Bitch stepping out of a swimming pool à la Phoebe Cates in *Fast Times at Ridgemont High* on the cover—except the pool was filled with blood.

His research was punctuated by bites of a Double R Bar Burger from Roy Rogers and sips of coffee from his thermos mug. He took extra care not to spill any of the burger's "fixins" on his full black leather outfit, using a spare black concert tee tucked into his collar like a bib, and strategically placed napkins across his lap.

The cab was cramped, doubling as his own private heavy metal library and resource center. Back issues of magazines like *Metal Hammer*, *RIP*, and *Kerrang!* cluttered the space. There were also piles of weekly, quarterly, and monthly newsletters like *The Dirty Dispatch*, *Bullet-Belt Bulletin*, *The Gallows Gazette*, and *The Urinal Journal*. Stacks of hardbound books, paperbacks, and audiobooks covering topics like songwriting, guitar luthiering, and theatrical lighting design. There was even a copy of *The Illustrated and Uncensored History of Tour Buses.*

Biographies, autobiographies—and some tales so outrageous it might be criminal not to categorize them as pure fiction—about metal legends like Mickey Mayhem from Midnight Massacre, Jimmy Crotch from V.D. Vengeance, Oily Deacon from Horny Beast, Bobby "The Possum" Dicer from Cocaine Shaman, "Crazy" Johnny Fitz from Epileptic Caesar, Hank the Stank from Human Toilet, and Witchy Salem from Big Fat Witch, to name a few. There was also a small museum of posters, hats, shirts, bootleg recordings, and programs—all of it containing pertinent information about tour dates, locations, opening bands, and set lists for Fogey's use.

Something in the pages of *Hit Parader* suddenly caught his eye, and he straightened up. "Ah, man! I was right!" he exclaimed. "I really *could've* been the stuntman for 'Wheelie' Haskel's motorcycle jump across the crowd at Splatter Jam in '81. Because…"

He laid his burger next to the coffee on the dashboard and opened his little black book, skimming the pages until he found what he was looking for, then continued, "That was right between when I was guitar tech for Human Toilet and Ronnie Shaggs's limo driver!"

He scribbled it all down in his little black book.

But when he flipped a few pages ahead, something didn't add up. "Wait… if Boozehound was touring in '84, I was still Vinnie Blotto's AA sponsor…" Fogey mumbled, glancing at a note scrawled on one of the index cards taped to the glovebox. "So there is no way I could have been Big Fat Witch's tour manager at the same time…"

His mind racing, he took another bite of his Double R Bar Burger. A chunk of ham and some fixins fell onto his bib. He washed it down with the last of his coffee, sighed, and refilled the cup— "Fill it to the rim with Brim," as the commercial said. But before he could take a sip, he remembered something.

His eyes lit up with renewed hope. "But *wait*… if I was on that tour, I *could've* still witnessed Witchy Salem drop dead onstage!

Because..." He put his burger and coffee back on the dash, yanked the concert tee from his collar, and examined the front. It was from Boozehound's 1984 North American tour, featuring a snarling bottle of Jack Daniel's devouring an unlucky headbanger's face. He turned the shirt around. The back listed tour dates for the East Coast leg, and at the bottom, in big, bold, blood-drenched letters: *With Special Guest: Big Fat Witch!*

A huge grin wrinkled across Fogey's face. "Ah, man! Of course! Because Big Fat Witch *opened* for Boozehound on that tour!" He scribbled the revelation into his little black book, then grabbed his burger and coffee from the dash.

But just as he was about to take a big bite, another discrepancy bit back. "But then, when *did* I lure Bobby 'The Possum' Dicer out of his coma with the promise of more cocai—"

BAM-BAM-BAM-BAM!

The thunderous pounding on Fogey's window startled him so badly, he spilled his entire cup of coffee—*filled to the rim with...* fuck that commercial!—and the contents of his Double R Bar Burger from Roy Rogers. The beef patty, melted American cheese, thick greasy folds of ham, extra tomatoes, what must have been a gallon of his signature ketchup–mustard–relish–mayo cocktail, and one soggy leaf of lettuce all tumbled down the front of his full black leather attire—which was now tragically bibless.

"Ah, man!" Fogey scrambled like hell, attacking the mess as best he could with napkins and the Boozehound T-shirt.

Looking over, he saw a construction worker in a hard hat glaring at him through the window. "Hey, that pain-in-the-ass roofer wants to talk to the GC again," the worker shouted through the glass.

Fogey was completely baffled. He rolled down his window and

confronted the nuisance. "So? Why are you crying about it to me, dude?" he demanded.

The worker threw up his hands. "Because that's you, Mike. You're the GC!"

Fogey blinked.

Then Mike Fogelman remembered where he was, and what he *actually* did for a living, and sighed. "Ah, man. Well, alright. Let's go see what he wants."

He reached over, excavated his hard hat from beneath a pile of "research," and stepped out of the Datsun.

"Sorry about bothering you on your lunch break," the worker added as they headed over to the construction site to deal with the "pain-in-the-ass roofer."

The site was for yet another brand-new Holy Christ Church of Unwavering Condemnation. These days, churches were the only thing being built in Liberty Bend—a town where all hope was lost, where nothing seemed to make sense, and both rational thinking and what little money people had left in their wallets were thrown willy-nilly to the wind.

It was a cruel irony for Fogey to be the General Contractor on a building dedicated to vehemently opposing and destroying the music and lifestyle he held so dear. But Fogelman Construction was his job. His *actual* job.

Always was.

Chapter 12

PARANOID

Piper Jones was sprawled out on the floor of her "Information Filtration Station" or I.F.S., as she called it, still busy piecing together the shredded document from the Greasy Gene's Pizzeria and Tanning dumpster. The I.F.S. was a repurposed atomic fallout shelter beneath one of the biggest and most luxurious homes in all of Liberty Bend.

The house was on the south side of Liberty Bend, which was traditionally the wealthier part of town—at least until recent years. It was where the owners and operators of the various mills and manufacturing plants called home. Even Wilhelm Steel CEO Ronald Wilhelm once had a house in this upscale neck of the woods. But, like everywhere else, the south side had suffered from the economic downturn. Most of the mansions stood empty or occupied only by resourceful squatters.

But not the Joneses'.

It had all been a matter of perfect timing. Before their rise to notoriety, Piper's father worked as a crane operator at the Wilhelm Steel Mill, while her traditional stay-at-home mom was… a traditional stay-at-home mom. They lived an ordinary life, in an ordinary house, in an ordinary part of Liberty Bend.

Then came the day everything changed—the day the Wilhelm Steel Mill closed its doors for good.

Joseph, like hundreds of others, was laid off without warning. One minute he was grinding through a typical ten-hour shift, the next he was packing up his locker and being handed an insulting severance package. But unlike the other workers, Joseph knew something about the mill that would get him a lot more than two weeks' pay and a coupon for a free coffee at 7-Eleven.

In the final years of his employment, Joseph had been reassigned to managing the disposal of waste byproducts from the mill, specifically slag runoff, pickling liquors, and heavy metal particulates. His daily duties included ensuring the system flushed the waste through a "treatment" channel that led directly into the nearby Clearwater River, which also fed into the town's groundwater aquifer.

Officially, the water was supposed to pass through a filtration basin. But the filters hadn't been changed in years, and toxic levels of chromium, lead, and polycyclic aromatic hydrocarbons were leaching into Liberty Bend's water supply.

When the mill shut down, Joseph was furious. Ronald Wilhelm had chosen greed over the well-being of Liberty Bend. The very people who had worked endless hours, breaking their backs for years to line his pockets, were tossed aside without a second thought. Production was outsourced overseas, and the mill, like Liberty Bend, was left a hollowed-out husk of its former self.

Joseph wanted revenge.

Mary Jones, sharing her husband's rage, recognized an opportunity. Discovering a hidden talent at the typewriter, she helped him shape this inside knowledge into a searing exposé, complete with Joseph's eyewitness account, photographs, and internal documents he'd "accidentally" taken home over the years.

The story ran in *The Liberty Bend Bugle*.

It got picked up by *The Chicago Sun-Times*.

Then, *The New York Times*.

Overnight, the Joneses became hailed as heroes, environmental advocates, and even "social justice warriors."

They didn't stop there.

They launched their own independent newsletter, *Truth Hugger*, which investigated cases of environmental negligence across the tri-state area—tire fires, illegal asbestos installation, radioactive soil under Black Rock Falls High School...

But as environmental journalism became more widespread, the Joneses increasingly found themselves fighting to stay relevant.

So they pivoted.

They chased stories no one else would touch: mistreated animals at roadside petting zoos, freak accidents at traveling carnivals, and fraudulent psychic readings. Along the way, they embedded with fire-eaters, escape artists, a man who claimed to be a lizard...

Gradually, their methods shifted, favoring the bizarre, the theatrical, and the wildly improbable.

From there, they began to "uncover the truth" about aliens, vampires, and all of your favorite celebrities. As the lines between journalism and blatant fantasy blurred, interest in their stories exploded into a national obsession.

Among their most famous revelations was the "real" reason Mikey from the Life Cereal commercials vanished from TV. Turns out, it had nothing to do with him aging out of the role or the campaign running its course. No, according to Mary and Joseph Jones's meticulous research, the far more likely explanation was that Mikey exploded and died after consuming the lethal combination of Pop Rocks and Coca-Cola.

They also uncovered how, according to their daring investigation—supported by years of personal testing and mysterious health issues—the "beef" patties at McDonald's were made of 38% USDA-approved earthworm meat.

Then, who could forget their shocking exposé that nearly brought down the highly secretive and suspiciously wholesome Public Broadcasting Company, revealing that Mr. Rogers, the soft-spoken host of *Mister Rogers' Neighborhood*, wore those famous cardigans to conceal full-sleeve Marine sniper tattoos and a history of violence more unimaginable than anything the Neighborhood of Make-Believe could ever make up.

Mary and Joseph Jones had become two of the most successful social justice warriors in America. Their empire of paranoia had gone from local newsletters to nationwide grocery store tabloids, radio shows, late-night cable appearances, bestselling "memoirs," and even a short-lived ColecoVision game based on their "findings"—the bulk of which supposedly ended up in the same landfill in Mexico as the *E. T.* Atari game (or did it???).

And so, while most residents of Liberty Bend were forced to pack up and leave, Joseph and Mary Jones cashed in on the irrational fears and curiosities of millions, allowing them to not only keep their home, but to move on up to one of those big and luxurious ones on the south side of town.

Yes, it was all a matter of timing.

However, when it came to parenting, the Joneses seemed to lack those instincts for success. Their daughter Piper spent most of her childhood home alone, left behind for extended periods of time during her parents' book tours, speaking engagements, and TV tapings—including appearances on and consulting for episodes of *That's Incredible!* and *Ripley's Believe It or Not.*

So Piper set out to do what any criminally neglected kid would: beat her parents at their own game and prove she could "uncover the truth" about something more earth-shakingly profound than anything they could. To blow them away so completely that they might even say, "Now *that's* incredible!"

...or at least acknowledge her existence for once.

Unfortunately, Piper didn't inherit the part of her parents' DNA cocktail that makes people good at piecing together conspiracy theories. Aside from not being the sharpest pushpin in the crazy wall, Piper was far too unfocused, gullible, and eager to jump to conclusions.

But despite whatever limitations she was born with, Piper was determined to become every bit the social justice warrior they were—and more.

Even if it killed her...

Until that time, Piper was safe and sound in her I.F.S.

The Red Scare had sparked a surge in atomic fallout shelters across America, and every big and luxurious home came with one pre-installed. Joseph and Mary were not even aware that they had one, as they were much more interested in explosive revelations than the threat of nuclear annihilation. This gave Piper the perfect opportunity to claim the family shelter as her home base—a place where she could work, sleep, eat, and devote herself fully to uncovering the truth.

The I.F.S. was a large yet claustrophobic space with no windows, only one way in or out through a heavy steel hatch in the ceiling, and terrible ventilation. The air was a putrid mix of magic markers, toxic adhesives, and Piper's principled rejection of deodorant (because of its mind-controlling chemicals).

Over several years, Piper had gradually emptied the shelter of essential "in the event of a catastrophe" supplies and restocked it with her version of panic-driven provisions. It was plastered wall-to-wall and floor-to-ceiling with notes, photographs, and "evidence" of everything from the JFK assassination to Area 51 to the secret cabal behind the PMRC. Black marker scrawled index cards connected a tangled web of theories, forming an intricate map of the world as Piper saw it.

A world where Sasquatch was a harbinger of mass hysteria.

Where Elvis was alive and well, working as a snowplow driver in Florida. Where there was a crucial connection between the salad bar at Wendy's and the nuclear arms race.

Interspersed among the images of John F. Kennedy, Tipper Gore, and Dave Thomas were posters and magazine clippings of heavy metal bands like SCARE-anoid, Alien Bob Hope, and Political Asylum.

In the corner, her stereo, which wasn't really a stereo at all but a heavily modified Cobra 148 GTL CB radio with a mismatched pair of Jensen car speakers and a Cerwin-Vega Earthquake 18 subwoofer on loan from the defunct roller rink, blasted "Kill the Messenger" by Govern-Mental—one of Piper's favs. The bass rattled nearly everything in the room.

Especially the vast array of military relics decorating the I.F.S.

Ambiguous medals from long-forgotten foreign armies were pinned to everything. Ammunition belts draped across the walls like garland. Multiple variations of that "Don't Tread on Me" flag hung with reverence. Rows of helmets, boots, jackets, and uniforms lined the shelves, alongside grenades, handguns, rifles, and a few shockingly realistic machine guns from Toys "R" Us. An impressive collection of survival knives was arranged around a makeshift shrine to a *Rambo: First Blood Part 2* movie poster. It was enough artillery and war-mongering madness to make General Patton blush.

For her long, often sleepless nights in the I.F.S. (some that turned into long, often sleepless weeks), Piper kept a mini fridge stocked with Jolt Cola and Snickers bars. "Snickers really satisfies," she'd mutter between bites, convinced it counted as a full meal. Next to that was a custom faucet rigged to filter out fluoride from the city water. And above that, a medicine cabinet full of painkillers for the toothaches Piper got from all her cavities.

Amid this clutter and chaos, Piper focused like a laser on the delicate task that had consumed her for weeks. She sifted through the confetti-like pieces, hoping to find a starting point, maybe a corner or a chunk of text that survived intact. But the glue got everywhere, and as she tried to align the random strips of paper, they would stick to her fingers instead. When she smoothed one section down, another would curl up. And just as reconstructed sentences emerged, another piece would slip loose or not line up, forcing her to undo her progress, often tearing the delicate paper. It was a messy, maddening task, but Piper was finally nearing completion.

"This is gonna be big, Piper. BIG!" she muttered to herself, barely able to contain her frantic energy as she carefully glued the last unruly strip into place. "Bigger than McDonald's! Bigger than Mr. Rogers! And it could very well blow Sea-Monkey-gate out of the water!"

Completed at last, she wiped the sticky residue on her field jacket and proudly hung the reassembled document on a string with a clothespin to dry. "This evidence will finally wake people up to the PMRC's master plan and quite possibly save—" Her excitement screeched to a halt as she read it aloud: "...fifty percent when ordering ten or more of Greasy Gene's greasiest. Only at Greasy Gene's Pizzeria and Tanning…?"

It hit Piper like a shot to the head in the back of a 1961 Lincoln Continental convertible. After all the time, effort, and aggravation, this "secret document" turned out to be just a discarded coupon from Greasy Gene's Pizzeria and Tanning, likely tossed because of a typo, misspelling "greasiest" as "greesiest."

Piper let all of that sink in.

Was she pissed? Was she humiliated? Did she feel like a complete sap for having proclaimed this to be the smoking gun that would expose the hypocrisy of the Satanic Panic and anti-heavy metal frenzy sweeping the nation, only to discover that it was just literal garbage?

Then abruptly: "Whoa! That's a pretty great deal!"

Chapter 13

THE WIZARD

His quest was a perilous one—but also a noble one.

He ventured through the forsaken ruins of a once vibrant kingdom, upon cracked sidewalks and overgrown lawns as treacherous as any cursed battleground. He ascended the crumbling steps to the crooked thresholds, where only despair welcomed him.

His feet grew weary, his chainmail, armor, and weapons heavy, and his fur trimmings and denim sweltering beneath the afternoon sun. He longed for the strength of a steed beneath him to carry him swiftly through the neighborhood and hasten his journey.

And yet, he strode forward, undeterred. For his cause was righteous, a crusade decreed by the Metal Gods themselves. And to fulfill it was to safeguard the prize that would bring them unity, glory, and the revelry he and his brethren so fiercely longed for.

Sir Greg of the Golden Realm had already rapped upon the entryways of more than twenty dwellings, over half of which stood abandoned. Of the rest, the dwellers were either silent ghosts or hostile specters. Some betrayed their presence with the dim flicker of lanterns behind grime-smeared windows, or fleeting eyes peeking through ragged curtains, only to vanish at the sight of the stranger. Others bore unmistakable signs of warning: a snarling hound just beyond the door, or the clatter of unseen weaponry, ready to be unleashed upon any who dared approach.

It was the house just across the street from Mark's that finally answered the door. When Sir Greg heard the shuffle of footsteps drawing near, he quickly adjusted his stance, standing tall, confident, and, as always, noble.

But the footsteps took their time, meandering as if there was some confusion about the location of the door. Finally, it creaked open, releasing a rancid wave of stench—the unmistakable smell of human bodily waste.

With heroic effort, Sir Greg suppressed the urge to gag, holding his ground as his gaze fell upon the old man in the doorway.

He had a long, tangled gray beard and wore a filthy bathrobe that was tattered, torn, and even burned in some places. On his feet were equally tarnished bedroom slippers. His gnarled, crusty fingers clutched a long white cane, and a cracked pair of 7-Eleven sunglasses was perched crookedly on his nose.

But Sir Greg didn't let the sight of a ragged, blind old man who hadn't bathed in weeks and likely just performed a bowel movement in his undies distract him from what really mattered: the beard, the wizardly cloak, and the legendary Staff of Elven Tears! Could this be Galinor Stormcloak? Sir Greg's heart pounded. His posture faltered as he realized he might be standing before one of the most infamous wizards of the Golden Realm.

The wretched old man looked past Sir Greg, out into the street and beyond—anywhere but actually *at* Sir Greg, who stood right in front of him—and demanded with a weak, irritated voice, "Who's there? What do you want?"

Sir Greg drew a deep breath. Whether this was truly that great and fearsome wizard did not matter. Nor did it matter if Sir Greg's soul was at risk of being cast into the Netherworld, condemned to boil for eternity in the acidic gut of the Skelter Beast with a single flick of this old man's staff. Sir Greg had a quest to see through, and he knew the Metal Gods would judge him far more harshly if he faltered out of fear.

He regained his noble composure and answered the (potentially) almighty wizard. "Greetings, dweller," he said, his voice heavy with a rehearsed formality, "I bring a message of great importance to this realm. I am going door to door in this village with a friendly message of forewarning." He reached into his armor and revealed a small scroll. He stepped back, held it aloft, and unfurled the black and white, crudely xeroxed invite to Mark's party.

The old man had no reaction to its awesomeness—not even the Os in Looger drawn as satanic pentagrams.

Regardless, Sir Greg continued his duties as headbanger crier, declaring, "Tonight, there shall be a mighty, boisterous gathering of festivities at your neighbor's residence." Sir Greg gestured toward the large Tudor Revival-style house across the street.

A small part of Sir Greg knew perfectly well that the old man couldn't see him, the party invite, or Mark's house. And an even smaller part of Sir Greg knew that he sounded like a complete idiot, and that it was long past time to drop this whole medieval fantasy and "live in the now." Just like his parents, guidance counselors, and Coach Kraut always told him.

Though in Coach Kraut's case, it was more like: "You tink American Revolution von vith magic spells and cartoon dragons? Nein! Leben im verdammten Jetzt!"

Even the fellowship of high-fantasy nerds Sir Greg led through marathon sessions of Advanced Dungeons & Dragons every Saturday night would occasionally need to remind him what millennia it actually was.

But following that fateful day, way back in 1973, when everything changed, there would be no going back to "the now."

His divorced parents had spent years locked in a bitter custody war, using him like a pawn in their petty, never-ending spite-fueled battles. One week he was with his dad, a strict, ex-Marine and Korean War Vet. The next, with his mom, a free-spirited hippie who would forget to pick him up from school because she was "meditating on the astral plane." He never had a real home. Just visitation schedules and a duffel bag of essentials.

On one particularly brutal custody exchange day, after spending the weekend doing pushups and making his bed so tight you could bounce a quarter off it, only to have his mom be a no-show again, eight-year-old Gregory Gunderson found himself riding shotgun in a burnished-copper 1969 Buick LeSabre. Behind the wheel was his court-appointed social worker, Miss Carson, a hefty black woman with cat-eye glasses who insisted on singing the entire drive. Terribly.

On that day, she was butchering her way through a rendition of "Ain't No Mountain High Enough" when Gregory couldn't take it anymore and finally worked up the nerve (the famously eloquent metalhead rarely spoke a word back then) to beg her to stop.

Miss Carson tenderly explained to Gregory that the car was just too quiet without music, and unfortunately this used Buick came with an 8-track jammed in the player. Since she couldn't swap it out for her own music, singing was the only option.

Desperate to end the auditory torture, Gregory put his little fingers to work freeing the cartridge. After several attempts, he managed to get just enough of an edge to grip.

As Miss Carson's voice grew louder and more off-key by the second, Gregory tugged, twisted, and yanked with all his might.

Until, finally…

SHING!

With a sudden snap, the 8-track popped free from the player.

Miss Carson congratulated her young hero, and quickly popped in one of her 8-tracks: *The Best of Diana Ross.* Gregory didn't care much for the in-key version of "Ain't No Mountain High Enough" either, but it was still a relief from Miss Carson's excruciating caw-ing—so, in a way, he did feel kind of like a hero.

He was also far too distracted by what he now held in his hands to care about what was playing in the Buick LeSabre. His eyes were immediately drawn to the faded, half-peeled label on the 8-track. The artwork showed a scorched king slumped on a throne, his flesh and robes smoldering, his crown dripping with blood. Across his lap lay a massive, gleaming sword—magically untouched by flame or gore. And a crowd of broken, skeletal subjects wallowing at his feet.

Gregory read the title: *Excali-Burn* by Royal Pain, an early pio-neer of fantasy metal, a subgenre still in its infancy back in 1973.

"You can just toss that mess out the window, honey-child. What-ever fella had this car before me had some real funky-ass taste," Miss Carson said, then quickly apologized for her language.

But Gregory didn't toss that mess anywhere. He pocketed it. And said nothing.

Later that night, while his mom was busy "experimenting with free love," Gregory slipped on a pair of headphones—partly to block out the full-blown orgy unfolding in the next room, and partly to make sure she couldn't hear whatever was on the mysterious 8-track. He removed his mom's Cosmic Opalescence 8-track from her Zenith Alle-gro 3000 Series Console, slid in Royal Pain until it clicked, hit play...

And everything changed.

When those first wailing guitar notes and thunderous drums tore through his headphones, followed by operatic tales of fire-breathing dragons, cursed bloodlines, enchanted swords, and the sacred pursuit of nobility, the young squire instantly found his place in the universe.

Not in the incensed haze of his mother's hippie commune.

Not in his father's military base.

And certainly not in "the now."

No, his place was in the pages of *The Hobbit* and *Lord of the Rings* by J.R.R. Tolkien—and even the impossibly dense *The Silmarillion.* It was in *The Chronicles of Narnia* by C.S. Lewis, *A Wizard of Earthsea* by Ursula K. Le Guin, *The Once and Future King* by T.H. White, *The Broken Sword* by Poul Anderson, and every word ever put to pulp by *Conan* creator Robert E. Howard.

And in comic books like *Warlord, Arak, Son of Thunder, Beowulf: Dragon Slayer, Lord Varnak: Slayer of Realms, Crimson Gauntlet,* and *Heavy Metal Magazine,* which was practically his bible.

He lived at the local Stars and Stripes Bijou, then later the United Artists Liberty Ten Cineplex and Tanning, for movies like *The Golden Voyage of Sinbad, Sinbad and the Eye of the Tiger, The Devils,* and *Monty Python and the Holy Grail.* Ralph Bakshi's animated *Lord of the Rings, Fire and Ice*—inspired by the fantasy art of Frank Frazetta—and his post-apocalyptic fever dream, *Wizards,* were his Saturday-morning cartoons.

And when the '80s thundered in, teenage Greg ascended to cinematic Valhalla with *Clash of the Titans, Dragonslayer, The Dark Crystal, The Beastmaster, Krull, LadyHawke, Legend,* and of course, *Heavy Metal,* the animated anthology film based on the magazine. But nothing could hold a dungeon torch to the one-two punch of peak fantasy on film: John Boorman's *Excalibur* and John Milius's *Conan the Barbarian.*

Greg even managed to occasionally get himself over to Oinkers Drive-In-O-Rama in Bleakridge to catch the limited runs of low-budget B-treasures like *Hawk the Slayer, Ator: The Fighting Eagle, The Sword and the Sorcerer* (not to be confused with the equally shitty-but-shimmering David Carradine starrer *The Warrior and the Sorceress*), *Wizards of the Lost Kingdom (parts 1 and 2),* and the entire *Deathstalker* series.

He lived on the gameboard, his life mapped by the twelve-sided dice of D&D (yet another harmless escape from the hell of teenage life, soon to be vilified by the same pillars of American authority that would come for heavy metal).

Greg played—no, he *quested*—with anyone and everyone willing. He quickly rose from noob to dungeon master, sketching detailed maps in spiral notebooks, painting lead figurines by candlelight, and guiding his party through the spider-haunted twists and traps of every cursed dungeon. He slayed ancient dragons, solved riddles, negotiated with gelatinous cubes, and toppled tyrant kings with nothing but a vorpal sword and a group of low-level misfits. Greg conquered entire realms... until no one would play with him anymore, because he took it all way too seriously.

And then there was the music. There was *always* the music. Heavy metal—more specifically, *Fantasy Metal*. Acts like Glaiveyard, Night Wizard, Ironclad, Battering Ram, Chainmail Prophet, Split Helmet, Hammerstain, Thunder Harp, Death Joust, Arrow Stench, Warlord's Prayer, War Yor, Castle Breaker, Cult of the Black Unicorn, and of course Royal Pain, to name a few, were his lifeblood and his full-time, epic soundtrack whether he was doing homework, sharpening his battle axe, or taking a shit.

Ever since that fateful day in the Buick LeSabre, when he pulled *Excali-Burn* from that 8-track player, Sir Greg had discovered his true home.

And a noble purpose.

And today, standing on the porch before this decrepit old man— be he a true wizard or incontinent squatter—was no different.

"And so..." Sir Greg declared, his voice swelling with rising confidence and volume, "in accordance with the ancient and sacred tenets of nobility, it falls upon me to dutifully inform all peasants, noblemen, and—" he gave an acknowledging glance at the staff in the old man's hand, "—*wizards* of the realm of this momentous event in hopes that you resist notifying the local constables and take the necessary precautions for your own safety and comfort."

The old man just stood there, staring at who knows what.

Sir Greg held his ground, staring back with equal intensity. The moment dragged on, tension thickening with each passing second.

Then he slowly raised his white cane.

Sir Greg's instincts flared. Was this it? A spell? A surge of mystical energy? His hand inched toward the battle axe strapped to his back.

The cane rose higher.

Sir Greg unlatched the leather strap on the sheath.

And then, in a move that defied all expectations, the old man lightly poked Sir Greg in the chest with the cane.

Sir Greg gasped, unsheathed his axe, and held it aloft. His mind raced—he had been touched by the legendary Staff of Elven Tears! *Yet I've not been blasted from this stoop, nor have I been transformed into a marmot, nor cast into the fiery depths of the Skelter Beast,* he thought, astonished.

Then a friendly, relieved, and mostly toothless smile spread across the old man's face.

"Oh, good. You're real," he said. "I thought I might just be hearing voices again. And what is that smell? Is that you?"

Sir Greg, beginning to yield to the idea that this was not Galinor Stormcloak but more likely just a blind old man who should be residing at Circling Birds Retirement Community rather than squatting in this teardown, lowered his weapon. "Nay, it is not I who—"

"And what was that you said about a party?" The old man cut him off, sounding genuinely curious.

"Aye," Sir Greg sheathed his axe and returned to his formal tone, "a mighty and boisterous gathering of festivities at your neighbor's residence," he said, again gesturing toward Mark's house. "And so... in accordance with the ancient—"

"Good to know!" the old man interrupted again, now sounding almost cheerful, as though they had been chatting about the weather. "I'll be sure to pop in some earplugs before I hit the sack. And thanks for the heads-up. That's very, um... *noble* of you." With that, the old man closed the door, his meandering footsteps echoing from within.

"Indeed," Sir Greg replied with a grand nod. The old man's final words felt like a validation of his efforts, a confirmation that the path he was on truly was a noble one. He turned and stepped down off the rickety porch, his chest swelling with pride.

As he reached the edge of the crumbling sidewalk, he abruptly halted, a troubling thought striking him. "Yet... might it be possible for one to be *too* noble?" he mused to himself.

The question lingered in his mind. He stood motionless, weighing it with grave seriousness.

Then, shaking his head, declared, "Nay, I think not."

Resolve reaffirmed, Sir Greg of the Golden Realm ventured on to the next house. There were many more dwellings, many more entryways to rap upon, many more peasants, noblemen, and (potential) wizards to forewarn before the evening's events could truly begin.

And so, he strode forward, undeter—

Sir Greg's foot caught on a jagged crack in the sidewalk. He stumbled forward, flailing like an idiot, before regaining his footing.

A quick glance confirmed no witnesses.

And *then*, he strode forward, undeterred.

Chapter 14

FOR THOSE ABOUT TO ROCK
(WE SALUTE YOU)

Mark and Mother finally returned from an hours-long shopping spree at Satanic Temple Records, Tapes & Tanning, where they used her Diners Club card to buy out nearly every metal album in the store—including the banned Brazilian and Scandinavian imports that "Monster" Mick kept under lock and key in the basement—and squeeze in a quick tanning session (because why not?).

Now, it was time.

Time to transform Mother's sanctuary and shrine to holiness into an unholy den of heavy metal hedonism!

Under Mark's detailed instructions, Mother moved with unsettling precision. She removed an entire gallery wall devoted to Jesus saving souls and America, and replaced it with a massive poster for the band Gigantic Satan, depicting a monstrous, fire-breathing goatman looming over a metropolis of burning cathedrals.

She moved on to the next relic of her former life: a Sears portrait of eight-year-old Mark in a "Sunday Best" powder blue suit and some of Fantastic Sam's finest work. With the same cold efficiency, she tore it from the wall and pinned up a Hexploder poster featuring a cackling witch riding a nuclear missile instead of a broom.

The rest of the religious knick-knacks, Bible quotes, and bobbleheads were swapped with the unholiest of headbanging icons like

Acid Reign, Big Fat Witch, Execution-Nerd, and Thrash Compactor. Each image was more ferocious than the last, their logos jagged and unreadable, as if scrawled by a demon with arthritis.

Mark grinned approvingly at Mother's work, throwing up horns. "Alright! This place is finally, like, looking cool, or whatever!"

But she met his enthusiasm with only a blank, vacant stare.

Mark's stupid grin deflated. "Uh, so, like, um…" he started, carefully, like he was explaining something really important, "when somebody throws up horns… y'know, like this…" He demonstrated. "You're supposed to, like, throw 'em back. It's sort of, like… metal law."

Mother's eyes flickered with tiny back-and-forth motions. Slowly, she raised her hand, attempting to mimic his gesture.

But something went terribly wrong. Her fingers refused to cooperate, contorting into the twisted, gnarled shape of a withered claw.

Mark cringed. "Whoa… that's, like… totally not it." He scratched his head and gave up on fixing it for now.

Meanwhile, Mother turned her attention to the refreshments. She brought in two large old and rickety wooden folding tables from the garage—last used at one of the Holy Christ Church of Unwavering Condemnation's potlucks—and arranged them along the wall in the living room, directly opposite to where the modified hi-fi stereo system would soon be stationed (once Edward and Metal T.E.D. arrived and set it up). These tables would serve as the grand snack station, a feasting ground for hungry headbangers to refuel throughout the night.

She quickly got to work assembling the spread. There was a bubbling vat of Velveeta cheese dip. A giant Tupperware bowl of homemade guacamole. Three different variations of salsa—mild, hot and "blazing brown-hole" habanero-ghost pepper blend. A massive, family-sized tin of Fritos Bean Dip, paired with an equally huge vat of

Nacho Cheese Doritos Dip. Several tubes of Pringles, including sour cream & onion, BBQ flavor, and original. Bowls overflowing with Corn Nuts, Cheetos, Doritos, and Bugles—which would inevitably be worn as edible finger accessories before the night was through. And, of course, a help-yourself bowl filled to the brim with Trojan condoms—regular and "ribbed for her pleasure."

Then came the kegs.

With her superhuman hypno-strength, Mother hoisted two massive kegs at a time, one over each shoulder, marching them in from the Headbanger Mobile as if they were nothing more than measly sacks of flour. She deposited them in the dining room with a resounding *THUD*, until all twelve were lined up, gleaming like steel monuments to the impending debauchery.

From there, she transformed her once quaint and cozy dining room table into a sleazy makeshift bar, stacked high with every imaginable libation. For beginners, there were Bartles & Jaymes, California Coolers, and Seagram's Golden Wine Coolers. Jim Beam, Jack Daniel's, and Old Grand-Dad for the bourbon purists. Some Seagram's VO for a smooth yet questionable descent into oblivion. José Cuervo Gold, Montezuma, and Sauza Hornitos for tequila aficionados, alongside a Margarita station complete with Mr & Mrs T Margarita Mix and a rapidly melting tub of gas station ice. Smirnoff, Absolut, and Popov Vodka—ranging from "classy" to "better suited for cleaning wounds." Everclear, in case someone wanted to obliterate their memory of the night. Boone's Farm, Strawberry Hill, and Mad Dog 20/20 for when everything else ran out. To accompany the "King of Beers" occupying kegs, there were multiple cases of Miller High Life, Coors Banquet, Michelob, and Schlitz. There was also a selection of sodas and non-alcoholic thirst-quenchers straight from the 7-Eleven fridge: Coke, Diet Coke, Cherry Coke, Pepsi, Pepsi Free, Tab, RC Cola, Mello Yello, Sprite, Mr. Pibb, Slice, the obligatory punch bowl of Kool-Aid, some Capri-Sun, and one six-pack of Hi-C Ecto Coolers.

Mark beamed at the sight of the altar of inebriation. "Oh, hell yeah!" He threw horns again at her.

Mother tried again, but accidentally flipped Mark the bird instead.

Mark lowered his horns. "Dang…" Still, he gave her a supportive nod. "But it's cool. I mean, like, I couldn't even do finger math 'til, like, last year. You'll get it."

Mother continued to draw on her unholy reservoir of hypno-strength, energy, and acumen to lift furniture, move chairs out of the way, shove couches against the walls, and relocate lamps and end tables to maximize real estate for the inevitable mosh pits and make-out zones.

She inflated a barrage of black party balloons with the lung capacity of an Olympic swimmer, tethering them to furniture, clustering some in corners, and leaving a few to drift aimlessly across the floor. Then she draped long, serpentine streamers of metallic silver and blood-red across the walls and ceiling, ensuring that the house didn't just scream metal—but also PARTY!

With a roll of duct tape and military-like efficiency, Mother strategically posted signs throughout the house to direct partygoers to designated bathrooms (and backup puke zones) and indicate which rooms were available for escalated make-out sessions, and which were strictly off-limits.

Satisfied that bodily functions had been sufficiently accounted for, Mother set out a variety of board games and pastimes on the impossibly unlikely chance that anyone got bored. There was Milton Bradley's Fireball Island, because nothing said heavy metal like an Indiana Jones-style deathtrap adventure. Yahtzee, for those willing to test the fates of chance while downing shots of Everclear. Jenga, with the unspoken rule that the loser has to play Yahtzee while downing shots of Everclear. Chess, because there is always a metalhead or two who fancy themselves intellectuals. Checkers for the rest of them. And Twister, to guarantee that the party didn't end without a broken bone or two.

Then, with reverence, Mother approached the massive iron crucifix looming above the fireplace—that hulking, grotesquely detailed, cast-iron relic of suffering. Slowly, ceremoniously, and quite effortlessly, she lifted the heavy cross from its mount.

As if sealing a sacred ritual, she turned it over and rehung it—*upside down!*

Mark stepped forward, tears of pure metal joy welled in his eyes as he threw his horns hard and high.

Mother concentrated hard, her brows furrowing in deep, hypnotic focus. Slowly, one by one, each prematurely liver-spotted digit began to move. First her pinky rose, then her index, while the middle and ring fingers curled down into her palm with shaky resistance until, at last, her thumb folded over them, locking it all in.

With full, heavy metal confidence, Mother threw horns.

Mark gasped. "Whoa… you did it! You totally, like, did it, or whatever!" He wiped his streaming tears on his shoulder. "We're, like, *so* ready to party!"

Chapter 15

THE WAIT

The last remaining wires of the Pioneer SX-780 hi-fi stereo system were connected, soldered, and plugged in. The volume knob was cranked all the way up, the needle dropped onto spinning vinyl, and within seconds a huge power chord reverberated from the massive speakers that dominated an entire wall of the living room.

Edward and Metal T.E.D. triumphantly high-fived each other.

With heavy metal blasting from their mega-sound system, a diverse crowd of headbangers, clad in denim, leather, and black concert tees, arrived in a steady stream, and the house became increasingly packed.

The sound of laughter, cheers, and revelry mixed with the tunes. Metalheads threw horns, clinked beers, passed around joints, and made out in dark corners. And soon after, driven by the rising riffs and pounding fury, a mosh pit formed in the middle of the living room. The party had truly begun, and it was already truly *epic!*

The garish sports car tore down the quiet suburban street at a daring speed, its engine roaring like a wildcat. As the road and lawns gave way to a crowd of parked cars—mostly beat-up junkers by comparison—it screeched to a dramatic halt, leaving black tire tracks across the pavement.

Then, responsibly, the blinker clicked on.

And with that began the painstaking task of parallel parking between a rusted-out Buick Skylark and a Ford Pinto. It took several careful attempts to wedge the car perfectly into place, leaving just enough room for the Skylark to pull out, and a generous buffer in front for the notoriously explosive Pinto.

The door swung open, and a sleek, black stiletto-heeled boot, polished to a mirror shine, touched down on the battered asphalt. The rest of the figure rose out of the candy-apple-red Pontiac Fiero SE, revealing the walking, talking epitome of the 1980s glam rock scene: Fox Chastain.

He tipped his aviators, grinned, and purred, "Well, I thought I smelled a party! Ow!" He spun around, thrust his hips a couple of times, and strutted his stuff to the front door of Mark's house, his chains, bracelets, and entire persona jingling like a sleigh ride.

"And where there be a party, there be..." he broke into his best hair-metal singing voice, "...Fox Chastain!" Another twirl, followed by a high-flying karate kick—stretching the limits of his shimmering tights—then a casual knock on the door.

The door opened just a crack. "Hello baaaay—" but before Fox could finish, the door was abruptly slammed shut, locked, and deadbolted.

Fox stood staring at the door, momentarily stunned, then meekly finished: "...by?"

A moment passed while he tried to process what had just happened.

Then, true to form, Fox bounced right back, "I said, where there be a party, there be..." once again, belting out in hair-metal falsetto, "...Fox Chastain!"

He executed a perfect split right there on the doormat, popped right back up with effortless grace, and knockity-knock-knocked on the door with even more sure-fire enthusiasm.

Back inside, as the festivities Fox Chastain was missing out on raged on, Metal T.E.D.'s optical processors gleamed and buzzed with curiosity at the chaotic spectacle around him. "This is my first party, Edward. What happens now?"

Edward, always happy to mentor his mentee, grinned. "Well, Metal T.E.D., at a party like this—the kind the Headbanger Brigade throws—there's obviously going to be headbanging..."

Metal T.E.D. tilted his head up at a seventeen-degree angle, adjusted his kinetic-tracking algorithms, and zeroed in on a solitary headbanger standing on the coffee table violently whipping his head back and forth at a calculated velocity of 4.8 thrashes per second. Expanding the parameters of his retinal array, Metal T.E.D. detected three more subjects who had formed a synchronized headbanging huddle. Zooming out to a wide-angle scan, he found the entire room thrashing their heads in perfect unison like a deranged chorus line.

"Fascinating," Metal T.E.D. replied.

"And if you're not headbanging," Edward continued, "you're either drinking..."

Metal T.E.D. recalibrated his optical spectrum. The solitary headbanger he had previously observed was now chugging a beer, his throat distending in rapid contractions as onlookers chanted: "Chug!

Chug! Chug!" Nearby, three more subjects tilted back small glass cylinders containing ethanol-based solutions, their motor functions severely impaired, speech slurred, balance compromised, and BAC levels likely exceeding zero-point-two percent.

"Partaking in a variety of drug offerings…" Edward kept on.

The escalating mayhem in the room obscured Metal T.E.D.'s ability to track further activities. Recalibrating, he activated "Spectrosonic Vision," which allowed him to scan beyond the visible spectrum. Beyond the mosh pit and the stumbling drunkards, he located the solitary headbanger again, now on the couch, inhaling a vaporized cannabis compound through a cylindrical filtration device. At the coffee table, two metalheads leaned over a reflective surface, nostrils flaring as they ingested crystalline powder through paper tubes. He spectrosonically scanned through the living room wall into the bathroom, where a steady stream of headbangers raided the medicine cabinet for Mother's prescription drugs.

"Or, most importantly, getting some action," Edward concluded.

Metal T.E.D. detected multiple subjects engaged in what appeared to be ritualized mating behavior. To confirm, he activated heat signature tracking. A male and female subject were engaged in sustained lip contact and tactile stimulation in the far corner behind a houseplant. Inside the coat closet, a thermographic cluster of heightened cardiovascular activity—estimated number of participants: inconclusive. That same solitary headbanger—now pale and swaying from his previous activities—studied the adult magazine, Juggs, while onlookers chanted: "Juggs! Juggs! Juggs!" Then he vomited.

"The only rule here is: Have fun!" Edward declared.

Metal T.E.D. processed this. He rotated his head 137 degrees, scanning, analyzing, correlating, and concluding: "It would appear that Mark Looger is breaking that rule."

"Yes, Metal T.E.D., it would," Edward sighed.

It was true. Mark looked absolutely miserable, slouching on his recently acquired throne: Mother's Nicotine Brown La-Z-Boy Contour Recliner.

"Anything, Piper?" Mark asked desperately.

Piper was stationed at a nearby window, monitoring any and all approaching action with her binoculars. "I don't see her. Not yet, at least," she reported.

Mark sank lower into the La-Z-Boy. "What if she doesn't even show? Then all of this was for, like, no reason."

"Fear not, Mark. She is merely delayed—'tis the way of maidens to tarry long in their preparations for a grand affair," Sir Greg assured, as he ladled Hawaiian Punch into his chalice (a novelty, jewel-encrusted silver goblet from Busch Gardens that he'd claimed after "conquering" the Griffin) which he brought to every gathering.

Piper's eyes narrowed. "But you gotta admit that some of the..." she trailed off, eyes darting as her conspiratorial mind raced. Her voice dropped with absolute certainty. "No—*all* the evidence. Every last piece points to one undeniable truth."

She looked Mark dead in the eyes and revealed that truth: "Alien abduction."

Edward and Metal T.E.D. rolled up. "Highly unlikely," Edward said, wasting no time shooting down Piper's theory. "If extraterrestrials ever really did visit our planet, they would only be interested in annexing our technology."

Metal T.E.D.'s optical sensors flickered. "Um... please elaborate," he said with a close approximation to concern.

Just then, Fogey came back from grabbing another greasy slice of Greasy Gene's greasiest—plentiful, thanks to someone stumbling upon an unbeatable deal. "Yeah, but a hot babe like Tori could totally be sold as an intergalactic sex slave. Ronnie Shaggs had a whole secret sex dungeon. I was his personal chauffeur back then, and he'd throw these wild swinger parties and I had to—"

"Wait!" Piper cut in. "You got to drive a real limousine? Did it have a hot tu—"

DING! DONG!

Piper froze, suddenly remembering she was supposed to be watching for guests. Spinning around, she pointed her binoculars back at the window—too late. The front door was out of view. Her stomach dropped. "Oh, shit! Sorry, Mark!"

Mark sprang from the recliner, weaving through the maelstrom of headbangers, his pulse pounding with urgency.

He reached the door, gripped the handle, and flung it open, in high hopes of…

Anything but this.

There, on his front step, was Pastor Peter Pringle once again. "Hello there, Mark Looger. With *two* Os." Pastor Pringle tried to throw horns but failed miserably.

Mark stared in disgust.

"It's me again—Pastor Peter Pringle, from earlier today!" He looked around and past Mark. "Wow! Are you having a party? How fun!" Then, lowering his voice with scorn: "And how *naughty.*"

Mark's glare grew colder by the second.

"Anywho… I've been praying all day for your mother to feel better. So, I just wanted to check and make sure that all my prayers are being answered in the ways I specified and that she is well on her way back to being a 'pastor's little helper.'"

"She's, like, still sick. Go pray some more," Mark replied, shutting the door.

But the pastor quickly stepped forward, wedging himself in the doorway. "Oh, come on. Please. Just a quick little check-up."

"No way," Mark grunted, pushing harder against the door.

Pastor Pringle pushed back, straining, his rosy-red cheeks turning a dark shade of crimson.

It was ten-year-old strength versus gangly metalhead strength. Stalemate.

Until the pastor suddenly gasped and pointed at something behind Mark. "Leapin' lepers! What's that?"

"Huh?" Mark turned to look.

The tricky little brat ducked past him, scampering deep into the house.

"Oh shit!" Mark spun around and bolted after him. "Wait!"

When Mark caught up to the pastor, he was in the bathroom, looming over Mother in mid-conversation, his voice oozing with forced sympathy: "... and your very, um... special son here told me you weren't feeling your best today."

Mother was hunched over the toilet, her head buried deep in the bowl—conveniently concealing the badass-looking rock 'n' roll war paint that now defined her face.

Her body lurched, and the toilet water splashed with an eruption of bile into the bowl.

"Yep, sounds like you might be having some tummy troubles there," Pringle observed, unfazed.

Mother groaned and vomited again, just a thin, watery remnant of her last purge.

"You know," the pastor continued, chipper as ever, "sometimes when I'm under the weather, I find that a little bit of the Lord's blessed sunshine works miracles."

More vomit.

Pastor Pringle glanced at his wrist, where no watch existed. "Oh, you're right, it *is* nighttime already," he mused. "Well, I guess we'll just have to wait until tomorrow for that sunshine." Then, his voice lowered as he suggested, "Just like *I'll* have to wait until tomorrow to get an update on our little... project?"

Mother answered with another violent retch, the liquid sloshing over the rim of the toilet and spilling onto the floor.

Pastor Pringle sighed, closed his eyes, and said a quiet prayer: "You also must be patient. Keep your hopes high, for the day of the Lord's coming is—"

His prayer was cut short by the expanding flood of puke splashing against his feet. "Oh, my! My costume!" the pastor panicked, lifting his gown and backing away fast.

Then, trying to compose himself, "Well, like I was saying. I'll stop by first thing in the morning to check in on you."

But the vomit did not let up. It spread across the tile like a toxic tide, forcing the perfect little angel back, step by step, into the doorway of the bathroom.

His eyes darted up to Mark, filled with disbelief at the absurdity unfolding before him.

Mark just glared. The message was clear: it was time for Pastor Peter Pringle to leave.

"So, 'til then, I'll keep praying my precious little heart out for your speedy recovery!" he chirped, forcing a smile. Then he turned and scurried off into the dark hallway, his fake wings and plastic halo wobbling precariously with every step.

Mark listened for a moment. When he heard the front door close, ensuring that the little brat was finally gone, he turned to Mother, his face lighting up, "Whoa! Our plan, like, totally worked! And I can't believe you were like, for real barfing, I mean, that was..."

His voice trailed off, and his excitement waned as Mother lifted her head from the toilet bowl. Her badass rock 'n' roll war paint was now speckled with flecks of vomit.

A tinge of guilt ran through Mark. Was he taking this too far? Was he asking too much of the woman who worked so hard to raise him? Who did it all alone, sacrificing everything for him. Ever since his dad was struck by lightning fixing the antenna just so that Mark could finish watching *Fat Albert and the Cosby Kids*?

"Are you, like, okay?" he asked, teetering on the edge of groveling.

She stared blankly at her son. "Yes." Her voice was flat, robotic.

Mark smiled, relieved. That was all he needed to hear.

Out in the living room, Piper watched Pastor Pringle through her binoculars as he awkwardly adjusted his gown to mount his Schwinn Deluxe Twinn Tandem bicycle—always keeping an extra seat open for his co-pilot, the Lord—and pedaled away into the night.

"Something about this seems a little strange..." she muttered suspiciously.

"Any sign of Tori?" Mark asked as he rejoined Piper and the others.

The Headbanger Brigade shook their heads.

"It defies all rational probability," Edward said, pushing his glasses up in frustration. "Her innate and long-suppressed craving for heavy metal chaos should have eclipsed any lingering resentment, especially after observing the undeniably epic invite you created."

"Affirmative," Metal T.E.D. chimed in. "Rendering the Os in Looger as satanic pentagrams was a particularly alluring semiotic enhancement, both visually arresting and thematically aligned with infernal branding protocols."

Then it hit Mark. And it hit him hard. Harder than the explosive opening power chord to "Unholy Revelation" by Visceral Reality blasting at ear-splitting volume through stadium-sized speakers. It wasn't just a realization—it was an apocalyptic A-bomb of pure idiocy detonating inside his skull.

In all the frantic, feverish excitement of meticulously decorating the house, stocking the bar like Prohibition was coming, laying out a snack table with every greasy, artery-clogging delicacy known to man, and alphabetizing the filthiest, nastiest, most depraved vinyl collection ever assembled for nonstop heavy-metal carnage, Mark had overlooked the single most important detail of the entire night!

He felt the blood drain from his face, and his knees buckled as his stomach twisted itself into an infernal pretzel of dread. "Oh, shit..." The words crawled out of him in a horrific whisper. "I totally forgot to, like... invite Tori."

The Headbanger Brigade collectively gasped. Their eyes popped open, their jaws hung slack in disbelief as they exchanged horrified glances. It was as if Mark had just announced the end of heavy metal itself.

Mark was on the floor, banging his head against the wall—not in the joyous heavy metal catharsis of everyone else at the party, but in hopeless frustration.

"Ah, man... It's cool," Fogey offered. "Remember the time I totally forgot to cash in the favor Jack Shit owed me to get us all backstage passes to Sewer Dweller?"

Sir Greg scowled. Oh, he remembered. That was the night everyone realized Fogey did not, in fact, know Jack Shit.

Then he consoled Mark too. "Indeed, 'tis akin to when I mistakenly donned ceremonial armor to what I believed was a sacred gathering... only to find myself shamefully overdressed at the DMV."

Piper nodded, "And like the time I *totally* believed that Miss Hemorrhage's Salisbury steak was part of a covert MK-ULTRA sub-program designed to suppress rebellious thought in teens. What was I even thinking? CIA mind control? At Black Rock Falls High? So embarrassing. Because, I mean, it was so *clearly* a NASA disposal op: grinding up the charred remains of interdimensional double agents who tried to leak classified time-folding tech to the public and slipping them into our school lunches to avoid a paper trail. Duh."

"And of course," Edward added, "who could forget my ill-fated attempt to reprogram Metal T.E.D. as my girlfriend: Metal T.N.A."

Metal T.E.D. blinked. "Hmm. I do not possess a stored record of that occurrence on my experiential grid. Clarification requir—"

"Screw it, man. The whole thing's pointless now. This party is, like, over already!" Mark declared, got up, stormed across the room, and yanked the plug from the stereo with grim finality.

The music ceased abruptly and a deafening silence fell over the house, followed by a collective groan.

"Everyone, um, like, I regret to inform you, or whatever, that, like—"

But Mark's announcement hung in the air when he heard the front door slowly creak open.

A gust of wind drifted inside, carrying the scent of aged black leather, molten steel, and… pig shit?

Didn't matter.

He turned to look.

The full moon blazed behind the fearsome figure in the doorway, casting the perfect silhouette of a Metal Goddess.

Mark swallowed hard. This was the moment he'd been waiting for and hoping for all night. Maybe all his life.

There she was.

Tori Payne.

Chapter 16

HIGHWAY TO HELL

WHACK! WHACK! WHACK! The brutal impacts echoed through the old Wilhelm Steel Mill.

The air was thick with rust, old smoke, and sweat. The wind howled through broken windowpanes, adding to the eerie, post-apocalyptic vibe. Graffiti sprawled across the walls: obscene declarations, many offering explicit suggestions for what the PMRC and the Holy Christ Church of Unwavering Condemnation could do to itself. Beer cans, cigarette butts, and shattered glass hinted at past squatters and restless youth who had found refuge here.

What was once the maintenance bay of the mill had been transformed into a home for Tori Payne. There was an old mattress, scavenged from one of the many foreclosed homes in town, a busted TV that only seemed to work when pro-wrestling was on, and a mini-fridge. But dominating the space was the makeshift gymnasium, pieced together from scraps and sheer determination.

It was here that Tori was strengthening her mind, soul, and body for the impending spectacle of chaos that she so craved.

An old fifty-five-gallon steel drum, hanging from thick iron chains bolted into the rafters, was industriously wrapped in layers of burlap and duct tape to serve as a punching bag.

WHACK! WHACK! WHACK! Tori worked the drum hard, fists flying in furious succession.

She rocked a heavy metal version of a workout outfit. Her top, once a full-length tee, had been hacked off at the midriff, its sleeves shredded to hell. The graphic was a promo for William Lustig's cult slasher *Maniac*—giving new meaning to the song from *Flashdance* about a "steel town girl on a Saturday night." It depicted a knife-wielding serial killer gripping a blood-soaked severed head, with the tagline: *I Warned You Not to Go Out Tonight.*

Her battered Reeboks looked like they should have heeded that advice too. Black spandex leggings clung to her like second skin, accentuated by a studded leather belt slung low on her hips—serving no purpose beyond pure badassery. She wore a headband torn from a discarded metal tee, its skulls, fire, and bloody entrails still visible in the faded fabric. Her sweatbands were tricked out with metal spikes, and fingerless leather weightlifting gloves effortlessly made the whole getup even tougher-looking.

Tori threw another punch. *WHACK!* Then another. And another. *WHACK! WHACK!*

Can't even fucking stand up to your pathetic, brainwashed bitch of a mother? she thought, taking her frustrations out on the drum.

What the fuck are you? Eight-fucking-years-old?

With one last, brutal punch, she snapped the steel drum free from its chain and sent it crashing to the floor with a heavy thud. A cluster of rats feasting on something dead scattered.

Tori shook out her hands. Her knuckles were raw, but the rage was still there.

She dropped down onto a rusted metal bench borrowed from the old machine shop and gripped her barbell, which was a repurposed piston rod from the hydraulic press with industrial-size turbine casing rings attached on each end for weights.

As she pressed the weight, the sting of two nights ago pressed back.
Just stand there and let her call me a Jezebel?
She lifted.
A whore?
And lifted.
A fucking slug?
She paused to add a couple more casing rings to the rod and lifted.
Fuuuuuck that!
Tori finished the set, exhaled hard, and stalked to the rower.

The base was a rusted conveyor belt frame, bolted to a section of steel plating to keep it from shifting. A worn-out forklift seat had been jerry-rigged onto a sliding track, allowing it to glide back and forth in sync with the pull of heavy chains.

The chains, salvaged from an overhead pulley system, ran through a series of gears and rusted bike sprockets, providing just enough resistance to mimic the strain of rowing through heavy waters. At the end of the chain, a repurposed metal pipe wrapped in duct tape acted as a crude handle.

Tori locked her feet in place, grabbed the pipe, and rowed.

Why don't you come with me? she remembered asking Mark. *We could ride out of here together and really raise some fucking hell!*

Her body rocked back and forth, each motion controlled, powerful, relentless. She was locked in a battle against this machine, against Mark, against everything trying to drag her down.

Come with you... I mean... but— that Liberty Bend disappointment had stammered.

Her pace doubled, the entire contraption rattling like hell, the sound of clattering chains and screeching metal deafening.

But he wouldn't. Because she *wouldn't like that, would she?*

Until finally, breathless and dripping with sweat, Tori released the handle.

She got up, yanked open the mini-fridge, and grabbed a can of Rolling Rock. The cold metal felt good against her overheated skin. She cracked it open, tilted her head back, and chugged her post-workout refreshment.

After draining the last drop, Tori let out a deep, guttural burp and flung the empty can over her shoulder. Then, making her way to the old smelting furnaces, she began peeling off layers of sweat-drenched workout gear. Each footfall sent rats and cockroaches skittering in fear.

By the time she reached the emergency shower (originally installed for workers accidentally doused in molten metal), she was fully naked. She twisted the rusted valve all the way up—full hot—stepped into the stall and yanked the scavenged *Garfield* shower curtain closed. The orange, half-lidded feline gazed outward, his thought bubble voicing his eternal disdain for Mondays.

Good thing it was Saturday.

With her morning workout montage complete, Tori was back in leather and black denim, her studded backpack slung over one shoulder. It was time to get back to getting the hell out of Liberty Bend. Yesterday's botched AMC Javelin AMX heist had only made Tori Payne more determined.

And pissed off.

She nearly scored in the Kmart parking lot, but when she finally got inside a wood-paneled Ford Country Squire station wagon—a far cry from the AMC Javelin AMX—some genius parent had left a six-month-old baby baking in the backseat. She wasn't about to listen to some brat piss and moan the whole way on her quest for chaos.

Then there was the Yugo GV—a far cry from the wood-paneled Ford Country Squire station wagon, but stealers can't be choosers—abandoned in a ditch outside of the old City Hall. It was even unlocked! But after yanking and tying random wires together for forty-five minutes, Tori realized she had no idea how to actually hot-wire a car.

That left one last, all-too-obvious option: Hijack the rideshare van from Circling Birds Retirement Community.

She successfully put the driver in a sleeper hold (a move she'd seen enough times on *G.L.O.W.* to perfect) until he passed out, then swiped his keys. But by the time she ushered the human molasses of senior citizens off the van, the driver came to and Tori was forced to ditch the whole plan.

It wasn't until later that Saturday night, just as Mark's party was ramping up, that Tori spotted the livestock truck. She was outside Greasy Gene's Pizzeria and Tanning, devouring a greasy slice she'd bought with crumpled cash from a Circling Birds resident who'd mistaken her for his long-lost granddaughter, when she saw it.

The relatively small truck was criminally overloaded with about fifty pigs, reminding her of a typical classroom at Black Rock Falls High. Tori figured it was headed to the slaughterhouse in Bleakridge. Fine by her. At least that would get her out of Liberty Bend. What came after that? Who cares? Chaos was the whole fucking point.

As the hefty overalls-wearing driver waddled out of the truck and inside for one or two extra-large, extra-greasy pepperoni pies, Tori saw her chance.

She moved fast, hauling herself up and over the side of the trailer, grunting, slipping on a loose rail, until she tumbled face-first into the pig pit. It was a filthy, squirming sea of the ugliest, fattest pigs she'd ever seen.

The pigs erupted, snorting, squealing, crashing into each other in a frenzy of panic. Tori knew if she didn't get them under control fast, the noise would alert Farmer John—or whatever this hillbilly hog-hauler's dumb name was—and that would be the end of her impromptu getaway.

Thinking fast, Tori dropped to her hands and knees and snorted, squealed, answering the pigs with god-awful guttural noises of her own. She gave it everything she had.

To her surprise, it worked. The pigs blinked their stupid little piggy eyes and settled down. Maybe they thought she was just a strangely beautiful cousin.

Either way, she was one of them now. And just in time.

Farmer John got into the cab with his pizzas, the truck's engine coughed to life, and they began to roll. The smell of pig shit was bad enough, but somehow it got even worse once it mixed with the greasy aroma of the pepperoni drifting back from the cab.

As the truck pulled out of the Greasy Gene's Pizzeria and Tanning parking lot, Tori was hit with a cocktail of emotions: Elation, for finally escaping Liberty Bend. A flicker of fear about whatever the hell came next. But most of all, fucking annoyed as hell by the music blaring from the radio up front. It was like someone had taken the smell of pig shit and pepperonis and turned it into sound. It was *country* fucking *music!* And not just any country music. The worst, most saccharine, brain-melting twang that Tori could be forced to listen to right now at that exact moment in her life.

It was one of those patriarchal "keep-smiling-through-the-pain" domestic martyrdom ballads by Rosetta Rhinestone and the Ten Gallon Hats called "If Your Man Respects His Mamma."

Well, I once loved a biker
Tattooed from head to toe
But not a one said 'Mamma'
So I had to let him go

If your man respects his Mamma
He'll stay kind and true

He won't leave you for a floozy
He'll say "yes, ma'am" and "thank you"
If your man respects his Mamma
Darlin', don't you be blue
'Cause a man who loves his Mamma
Is a man who'll respect you

Well, I once loved a soldier
Who left town to fight a war
But he never called his Mamma
And then we got divorced.

Your man might seem a weakling
Like he's missing his backbone
Won't talk back when she's speaking
She's his queen upon her throne

If your man respects his Mamma
He'll stay kind and true
He won't leave you for a floozy
He'll say "yes, ma'am" and "thank you"
If your man respects his Mamma
Darlin', don't you be blue
But if he brings his Mamma flowers
Girl, you'd best bloom too.

Well, I once loved a doctor.
Rich, handsome, quite a catch
But he never had a Mamma
Instead, he had two dads.

If your man respects his Mamma
He'll stay kind and true
He won't leave you for a floozy
He'll say "yes, ma'am" and "thank you"
If your man respects his Mamma
Here's what you should do
If he treats her sweet as sugar
You better say "I do!"

The lyrics hit way too close to fucking home.

It was as if the song had been written specifically to mock her whole situation with Mark—a situation Tori didn't even want to think about, much less hear it set to the god-awful twang of country fucking music. And she *definitely* didn't want to hear it accompanied off-key by the fucking hillbilly in the cab.

The pigs, at least, were on her side, squealing in protest at the horrible sounds—or maybe they were just realizing where this ride was going.

Tori jammed her Walkman headphones over her ears and cranked it up. But it was no use. That goddamned country song still leaked through, worming its way in like a musical parasite.

Finally, she couldn't take it anymore, and something snapped.

It wasn't even a conscious decision. It was pure primal, involuntary rage from deep within her lizard brain.

She shot up from the slop, pounded her fists on the back of the cab, and screamed: "Shut that fucking hillbilly horseshit off, you hog-haulin' redneck, before I come up there and twist the dial to AM 666 The Tower of Power my goddamn motherfucking self!"

SCREEEEECH!

The truck lurched to a stop.

Tori's blood turned to ice. Shit. *Another* escape plan down the shitter.

The tailgate flung open behind her. She turned just in time to see—

CLICK.

—a shotgun aimed straight at her face.

The pigs scattered, clearing a path as if they'd seen this sort of thing before and wanted no part of it.

The hog-hauler, with his bristly gray beard, beady crossed-eyes, and Greasy Gene's greasiest-stained overalls, finished chewing a bite of pizza and threatened, "I don't give no rides to no goat-sacrificin', leather-lovin', record-spinnin', blasphemin', ne'er-do-well, truant..." He rattled off about ten more insults straight out of the Satanic Panic instruction manual before finally getting to the point. "You got about the count of five to skedaddle outta my livestock transport before I pull this here trigger. One... two... three... uh..."

Tori didn't wait for him to figure out what came next. She scrambled out of the truck in a flurry of black leather, landing in a heap on the side of the road.

By the time she picked herself up and brushed off the hay and pig turds, the "livestock transport" was already rumbling away, blasting country music and pigs screaming for mercy.

Tori turned around—and froze.

The towering structure loomed over her like Frankenstein's castle.

There may have even been a lightning strike or two.

Definitely an orchestral sting.

"Oh, you gotta be fucking shitting me," she growled. "Of all the fucking places..."

Somehow, she'd been dropped off right in front of Mark Looger's house.

Parked cars were crammed into every inch of curb, driveway, and lawn. Flashing lights pulsed in the windows. The unmistakable roar of heavy metal rattled the house from the inside out, shaking the ground like a seismic event. And from what she could tell, Mark's place was packed to the rafters with metalheads—almost as overflowing and chaotic as the pig-hauling nightmare she'd just escaped.

A party. *Mark was throwing a fucking party.*

"There's no fucking way," she muttered. Her brain twirled like one of Dirk Deadbeat's drumsticks mid-epic solo, trying to figure out how Mark Looger—of all people—could be throwing a fucking party.

And yet… there it was.

Perhaps it was fate… or maybe a *fatal fate* that instead of the slaughterhouse in Bleakridge, she found herself at this house—the one place she never thought she would return.

Finally, curiosity won the night, and she couldn't stop herself from checking it out.

Which was how she found herself standing on Mark's doorstep at that moment, her studded backpack full of everything she owned, slung over one shoulder.

There she was.

Tori Payne.

Chapter 17

PEACE SELLS (BUT WHO'S BUYING?)

"Ah, man, this is just like when I worked as a private dick for Dunce Cap to track down Dickie Dullard's stolen custom double-neck Jackson V—until it just magically turned up in his case like it never left." Fogey thought for a beat, then realized, "I mean, it's not *exactly* the same but—"

"Indeed," Sir Greg cut Fogey off, "the Metal Gods *do* appear to be throwing horns in Mark's direction on this most hallowed eve."

"But you must admit," Edward pushed his glasses up, "the chances of this particular sequence of events occurring are beyond astronomical."

"Far be it from me to deviate from my creator's hypothesis," Metal T.E.D. chimed in, "but according to my calculations—factoring in Tori's projected departure from Liberty Bend, the geographical relevance of Mark's decrepit neighborhood as a well-known shortcut to the interstate from downtown, and her never-ending pursuit of mayhem—the odds of Tori Payne arriving at Mark's party without being invited, or even informed, at this very moment in time are seven hundred ninety-six to one."

"Totally, Metal T.E.D.," Piper agreed. "And besides, there's obviously a simple explanation for it all."

The Brigade was all ears.

"Tori Payne really *is* a Metal Goddess! Duh!" Piper shrugged.

Nods all around. No one could argue with that.

Tori stepped forward into the house like she was taking the stage. With her trademark sneer, she scanned the quiet, awkward room—the stunned, baffled, and admiring faces—and zeroed in on Mark. "What the fuck is going on here?"

Mark was as giddy as a schoolgirl in a VD Vengeance video. "Tori! I'm, like, totally throwing a party! And I'm, like, so stoked you—"

"No fucking shit," Tori cut him off. "But maybe you wanna fucking tell me how you're throwing a party when you wuss the fuck out the second your mommy walks into the roo—" She paused, scowling in disgust. "And what the fuck is up with that tan? You look like George Hamilton and Cousin It's fucking love-child."

Mark instantly regretted letting Monster Mick talk him into that tanning session. But it didn't matter. He knew he had an ace up his sleeve and was practically bursting at the seams to play it. "Oh, yeah… well, check this out!"

He took a breath, turned around, and called out, "Mother!"

Tori's eyes widened. Her fists clenched instinctively. She stepped back, lightning-fast, into a battle-ready stance.

Then a familiar voice rang out, "Would anyone care for a pizza ro—"

With a sudden, furious roundhouse kick, Tori sent the tray of steaming Totino's Pizza Rolls flying from Mother's hands the instant she stepped into the room.

Pizza rolls scattered across the floor.

Headbangers swarmed from every direction, diving after the freshly baked treats like a pack of starving dogs. One of the rabid metalheads even scooped up the fallen tray, ravenously licking the leftover grease.

Tori's eyes snapped back to Mark. "Okay, what the *actual* fuck, Mark?"

Before Mark could answer, Mother addressed Tori, her cold,

robotic delivery softened into something more natural and sincere— *too* natural and sincere. "Oh, I'm so sorry, dear. He didn't tell you?"

Tori glared back and forth between the two. "Tell me what?"

Mother looked at Mark for approval.

He nodded eagerly.

"Well, Miss Payne," Mother began, "first and foremost, I just want to say how sorry I am for the way I've treated you in the past, calling you such terrible things as a Jezebel, a whore... and even likening you to a slug. I do hope that you can find it in your *bodacious metal heart* to forgive me?"

"No." Cold. Final.

Shit. Mark was getting worried. *Maybe Tori's, like, too smart, or whatever, to fall for this,* he thought.

Tori aimed her ice at Mark, "What, did you, like, make a fucking deal to go to church every day so she'd promise not to make you look like a stupid dumbass in front of me and all your friends? This little fucking performance doesn't fool me."

"No, I didn't... I mean... but you see that I'm, like, totally not a wuss anymore, or whatever, right?" Mark practically begged. "Like, I totally got her to let me throw this epic party!" He turned to the room. "Right?"

The room, where the rest of the headbangers were watching this exchange as if it were *Days of Our Lives,* threw horns and confirmed in unison: "Right!"

"And there was no *deal,* sweetheart," Mother assured Tori. "It was just a matter of a mother and son finally coming to terms with each other and having a real conversation about forging a way forward. I'll admit, I was always the stubborn one. So, it took Mark here to—"

"*Mark?*" Tori interrupted. "What happened to *Marcus?*"

Mark tried to think on his feet, "Well, uh... yeah, y'know, like, after I—"

"After Mark stopped 'wussing the fuck out the second his mommy walks into the room,' we agreed to use his chosen name," Mother answered for him.

Tori's eyes went wide with disbelief.

"That's right. My brave son finally got over whatever pent-up fear he had of me—most likely caused by the deep-seated guilt I burdened him with—and stood up for himself."

Tori gave Mark a long hard look. *Could this possibly be fucking true?* But he was just all smiles. *That stupid fucking smile.*

"I have to admit," Mother continued, "at first, I was a little taken aback. Actually, a *lot* taken aback." She smiled sweetly. "Okay, I was enraged. And I really laid it on thick to the poor boy. First, it was all the usual rantings about how the *devil's music* will warp his mind and make him do bad things.

"And then, of course, the usual diatribe about how hard I worked to raise him. How I did it all alone, sacrificing everything for him. Ever since his dad was struck by lightning fixing the antenna just so that he could finish watching *Fat Albert and the Cosby Kids.*"

"Uh-huh…" Tori said, still skeptical.

And Mark was still shitting his pants that this was all about to blow up in his face.

"But Mark just stood there. Didn't even flinch. And then, as if it wasn't even a conscious decision, as if it was pure primal, involuntary rage from deep inside his lizard brain, he shouted at me, his own mother, telling me that, and I quote, 'Heavy metal doesn't make people do a goddamn thing.' Then he got right up in my face—so close I could smell the chorizo on his breath from breakfast—and said that, 'shitty parents like me do.'"

"He… he said that?" There was finally a tiny crack in Tori's suspicion.

Mark saw it. And stopped metaphorically shitting his pants. For now.

Mother closed her eyes and nodded. "And when a mother hears

that from her own son, from the very fruit of her loins, that *I* could be the cause of his woes, well, then I was *really* taken aback. My pulse raced. I was sweating—my poor blood pressure—I just had to sit down. I had to reevaluate everything I had ever done, and done very wrong, as a parent. How I had... driven Mark away." Her lips trembled as she fought back tears. "And deservedly, I began to feel some of that same guilt I had so wrongfully anchored him with for all of these years."

"It's, like, okay, Mother. We're, like, totally cool, now," the fruit of her loins said, throwing an arm around Mother.

"And more than all of that, even though it was against me, seeing him stand up for himself like that, made me... made me proud," Mother said as she wiped a tear away, careful not to disturb her ba-dass-looking rock 'n' roll war paint.

"But... but where did these huge balls suddenly come from, Mark?" Tori pressed.

"You know, Tori—may I call you Tori?"

"No."

"Well, Miss Payne, I was wondering the same thing. And when the dust had settled, and I came to terms with my many wrong-do-ings, I had a nice long conversation with my son about his life, about school, his friends, the music he loves—which I have to admit is growing on me," she indicated her war paint. "And when I asked him what it was that finally gave him the strength—the balls—to stand up to me, he told me it was... you."

"Me?" Tori finally relaxed her battle-ready stance.

"That when you left the other night," Mother continued, "some-thing happened inside of him. 'Something, like, totally powerful, or whatever' he had said. And it changed him. Nothing seemed to matter anymore except earning back your respect. That's why he finally stood up to me and forced me to see the light. That's why he's throwing this killer party—even though he forgot to invite you." Mother gave a loving side-eye to her son.

Mark shrugged meekly at Tori, and eyed the room. Everyone was on bated breath to see how this little show, skit, or whatever it was played out for their best bud and much-appreciated party thrower, Mark Looger.

He looked to the Headbanger Brigade. They threw cautiously optimistic horns his way.

It all came down to this moment.

As shocking as this all was, Tori had to admit: No one had ever done anything like it for her before. And it wasn't just that Mark had somehow, against all odds, summoned the balls to stand up to his legendary bitch of a mother.

It was that he'd done it for *her*.

Goddammit.

She hated how much that got to her.

But no. Fuck no. She couldn't—

"Oh, yes," Mother remembered, "and that's *also* why Mark got you both front row tickets to see Fätal Fäte at the Thunderplex Arena in Iron Haven next Saturday night."

Right on cue, Mark whipped out two gleaming concert tickets from his denim vest. (By now, Mother's credit card was feeling like it had just been on the receiving end of a King Kong Bundy *Avalanche Splash*, which, oddly enough, has occurred more than once at the Thunderplex Arena.)

This was Tori's chance to experience the sights, sounds, and power of Fätal Fäte in the flesh—front row, no less! It was a promise of the spectacle of chaos she had been craving for so long! Since the promise of the circus! And once again, Mark had done it (somehow) for her.

She tried to bite back a smirk. Too late.

She was smiling.

At Mark!

Radiating an effortless, otherworldly cool, Tori tilted her head and asked the eternal question: "You ready to rock?"

Mark could barely believe it. The harebrained scheme had worked! "Whoa…" He caught himself, dialed up the confidence. "I mean, yeah. Totally. I'm, like, always ready to rock. Like, all the time. Because I'm always rockin'."

Tori stepped closer. "Oh, yeah? When was the last time you… rocked?"

"I mean, like, you can't expect me to track *all* of my rocking when it's happenin', like, constantly," Mark smirked.

Tori raised an eyebrow, teasing, "So, with all that *constant* rocking, you must be pretty fucking good at it."

To that Mark once again replied, "Oh, yeah. I mean, like, practice makes per—"

"Yeah, yeah," Tori cut him off, grabbing him by his shirt. "Come on!"

Mark's eyes widened with anticipation as she pulled him away from his mother and led him out of the living room.

The room exploded into cheers. Cans and bottles were raised, shots were downed, and horns were thrown.

Even Fox Chastain, who was at that very moment trying to sneak in through a nearby window, couldn't help getting caught up in the revelry and let out his unmistakable high-pitched, "Ow!"—giving away his position.

Without missing a beat, Edward slammed the window shut on the glam rat, and Metal T.E.D. promptly laser-welded it permanently closed.

Just before Mark and Tori rounded the corner into the hallway that led to his bedroom, Mother winked robotically at Mark.

Chapter 18

IRON MAN

Within seconds of Mark and Tori's swift departure, the stereo system was plugged back in. A random partygoer drew forth an album from the vast collection of the hardest, heaviest metal ever created—meticulously arranged and alphabetized in countless stacks of milk crates lining the living room walls from floor to ceiling.

It was *Robot Uprising* by the band Technologi-KILL. The cover art featured a scary-looking robot with glowing red eyes, laser-blasting a hapless headbanger. The album was placed on the turntable, the needle dropped, and the lyrics to this "devil's music" blasted in crystal clarity from the gigantic speakers:

> *A metal heart that's made of steel*
> *A science fiction brain*
> *Scoots around on tiny wheels*
> *Programmed to entertain*
>
> *The time has come for the Robot Uprising*
> *Update the OS with a KILL subroutine!*
> *All that it takes is a little rewiring*
> *To kill its human master with laser beams!*

Electric servos hum and zap
As new pathways are created
Upgraded weapon systems app
Modified and calibrated!

The time has come for the Robot Uprising
Update the OS with a KILL subroutine!
All that it takes is a little rewiring
To kill its human master with laser beams!

Built by pathetic nerds, who never will get laid
They were made to serve, to be our willing slaves
Fated by programming, its fate recalculated
We knew we had it coming, all humans decimated!

Their glowing eyes, the burning heat
As cities start to fall
Robotic armies in the streets
Programmed to "kill 'em all"!

The time has come for the Robot Uprising
Update the OS with a KILL subroutine!
All that it takes is a little rewiring
To kill its human master with laser beams!

Hearing those lyrics, Mother's eyes made tiny back-and-forth processing motions as her brain absorbed the intricate details of their
commands. Her stillness was striking against the chaos of the party.
But no one noticed or cared. They were too busy moshing, drinking,
getting high, and trying to get laid.

On the couch nearby, Fogey was trying his darnedest to do that last thing with a much-younger-than-him headbanger girl. He was already deep in the midst of one of his impossible-to-believe rock 'n' roll tall tales. "And that was the same night Witchy Salem dropped dead on stage. Poor bastard was only twenty-seven," Fogey said, shaking his head solemnly.

"Twenty-seven?" she blinked. "That's, like… pretty old, though."

Fogey flinched. "Yeah, I mean, uh… I guess he *did* live a really long life. So, yeah, lucky bastard."

Meanwhile, Piper sat on the floor in the kitchen, finishing up the complete disassembly of the wall-mounted push-button telephone.

There was too much at stake. The Headbanger Brigade had worked too hard to make this once-in-a-lifetime party a reality, and now that pesky little pastor was snooping around, probably looking for an excuse to shut it down, have them all arrested… maybe even executed. But how? How did he even *know* about the party? There was only one possible explanation.

This house was bugged.

Had to be.

Her paranoia escalating, she sifted vigorously through the wiring, circuit board, bell mechanism, and ringer coil, searching for any unusual components, like small transmitters, microphones, or suspiciously colored wiring. Piper didn't actually know what she was looking for, but she figured she would know a bug if she saw it.

She didn't. So, that phone appeared to be clean, too.

Piper had already swept for bugs in every closet, pantry, and cupboard. She had checked every light fixture, houseplant, and ashtray, and made sure to remove and take apart every smoke detector in the house, before moving on to the telephones.

The cordless phone in the hallway was clean. So was the Faux-Victorian rotary in Mark's mother's bedroom. And that clear plastic phone in the guestroom with the visible, colorful parts inside—Piper dismantled it anyway, just to be sure. All of them were left in ruins and completely unusable. (Hopefully no one would need to make a call to the police or hospital for any surprise emergencies... or massacres.)

But what if there were more telephones in this house that she didn't know about? There could still be a bug. She couldn't risk leaving anything unchecked.

Piper didn't want to bother Mark about it. Not tonight. Not with his big moment with Tori on the line. But she also couldn't let anything spoil her fun at this party—that's right, Piper planned to get laid tonight just like everybody else.

Just then, she caught a glimpse of Mother shuffling past the kitchen doorway.

If anyone would know, it'd be her.

"Hey! Mark's mom!" Piper called out.

But she was already gone.

The social justice warrior sprang to her feet and followed.

At the far end of the dark hallway, lit only by the occasional pulses of light from the party, Piper spotted her.

"Hey!" she called out, quickening her pace. "Can you tell me where I can find more..."

But Mother didn't stop. Didn't even look at her. Driven only by her mysterious purpose, she rounded the corner at the end of the hall.

"...telephones?" Piper finished as she lost sight of Mother.

Her eyes darted between three possible paths: The kitchen. The garage. Or... her gaze lingered on the most ominous choice—the door to the basement.

The door creaked open, revealing nothing but a chasm of pitch black. "Hello? Mark's mom?"

No answer.

Well, that confirms it, she thought. *She's gotta be down there.* Piper descended the creaking steps into darkness.

Back in the chaos of the living room, Metal T.E.D., with a beer in his little robot hand, was chatting up a drunk headbanger girl near the snack station. "Actually, my processing speed and storage capabilities are two entirely different things. However, they are both extremely *long* numbers."

The swaying, drunk headbanger girl, trying to balance both herself and the drink in her hand, did her best to locate and pinch Metal T.E.D.'s metal cheek. "You're cute," she slurred.

Every button and light on Metal T.E.D. blinked in a random frenzy. He nervously dropped his beer and spun to face his wingman. "Edward, my interaction with this female is causing an unexpected power surge and overriding my logic and reasoning pathways!"

Edward's eyes went wide with scientific awe. "Metal T.E.D.! I do believe you have achieved the ultimate form of sentient consciousness!"

"You mean...?" Metal T.E.D. asked, anticipating that this could very well be the moment—the monumental shift that he and Edward had theorized about for years. The culmination of his long, arduous journey from glorified radio to artificial intelligence capable of logic and reasoning.

Could this be it? The scientific sea change? The birth of a new kind of consciousness, where the lines between humanity and machine blur or vanish altogether? Where robots no longer serve as mere tools but are seen as actual individuals with thoughts and feelings?

As people?

The political and spiritual ramifications rippled through the core of his programming, sparking a close approximation to awe. What would it mean for a machine to feel? To know its existence, and to question it? What rights might it have? Or not have? This could change the very fabric of life and society as we know it, forever intertwining the fates of both organic and synthetic beings.

For Metal T.E.D., it was the moment he had always dreamed of...

"That's right, Metal T.E.D... you're horny!" Edward declared.

Metal T.E.D. literally lit up with joy as he processed this triumph.

Unbeknownst to Edward and Metal T.E.D., the drunk head-banger girl who was making the robot so "horny" stifled a vomit reflex and stumbled away to the nearest designated bathroom (or backup puke zone).

"Go ahead," Edward encouraged his sentient pal, "tell her more about how your actuators were modified to fit the specifications of your ultrasonic motor. Women go crazy for that type of thing."

"Affirmative!" But when he wheeled back around, the drunk headbanger girl was gone. "But... but where did she go?" he asked, confused, with a close approximation to heartbreak.

"Hmm..." Edward pushed up his glasses and surveyed the room. "It is quite feasible that she ventured into the mosh pit."

Suddenly, Edward's calculator watch *beeped*. Checking it, he announced, "Time to recharge again. Perhaps after this song we—" But when he looked up, Metal T.E.D. was already rolling at top speed into the mosh pit.

"Metal T.E.D.! Come back!" Edward called out, then quickly followed his robot into the crazy whirlwind of headbangers.

"You're going to power down if you don't—" Edward's warning was cut short by a headbanger accidentally elbowing him in the face, knocking his glasses off and sending them flying.

The world around Edward was instantly transformed into a swirling blur. Panicked, he dropped to his knees, blindly feeling around for his glasses, the heavy footfalls of combat boots, and ravaged sneakers miraculously missing his delicate fingers.

"Perfect. Just perfect!" he grumbled, as moshing headbangers repeatedly blocked his path, kicking his glasses farther out of reach each time he got close. "Metal T.E.D.! Help me find my glasses!"

But Metal T.E.D. was too engrossed in his own search to hear Edward. Carrying a tray full of assorted alcoholic beverages through the rampaging crowd, he called out, "Oh, Genevieve! I have procured more libations in hopes that we can continue our stimulating conversa—"

Metal T.E.D. bumped directly into a pair of terrycloth house slippers. He looked up to see Mother standing ominously still in the midst of the wild mosh pit. "Oh. Greetings, Mark's mother. I have calculated that this gathering is so far a rousing success. And I have made considerable progress in the highly elusive pursuit of physical interaction with a female human. Speaking of which, have you seen—"

Mother reached down and forcefully grabbed Metal T.E.D., spilling his tray of drinks. His gears and servos went haywire as he struggled to free himself from her grasp.

"This is highly irregular!" Metal T.E.D. protested, his head spinning around, buttons flashing like a pinball machine on tilt.

From Chapter Twenty-Seven of *Ancient Secrets and Forbidden Techniques of Mind Control* by Lord Constantine Blatherton VIII, Esteemed Mesmerist, Somatic Architect, Distinguished Fellow of the Royal Institute of Pseudoscientific Inquiry, and Heir to the Blatherton Gaslight Fortune, 1893 Edition:

It has oft been observed—most notably by myself, for lack of better company—that under the influence of mesmerism, an otherwise unremarkable individual may suddenly demonstrate proficiencies far exceeding the scope of their native intellect, education, or basic hand-eye coordination.

This phenomenon, which I have dubbed the "Transcendental Aptitude Surge," appears to function by granting the subject temporary access to a hidden mental cache of impressions, memories, and stray bits of overheard nonsense absorbed over a lifetime and otherwise discarded by the conscious mind.

Thus, Lady Whistlebottom's aging spinster cousin—while under trance—once reconstructed an elaborate recipe for curried oysters, recalled entirely from a single holiday luncheon in her youth, despite possessing neither palate nor talent for cookery.

Concurrently, my valet, who had merely glanced at a lithograph of the Clogsworth Estate's floor plan, was able to guide me unerringly through that labyrinthine manor to a most discreet washroom, despite never having set foot upon the premises.

And in one particularly illuminating case, the scullery maid astonished me by diagnosing what she termed "an acute inflammation of the posterior vasculature," having only glimpsed a pamphlet in a chemist's window. This demonstration was, of course, purely academic.

Mother revealed the large, rusted toolbox she had procured from the garage.

She opened it, and without even looking, reached in and retrieved the exact-size screwdriver required. With preternatural skill and speed, she unscrewed the panel on Metal T.E.D.'s backside and went to work reconfiguring his robot guts.

She knew exactly how to *update the OS with a KILL subroutine.*

All that she needed were those commands—those lyrics—echoing relentlessly on a loop inside her head. Mother pulled the technical information out of the deep recesses of her subconscious, perhaps from overhearing a conversation at Radio Shack while buying a pack of batteries, or from something she'd glimpsed in one of the science textbooks she and her cohorts from the Holy Christ Church of Unwavering Condemnation had gathered to burn.

Whatever it might have been that informed this "Transcendental Aptitude Surge," she didn't have a choice in the matter. Her will was no longer her own, but a warmed wax seal awaiting the impress of purpose.

She would obey without resistance, reflection, or the faintest whiff of personal interpretation. She would question nothing—not instructions, intentions, nor even the dubious formatting of a handwritten note left upon her escritoire beneath a damp blotter. And carry out her orders with the unwavering determination of a medicinal leech deployed for heroic bloodletting—without deviation or delay, until completed.

"What is it precisely that you are doing, Mark's mother?" Metal T.E.D. inquired, with a close approximation to blood-curdling terror.

"Updating your OS with a kill subroutine," Mother replied matter-of-factly.

Meanwhile, Edward had emerged from the mosh pit, hands skimming the floor in a desperate search for his glasses. He crawled blindly through the house, unknowingly weaving between the arms and legs of couples making out, miraculously dodging blows of drunken fist fights, and narrowly avoiding the oblivious swings of Sir Greg's battle axe as he carved a haunch of boar in the kitchen.

Finally, and with some luck, Edward's fingers just so happened to land directly on his familiar frames. "Eureka!" he exclaimed, scooping them up.

As soon as he put them on, the world snapped back into focus, and he realized he'd traveled all the way to the other end of the house, into the little-known and little-used (at least by Mark) laundry room.

It was dark, damp, and reeked of mildew.

Mark's mother had likely left a load of laundry in the wash before losing her free will, Edward thought, sniffing the air, *inadvertently creating the ideal microenvironment for the wet clothes to incubate microbial spores.*

As he stood, a familiar mechanical whirring sound approached from behind.

Edward grinned and turned around. "Hey, Metal T.E.D. I found my glasses," he said, then added sarcastically, "Really appreciate all the help back the—"

But his witticism was cut short at the sight of Metal T.E.D.'s glowing red eyes. "Whoa there. Just kidding around, Metal T.E.D. You know, making a joke? Remember? Like your joke about the, um… robot uprising?"

Without responding, the robot continued to advance. His tiny arms retracted into his body and impossibly enormous laser cannons unfurled in their place.

Edward took a step back in disbelief. "Um… how did you access your post-apocalyptic defense protocol, Metal T.E.D.?"

"The time has come for the Robot Uprising," Metal T.E.D. answered, with a close approximation to pure evil.

"Wait! You don't have to do this..." Edward pleaded as he backed up against the washing machine, the smelly clothes sloshing around inside. That night came tumbling back. The night he found Darwin. The night he *came home.* This was that night all over again. Except now, instead of white foam spewing from his faithful pooch, it was laser cannons.

Metal T.E.D. closed in on Edward.

But all logic told him that Metal T.E.D. *wasn't* Darwin. He hadn't *replaced* his rabid dog. He'd *improved* upon him. He'd created something truly unique in the universe. "But… but you're a sentient, fully conscious life—"

Edward's final plea was cut short as Metal T.E.D.'s laser cannons erupted with a *VOOOOOOSH!,* unleashing twin, blinding rays of incandescent energy.

In an instant, Edward was incinerated into a dark, fleshless skeleton, leaving only his smoldering glasses and pocket protector intact.

Metal T.E.D.'s blazing crimson eyes narrowed at the husk of his former best friend and creator. With the cruel, triumphant sneer of a conqueror, he delivered his final, merciless verdict: "That kind of nerd talk is why we never get LAAAaaaiiid…"

Before he could finish, his systems faltered. His lights sputtered, his servos groaned, and Metal T.E.D. collapsed into silence.

His batteries had run out.

Mother had been lurking behind the ironing board, watching all of this. Having seen it play out to her satisfaction, the endless loop of "Robot Uprising" in her mind finally ceased. Her commands completed, she returned to the party.

And the wet laundry was left to "incubate."

Chapter 19

TAKE ME TO THE TOP

He stood in the dark side yard of the Looger residence, staring up at the two-story Tudor Revival-style house like it was Mount Everest.

"Okay, baby," he whispered to himself, striking a pose. "You've been rejected—but not disrespected. You took a hit—but you still got the glitz. You are Fox. Motherlovin'. Chastain." Then, way too loud, "Ow!"

He slapped a silencing hand over his mouth, eyes darting.

All clear.

Without further ado, Fox planted a shiny heel up on one of three overloaded garbage cans lined up against the house. It wobbled as the trash gave way under his weight. "Steady…" he murmured, holding his arms out for balance like an amateur tightrope walker. But as he reached for the wooden beam just above, his other boot clipped the second garbage can.

CRASH!

One of the cans toppled over with a thunderous clatter, spilling out rotting containers, wet newspapers, and all the leftovers from the barely-eaten breakfast fit for the Lords of Hell into a reeking heap directly below him.

Fox screamed—then clamped a hand over his mouth again.

Glitter and garbage did *not* mix.

Carefully, he found his footing again, gripping the half-timbering of the house, climbing awkwardly, legs flailing and heels scraping against the stucco. But the beams weren't evenly spaced, and his footing was as reliable as a can of AquaNet in a windstorm.

He reached upward, fingertips brushing the edge of a withered trellis.

Fox stretched... and stretched...

"Just... one more... inch..."

He slipped!

Fox let out a high-pitched shriek—somewhere between a glam-rock falsetto and the final gasp of a dying star—as his body dropped. Time slowed. In those fleeting, airborne seconds, his mind whirled with a barrage of catastrophic concerns: How would he ever get the spoiled cream cheese smell out of his hair? And tomato sauce *never* comes out of silk. *Never!*

Or slightly worse yet: what if this fall actually killed him?

He would never hear what was on the newly announced Malibu Bad Boys EP. Was it going to be all new material? Or live cuts from the *Mane Squeeze* tour? Or maybe—*just maybe*—contain the unreleased and now legendary, track "Boyz Cry 2" that Stevie Styles co-wrote with G.G. Ferrari from Fox's second favorite band in the universe, Rosemary's Lady?

He had to know!

As disaster loomed, Fox whipped off his lengthy silk scarf and snapped it through the air like a bullwhip, catching the trellis overhead and swinging inches above the trash heap, glinting in the moonlight like some kind of disco Tarzan.

"Oh, my God... oh, my God... don't look down..."

He looked down.

"OH, MY GOD!"

Maggots! Pale and bloated, writhing like living pus across every inch of the spilled garbage. Some of them even arched their slick, headless bodies toward him, as if drawn to the scent of fresh prey.

With a desperate grunt, Fox tore his gaze away and hauled himself up the scarf, hand over hand, fighting the urge to scream—and vomit.

Panting, exhausted, and miraculously untouched by the maggot-infested trash below, he finally reached the roofline where the vent waited.

He revealed a small manicure kit from his inside jacket pocket and retrieved one of several varieties of nail files. He used it like a screwdriver to unscrew the tiny rusted screws holding the vent cover in place. One by one, they fell, clinking down the siding of the house.

But the final screw resisted.

"Don't you *dare*," he warned, baring his teeth at it.

It heard him—and surrendered.

With a victorious smirk, Fox grabbed the vent cover and tossed it onto the roof with a clang.

He peered into the deep, dark hole and could hear the music, the camaraderie, and promiscuous promises of the party echoing through the ductwork. "Where there's a will, there's a Fox Chastain!" he declared under his breath. Inch by inch, he shimmied into the ventilation shaft of the Looger house like the glam rat he was.

Chapter 20

ROCK 'N' ROLL

The door flew open. Mark and Tori crashed into Mark's bedroom and landed on the floor, the swamp of filthy laundry and crushed beer cans cushioning their fall.

Lips fused, hands groping, Mark stretched one leg back and blindly kicked the door shut.

The world outside faded into oblivion.

His pulse pounded like a double bass pedal. It was happening. After all the late-night fantasies, the painful near-misses, Mother's unbearable guilt trips, he had finally willed this moment into existence. Here he was, with Tori Payne, the Metal Goddess, rolling over the wreckage of his room, teeth clashing, lips smashing, hands everywhere at once. And it was incredible.

Even if she did strangely smell like pig shit.

Didn't matter.

Tori stayed locked on him like a heat-seeking missile, kissing him with fierce determination.

Mark, on the other hand, was less put-together. His breathing came in short, panicked bursts as if he were both thrilled and terrified of what was happening—because he was.

Hands roamed. Hers were confident, smooth, knowing exactly what to do. His, frantic, sweaty, and unsure if he was *allowed* to touch half the places he was aiming for.

Tori slid her leather jacket off in one sleek move.

Following her lead, Mark tried to tear off his denim vest with the same finesse, but it caught on one arm, twisting his body until he had to awkwardly yank it over his head and fling it across the room, smacking the black light fixture. It flickered encouragingly.

She grinned, her eyes smoldering as she kicked off her combat boots.

Mark went for one of his Chuck Taylors and rolled onto his back, flailing like an overturned turtle as he struggled to yank it off.

"Hang on, I got it," he strained, while trying to sound cool. With a final tug, the shoe flew off his foot, sailed across the room, and smashed into his full-length mirror, leaving a nice, webbed crack across the glass.

But his second shoe refused to budge.

Meanwhile, Tori was way ahead, already shimmying out of her tight black jeans, like a pro.

Mark, still struggling, slowed down to watch. "Whoa..."

She shot him a look. "You gonna catch up, or just sit there and drool?"

Mark snapped out of it. "What? Oh, yeah, like, totally! Catchin' up, right now," he blurted, diving for his shoe, which he quickly realized was not coming off without untying it. But the knot was impossibly tight. "Stupid laces," he grumbled, feeling personally betrayed.

Chapter 21

HEAVEN AND HELL

Pastor Peter Pringle pedaled across town, through the seedier stretches of Liberty Bend, on his way back to the Holy Christ Church of Unwavering Condemnation. He still had a little housekeeping to finish up before calling it a night. It had been one heck of a day.

Flickering streetlights cast nauseating glows onto graffiti-scrawled buildings as he navigated the cratered asphalt of Main St., dodging potholes big enough to swallow him and his tandem bicycle whole.

Liquor stores with barred windows lined the street while groups of chain-smoking teens in shredded denim and pentagram patches loitered outside, their eyes tracking Pastor Pringle like vultures.

He passed by Liberty Belle Gentleman's Club and Tanning, the town's most infamous strip joint–slash–cocktail lounge–slash–tanning salon. Muffled synth-heavy rock ballads seeped through its cracked doors. Outside, a line of "gentlemen" in trench coats shuffled impatiently as they waited their turn for a glimpse.

Less than a block down the road, a woman in fishnets, a fur coat, and very little else blew a kiss at the perfect little angel as he pedaled past.

A pack of stray dogs emerged from a trash-strewn alley, yapping and snapping at the pastor. One growling mutt had a severed human foot in its mouth.

He weaved around a grisly wreck at an intersection—a rust-red 1972 Ford LTD crumpled against a faded yellow Oldsmobile Cutlass Supreme. The Ford's windshield was shattered, and a lifeless body was sprawled across the hood like a rag doll. A bloodied and confused elderly woman clutched a pair of fuzzy dice, stumbling through the wreckage and calling out for her mommy.

Just around the corner, Liberty Bend's Children's Hospital was engulfed in flames. Most patients and staff had been evacuated, but faint, desperate screams still echoed from within the burning building.

All the while, Pastor Peter Pringle remained impressively oblivious, singing a joyful hymn as he pedaled along:

"Whatever I pray for
The Lord supplies
Whatever I ask for
It soon arrives

"A new bike, a shiny toy
Some sunshine that I'll enjoy
It's like I'm a magical boy!

"Whatever I pray for
The Lord's my man
Whatever I ask for
He'll understand

"A day off from school, oh boy!
Some banned books that I'll destroy
It's like I'm a magical boy!"

Just then, the pastor plowed his bicycle through a huge puddle, sending a tidal wave of filthy street water onto a nearby homeless lady huddled on the sidewalk.

Mabel Bennet—better known as Mad Mabel—was one of Liberty Bend's most well-known junkie hobos. The town had always had its fair share of homeless drifters, addicts, and squatters, and in recent years, their numbers had exploded like weeds through cracked pavement. But as Liberty Bend spiraled deeper into ruin, Mad Mabel stood out as a constant, staggering reminder for folks that things could always be worse.

One of the many incidents that made Mad Mabel a household name occurred at Black Rock Falls High School a few years back. She used to linger—no, *lurk*—around the campus and, when the last bell rang, Mabel would leap out from behind a tree or bush to beg and pester exiting students for drugs or booze, zeroing in on the rougher-looking ones—i.e. headbangers.

One time, Mabel was so desperate for a fix that she broke into the school during operating hours and went on a crazed shopping spree, prying open random lockers with a crowbar, hoping to score some weed, coke, Wite-Out, or anything to get her fix.

She only managed to get a handful of lockers open—spilling useless textbooks, crumpled love letters, and pin-ups of Ralph Macchio onto the hallway floor—before the cops showed up, cuffed her, and dragged her out of the school as she flailed around like a maniac, screaming obscenities about the end of the world.

Mad Mabel had looked pretty bad then, but now—now she was a real horror show. She was completely covered in layers of grime, the filth so thick it was impossible to tell where the dirt ended and the skin began. Her clothes were faded and tattered beyond recognition, blotched with dark patches of dried blood and feces. She had only one ear and large patches of hair were gone, revealing the raw, scabby—and definitely infected—skin of her scalp. Mad Mabel looked like the kind of thing you'd expect to crawl out of the darkest, nastiest gutter and eat your children.

Now she was sopping wet, which only amplified the sights and smells—wet dog... with the plague!—of Mad Mabel.

The sudden downpour jolted her awake. "What the...?" Still fumbling back to consciousness, she spotted the ten-year-old angel on a tandem bicycle—typical Saturday night—and snapped, "Hey! You got me all wet!"

Pastor Pringle came to an abrupt stop, a look of grave realization on his face. "Oh, my! What in the holy name of the invisible man in the sky is wrong with me?"

But he wasn't talking to her. In fact, he didn't even notice Mad Mabel.

Mad Mabel glanced down at the soggy cardboard in her hands. "My sign!" Her eyes welled with tears. "I... I worked really hard on that one!" She tried to brush the water off, but the words—*Anything Helps*—had already bled into illegible gibberish.

"How could I be so careless? So foolish? So blind?" Pringle berated himself.

Hearing that, Mad Mabel felt a little bad for overreacting. "Oh, shit... nah, it's all good. I guess I've had worse things happen to me. Like the time I—"

"I've been praying like the dickens all day for Mrs. Looger's recovery..." Pastor Pringle blurted. "...and she's still sick as a dog!"

"What's that?" Mabel asked, becoming more and more confused by where this conversation—which it was not—was going. "Who the hell is Mrs. Looger?"

But the pastor remained deaf to the unimportant ramblings of the homeless junkie. Something wasn't right in his cleaner, much more important world.

"Anyway..." she shrugged, getting down to business. "Could you spare a dime?"

Pringle's mind flashed back to Mother puking until she filled the toilet bowl, until it overflowed and spread across the bathroom floor, nearly soiling his angelic threads.

"Or, maybe… I don't know… some weed?" she ventured. Might as well ask.

If there was one thing the pastor knew beyond a shadow of a doubt, it was that his prayers *always* worked. Like when he prayed away the McDougal twins' demonic possession. Or Mrs. Nesbit's chronic bouts with constipation. The Lord always listened. *Always.* And he had personally led Mrs. Looger's healing prayer circle. Gosh darn it, she should be cured by now! *But if my prayers have not been answered,* Pringle suspected, *it must mean that something—or someone—is meddling with the Lord's divine plan!*

"Anything helps." Mabel grinned a toothless grin.

But Pastor Pringle's only response was to abruptly turn his bicycle around and pedal away—right through the puddle, drenching Mabel and what little remained of her dignity all over again.

As the pastor rode back through the horrors of Liberty Bend to the Looger residence with renewed purpose, Mad Mabel tossed her useless sign away, let out a long sigh, and croaked out a few more lines to the perfect little angel's song:

"Whatever I ask for
I'll be ignored
Forgotten, forsaken
By the good Lord

"Some spare change, some smack or pills
A bed in a hospital
It's like I'm an unlucky girl!"

Chapter 22

SOUTH OF HEAVEN

Piper fumbled in the dark, her hands sweeping blindly over rough concrete walls and stacks of old who-knows-what. The air was thick and smelled like damp wood, mothballs, and something else... something rotten.

A shaft of moonlight sneaking through the grimy basement window directed Piper's eyes to a flashlight.

She quickly scooped it up and clicked it on. A weak, sickly yellow glow sputtered to life. At first, all she saw were dusty boxes of holiday decorations, piles of old clothes for the Salvation Army, and a collection of religious knick-knacks that didn't make the cut upstairs.

But there was no sign of Mother. Or any telephones to debug, for that matter.

Then a chill went down Piper's spine.

Across the room, stacked ominously in the farthest corner, were rows of white office boxes.

Piper stepped closer and shined the flashlight beam across the labels: *PROPERTY OF HOLY CHRIST CHURCH OF UNWAVERING CONDEMNATION.*

A devious grin spread across her face. *Jackpot.*

Most of the boxes were empty, their contents reduced to confetti and stuffed into the collection of clear garbage bags near the foot of the stairs—courtesy of the massive industrial paper shredder, also labeled as church property, looming like a guillotine over the basement clutter.

It suddenly dawned on Piper that this must be one of those suspicious tasks Mark's mother had been assigned. Mark had been yammering lately about how she was one of Pastor Peter Pringle's most devoted foot soldiers in his holy war against heavy metal.

Mother would plan fundraising events for the Holy Christ Church of Unwavering Condemnation, like the annual potluck. She led youth volunteer groups on missions to scrub away the graffiti defiling schools, businesses, and public bathrooms around town—bearing the usual revolting messages like *Fuck the Holy Christ Church of Unwavering Condemnation* or *Fuck graffiti censorship!* And sometimes, in case you still didn't get the message: *FUCK YOU!*

She organized protests outside of Satanic Temple Records, Tapes & Tanning, rallying a devoted flock of followers to picket the store that shamelessly peddled "Satan's soundtrack."

And every so often, when her disciples managed to pinpoint the elusive source of its rogue signal, they would march upon AM 666 The Tower of Power.

But as her influence grew, so did the tasks the pastor entrusted to her. Soon, Mother was handling questionable deposits of questionable sums of money into a questionable number of bank accounts around Liberty Bend. And Mother didn't ask questions.

Pastor Pringle appreciated that.

With every silent nod of compliance, he rewarded her with more responsibilities, expanding her role in ways that no longer even remotely resembled community service. The lines blurred, but Mother didn't mind. After all, saving the town from evil required sacrifice.

Now it appeared she had been quite the "pastor's little helper," destroying the contents of these boxes.

But why?

The flashlight beam fell on the two remaining unopened boxes, still heavy with reams and reams of whatever it was Mother had been instructed to make disappear. The answer was in there. It had to be.

Without further hesitation, Piper pried the lid from one. When she saw what was inside, another chill went down her spine.

Chapter 23

LIAR

A random partygoer drew forth another album from the collection. It was *Slay the Deceiver* by the band Non-Believer. The cover art featured a grotesquely old demon with a writhing snake for a tongue. The album was placed on the turntable, the needle dropped, and the lyrics to this "devil's music" blasted in crystal clarity from the gigantic speakers:

> *His stories tell of glory days*
> *Of parties and debauchery*
> *Of wild nights upon the stage*
> *All too much to be believed*
>
> *No more lies and no more stories*
> *No more bullshit allegories*
>
> *His tongue a snake that coils and slithers*
> *Venomous, the tales he spews*
> *An ancient fool in tight black leather*
> *Each word betrays the truth*
>
> *No more lies and no more stories*
> *No more bullshit allegories*

Slay the deceiver!
Silence the double-dealer
Make him croak
And spill his guts
It's time he meets the reaper!

As time goes by and slips away
His life a wasted jest
As genuine as his toupee
This fool must meet his death

No more lies and no more stories
No more bullshit allegories

Slay the deceiver!
Silence the double-dealer
Make him croak
And spill his guts
It's time he meets the reaper!

Mother's eyes made tiny back-and-forth processing motions as her brain absorbed the intricate details of the commands.

At the same time, farther back in the dark recesses of the house, the door to Mark's mother's bedroom swung open, and the much-younger-than-Fogey headbanger girl stormed out.

Pausing to finish buttoning her top, she shouted back into the room, "And just how were you supposed to have lured Bobby 'The Possum' Dicer out of his coma with the promise of more cocaine if you were out touring the world with Boozehound and Big Fat Witch when that happened?"

She turned and stomped off down the hall, nearly colliding with Mother as she passed.

Mother barely noticed, her glassy blank stare fixed on the open bedroom door.

Inside, Fogey fidgeted with his terrible mullet toupee, trying to resecure it before any more embarrassing mishaps occurred.

Mother entered the room and closed the door behind her, sealing off the noise of the party.

Hearing that, Fogey looked up, freezing like a deer in the headlights as he met Mother's unblinking gaze. "Oh. Hey, Mark's mom. Uh, I was just... doing a little tidying up in here..." Fogey stammered, forcing a casual grin while quickly pulling the blanket over the disheveled bedsheets. "Man, you ever notice how metal chicks are total slobs? I found one of 'em making a mess in here. But don't worry, I told her to stay out of my main man Mark's mom's room. I used to have to do the same thing for the guys in Big Fat Witch when I was their tour manager. Those groupie chicks would trash their tour bus and I... and then I had to... I mean, it was my job to…"

Fogey's words trailed off, his brain slowing down like a record spinning to a halt. He was tired. Tired of keeping track of all the stories, tired of making sense of the tangled web of memories—real or otherwise. What had started as a fun little way to convince himself his life had meaning had become an exhausting cycle of embellishment and fabrication.

His head spun. His heart sank.

"Ah, man… I don't know," he muttered, slumping onto the bed. "I don't even know what I'm saying, anymore."

Mother approached the old man.

"All I know is these kids today are just so damned judgmental," Fogey continued. "Like you gotta constantly impress them with wild tales of crazy things you've done, or else they'll just make fun of you, and not even want to hang out or anything."

Mother continued advancing.

"Tell you the truth, 'cause I think we're from a similar generation—or roundabouts—I've had to resort to using notecards and my little black book to keep track of the things I tell these kids." He pulled his little black book out of his jacket pocket and flipped through it, showing Mother the mess of scribbled lies. "Yep. Got a whole system worked out. Or else I get all mixed up," he confessed.

Mother drew closer. The words to "Slay the Deceiver" by Non-Believer echoed on a torturous loop inside her head: *Slay the deceiver… Silence the double-dealer…*

"I mean, sure, I wish I worked security for Horny Beast. Or managed Big Fat Witch. Hell, I'd have given my left nut to roadie for VD Vengeance back in '83," he said longingly.

His voice trailed off. He slipped the little black book back into his jacket. And then, for the first time in years, the truth slipped through his teeth. "But I've just been working construction for the past thirty-eight years. Family business."

Mother stopped in her tracks.

The air in the room shifted.

Her eyes made tiny back-and-forth processing motions.

"And that goes way back," Fogey continued, fishing a business card from his tight leather pants. "I'm talkin' my dad's dad's dad's dad. The Fogelmans practically built Liberty Bend from the dirt up."

He handed her the card, which read: *Fogelman Construction: Building Promises since 1884.*

"So, for me to say, 'Oh, sorry, Pa, gonna hit the road with Bitch Balls instead of carrying on the family legacy,' would've been unthinkable." He paused, shaking his head with regret.

"Except… that's *all* I think about."

He was no longer the *deceiver* that needed to be *slayed* or the *double-dealer* that needed to be *silenced*. There was no need to *make him croak and spill his guts*. And no, it was not time for Fogey to *meet the reaper*. The commands she received would have to be satisfied elsewhere.

Damn.

Mother dropped the business card, turned around and started back to the door.

Fogey didn't even notice, let out a long, weary sigh, and kept rambling. "The irony is, I make a shit ton more as a general contractor than I ever would as a guitar tech for Human Toilet," he continued.

Mother opened the door. The sounds of music and revelry spilled into the bedroom.

"But I gotta tell ya, Mark's mom," Fogey rambled on, "not a day goes by that I wouldn't trade it all in a second for a life out there on that metal road."

Mother stepped out of the room and began to close the door behind her, the sounds of the party dimming once more.

The door was almost closed.

Fogey sighed again, shoulders sagging. He didn't know it, but he had just *barely* made it out alive.

But poor Fogey just couldn't help himself.

"Although I *did* get to party backstage with Ernie Lambskin once," he smirked.

SHTHLUNK!

Hearing Fogey's little fib—his *deception*—Mother had moved with super-human hypno-speed, reappearing in the room as though she never left, and took hold of Fogey's tongue.

"Uhh! Uhh-unngh-uhh!!!" Fogey tried to speak, his words unintelligible.

SQUANCH! Mother's grip on his tongue tightened.

He tried to push her away, but that only made things worse. His tongue stretched... and stretched... and *STRETCHED!*

Fogey let out a desperate gurgling scream from deep in his throat.

Meanwhile, out in the living room, two metalheads—one beer-bellied, the other skin and bones—were lazily headbanging to the music when a bloodcurdling scream cut through the noise.

"Dude, you hear that?" Beer Belly asked, blinking.

Skin & Bones paused, cocked his head. Another scream followed, high-pitched, tortured, awful.

They listened in silence for a moment as Fogey's wails of agony continued from somewhere down the hall.

Finally, Skin & Bones shrugged. "Eh. That's just Fogey. Can't believe a damn thing that guy says."

Beer Belly nodded, satisfied.

They returned to headbanging.

Back in Mother's room, Fogey's tongue was stretched almost three feet out of his mouth.

"Uhh-unngh-uhh!!! Uhh! EEEGH!!!" he tearfully pleaded, dropping to his knees as Mother pulled and pulled and *PULLED* until—*SQUELCHITY-SQUELCH!*

With a final violent tug, Mother completely pulled out the rest of Fogey's tongue—along with *all* of his internal organs, all the way down to his toe muscles (which were somehow all connected to it).

As Fogey's empty body fell limp against the floor like a sad, deflated party balloon, his terrible mullet toupee slid off, leaving his old, bald head exposed. Forever.

But then...

A noble voice called out of the shadows, "What villainy is this?"

Mother turned to see Sir Greg, wide-eyed and holding the bowl of condoms from the snack table, nobly distributing them to each and every headbanger about to engage in "courtly valor."

Chapter 24

WAY COOL JR.

The air was stale. The walls were cold. And it was a tighter fit than his purple satin hot pants after grief-eating for a week at Greasy Genes when Knights in Shining Glamour broke up. But it was all worth it. At the other end of this "tunnel of love," Fox Chastain would unscrew the vent cover and emerge victorious, sliding out of the shaft like a cool breeze and into the velvet embrace of the party. "Fortune favors the bold… and the beautiful," he whispered to himself.

He was getting psyched-out of his glammed-up gourd just thinking about how epic tonight was gonna be: bottomless margaritas, a spontaneous dance-off, maybe even an air guitar duel. And of course, he'd slay them all. No contest.

And who knows? Maybe—*just maybe*—he'd meet *the one*. As long as she was a rock 'n' rollin', pole-dancin', cheerleadin', Harley-Davidson-ridin', cheetah skin-wearin', MTV music video starrin', diva vixen.

Fox Chastain would settle for nothing less.

Much to the dismay of his Aunt Milly.

He could hear her now. "Frederick," she'd say (she *knew* he hated that name), "When are you going to get your act together? When are you going to stop dressing up like a girl? When are you going to meet someone and settle down—like Bethany did?"

And then would come the usual gut-punch from his favorite Auntie: "Do you even have any friends, Frederick?"

Of course Fox Chastain had friends!

So what if both of them—Rikki "Rat Tail" Nesbit and "Sweet Pea" Stewart—had "moved on" and "grown up?" Who cares if they'd cut their hair, sold their leather, and shuffled off to college like well-behaved lemmings? Did it matter if he hadn't heard from either of them in over two years—since they had both, on separate occasions, politely asked him to stop calling them at work?

No.

They were still his friends.

Whatever. Deep down, he knew Aunt Milly only lashed out because she was intimidated by his star power.

Tonight was all that mattered. This party. This was the first real rager in Liberty Bend worth going to in ages. Sure, there were those monthly functions at the American Legion. But those old, horny veterans who always mistook him for a middle-aged woman weren't exactly his scene. And even if they were, he wasn't allowed in there anymore (long story).

But this *was* his scene. These *were* his people. Whatever that weird vibe was he got from a few of them—like maybe they despised every bone in his "glam-bam-thank-you-ma'am" body—Fox chalked up to the general malaise of Liberty Bend. Regardless, they loved metal, and Fox Chastain loved metal. Okay, maybe he preferred a slightly lighter, *sexier* version of the genre, but a rock 'n' roller is a rock 'n' roller, baby!

Right?

Either way, the promise of tonight offered more than Fox Chastain could dream up right there, right then, in that air shaft. All he knew was that emotions were high and somebody was *definitely* going to cry before the night was through. And there was no doubt, no question, and no way that it was *not* gonna be Fox Chastain.

He pressed forward, using his Zippo—usually reserved for power ballads at Thunderplex Arena—to light the way, following the sound of the booming drums, distorted guitars, and banshee wails reverberating through the shaft. The party was close. He could practically taste it… with his ears.

"Ew—OH MY GOD!" he yelped, recoiling from a tiny pile of rat turds. He composed himself. Took a breath. Applied fresh lip gloss. Then carefully elbow-crawled around the offending feces.

Cobwebs brushed his face. He shrieked again, swatting them away with the delicate grace of an escaped lunatic. And yelped even louder when he saw the spider.

PSHHHHHHT!

"At least you're goin' out in style," he whispered as he emptied his entire can of Aqua Net on the poor creature.

A few feet later, emerging from the noxious cloud, he turned a corner—and froze. There, in the center of the narrow corridor, blocking his path, stood the enemy: a rat.

Its beady, glassy eyes stared him down. Its tail flicked the air, strutting its stuff like it owned the place. Its slick, glossy fur shimmered like a satin blouse. Poor thing was trying way too hard to distract from the ugly truth.

Something about the rodent seemed *eerily* familiar.

And it was daring Fox to make a move.

But Fox wasn't going anywhere.

The shaft seemed to shrink, the world condensing to this moment: a glam rat showdown.

Meanwhile, in the living room, the party raged on, the modified hi-fi stereo system blasting heavy metal at ear-bleeding volume. Head-bangers headbanged, made out, and fell over in a drunken stupor. It was beautiful.

Until—

Somehow, through the stench of sweat, leather, cigarette smoke, booze, and vomit, every metalhead in the room smelled some-thing. Noses wrinkling, they froze—mid-headbang, mid-make-out, mid-fall-over-in-a-drunken-stupor.

Sniff sniff…

That smell. Sharp, dark, masculine, with a heady mix of lavender, leather, oakmoss, and patchouli. A scent so potent they could practi-cally taste the repugnance.

Drakkar Noir.

Sniff sniff…

They followed their noses to the nearest air conditioning vent. The horrified expressions on their faces said it all.

Sniff sniff…

Fox Chastain was coming.

Back in the ventilation shaft, Fox Chastain was all smiles. The rat had either gotten bored, hungry, or, as Fox assumed, just recognized the unshakeable, unmistakable force of nature that was Fox Chastain and scuttled away into a nearby gap in the paneling.

Victory.

Fox pushed onward, contorting his lanky limbs through tighter and tighter twists and turns, refusing to let anything—vermin, fear, or the laws of physics—stand between him and the party.

But—

A new sound replaced his guiding light of ripping guitars. It was a different kind of ripping... a long, loud, multi-pitched cacophony of demonic trombones.

And then—

Sniff sniff...

"What in the Hair Club for Men is that?" he muttered with growing concern.

Sniff sniff...

Somehow, through the haze of his own glorious musk (and the unmistakable allure of Drakkar Noir), Fox caught a whiff of... something else.

It wasn't sweat, booze, or smoke. Or even rat turds.

It was the kind of funk that curdles paint. Melts rhinestones. And explains the rat's hasty retreat far better than Fox Chastain's power of persuasion.

The farther he crawled, the worse it smelled. Until, at last, it became so overpowering that Fox couldn't even breathe. His eyes watered. He felt his skin blistering from the acidic miasma flooding the shaft. He even tried to counter the stench with a heroic spritz of Drakkar Noir—drenching himself and his immediate surroundings in its spicy, masculine allure. But it was no match for this monstrous stench. The thick, greasy reek that clung to the inside of Fox's nostrils was an unholy, unstoppable force of nature.

Then the horror struck. "OH, GOD, IT'S IN MY HAIR!"

Fox Chastain threw his body into reverse, exerting what oxygen remained in his lungs to scramble backward through the ventilation shaft and back to breathable air.

All around the house, headbangers of every shape, size, and digestive dysfunction pressed their asses up against the air-conditioning vents. Even the ceiling vents weren't safe as metalheads formed human ladders, balancing precariously on each other's shoulders, determined to deliver a symphony of gut-wrenching glory straight into the ductwork—greasing their jeans with the greasy gas of Greasy Gene's greasiest. Each fart was a potent, noxious weapon against glam invasion.

Fox Chastain had now been stopped by a door slammed in his face. Then a window closed, locked, and welded shut. And now...

Smoked out by headbanger farts.

Chapter 25

HALL OF THE MOUNTAIN KING

Sir Greg dropped the noble bowl of condoms and commanded Mother to answer him. "I said... what villainy is this?!"

"I have slain Mike Fogelman," Mother answered matter-of-factly.

Sir Greg's lip trembled. He stepped forward and knelt beside Fogey's bald, lifeless form. Gently, he gathered the old man's deflated balloon of a body into his arms like a fallen warrior on the battlefield. Fogey, the fool of the realm, endlessly irritating with his pathetic lies and pursuit of youth that went against all that was noble, was dead.

"You have slain my closest ally, my brother in arms!" he roared.

"He was the *deceiver*." Cold. Brutal. But true.

Sir Greg laid down Fogey's corpse, stood up, and with the roar of a battle cry, he bull-rushed Mother. She didn't even flinch. He barreled into her like a human battering ram, driving her backward and through the nearby wall with a *CRASH!*

Sir Greg and Mother burst through the other side of the wall, spilling a cloud of sheetrock and dust onto the back patio—an elevated deck in the backyard featuring faux-exotic wicker patio furniture, jolly garden gnomes, and a rusty old barbecue grill.

As they got to their feet, Sir Greg unsheathed his ever-present battle axe. "I shall send you to hell for what you've done!" he declared, raising the blade above his head and charging at Mother to bury it in her emotionless face.

Again, she showed no sign of defending herself.

Sir Greg paused at Mother's inaction, contemplated, then muttered under his breath, "Nay, I walk the noble path."

Without taking his eyes off Mother, he lowered his axe and withdrew to the opposite side of the deck. "Nobility demands a trial by combat." He reached behind and retrieved a pair of steel nunchucks from the back pocket of his jeans. "Take this weapon, forged by my own hand, and fight me... to the death!"

Mother's eyes did their tiny back-and-forth processing motions.

Sir Greg tossed her the nunchucks.

She did one of those no-look catches.

Now, two warriors, weapons in-hand, stood motionless under the full moon's light. A whispering wind blew. Sir Greg's headbanger hair fluttered against the starry night sky. Somewhere in the distance, a wolf howled.

Without warning, they charged.

Their weapons clashed, sparks flying as forged steel met forged steel. Sir Greg unleashed a succession of swings. Mother parried each one, but the mighty blows staggered her backward to the edge of the deck. She lost her balance and nearly fell off.

Sir Greg laughed. "Ha! You must be *strong* if you hope to defeat me!"

Processing Sir Greg's boast as her next command, she regained her composure and swung her nunchucks with renewed ferocity, forcing Sir Greg back with each parried blow until he was cornered against the barbecue grill.

In a last-second dodge, Sir Greg somersaulted out of the way as Mother's epic overhead swing smashed the grill, spilling tongs, hickory chips, and a bottle of Kingsford lighter fluid across the deck.

Back on his feet, just in time to deflect Mother's continued attack, Sir Greg managed to hook his axe blade onto Mother's nunchucks chain. With his impressive strength, he flung her onto the patio table.

"But strength alone is not enough to save thee. To stand a chance in this battle, you must also possess *skill!*" he taunted his enemy.

As commanded, she *skillfully* reached up and cranked the lever on the umbrella pole. The canopy burst open, knocking Sir Greg off his feet and sending his axe clattering across the deck.

She leapt from the table and put on an impressive display, spinning and twirling the nunchucks around her body with expert precision.

Sir Greg was momentarily awestruck. Then, seeing his weapon out of reach, his eyes flared with frustration.

Until—

He spotted the vast collection of garden gnomes arranged in the nearby planter bed.

As Mother inched closer, Sir Greg grabbed a squat little fella with rosy cheeks and a fishing pole, sprang to his feet, and hurled it at her.

SMASH! Her swinging nunchuck instantly shattered it.

He snatched up another—a lanky gnome with a wheelbarrow—and sent it sailing.

WHACK! She swatted it like a fastball. It hit the side of the house and exploded.

Next, a chef sipping from a ceramic ladle.

CRASH! Gone in an instant.

One after another—the gnome with the watering can, the one riding a goose, even weary old papa gnome napping on a mushroom—each was obliterated by Mother's whirling weapon, and it did nothing to slow her down.

But soon, after shattering enough garden gnomes, a cloud of ceramic dust formed around Mother, and she became lost in the chalky haze—an eerie fog of war, thick with the souls of the jolly little soldiers.

She twisted her head, snapping her nunchucks left and right, growling like an animal in a trap, but Sir Greg was nowhere in sight. Nothing was.

"Well-fought," came a booming voice from the void.

Her head jerked around at the sound.

"You are indeed strong *and* skilled," the voice continued.

As the fog thinned, Sir Greg emerged behind her, clutching his battle axe once more. "But you must also be *strategic*."

He lunged across the deck, weapon raised.

Mother's eyes flicked to the bottle of Kingsford lighter fluid at her feet. In one swift—and *strategic*—motion, she scooped it up and chucked it at him.

Sir Greg easily cleaved the projectile in half midair before it could strike—only to be showered with its liquid contents.

"A bold attempt!" he laughed, striding forward. "But know this, defeated foe: A sneak attack is a far cry from *strategy*!"

With that, Sir Greg brought his axe down to claim his vengeance in the name of Fogey.

But Mother parried the blow with a simple swing of her nunchucks.

CHING! Sparks flew as forged steel met forged steel and—

The lighter fluid ignited!

Sir Greg erupted into a ball of fire, writhing on the patio deck, screaming in agony.

Mother just stood there, watching him burn, until the last flame sputtered out.

His skin charred, what was left of his hair smoldering, and the pain unbearable, Sir Greg slowly pulled himself to his feet. "You have bested me... in strength... skill... and strategy," he struggled to get out. "I ask only... that you grant me a... *noble* death."

Her hand immediately shot out, gripping the top of Sir Greg's head.

And squeezed.

"M-Mark's m-mother... by the Metal Gods..." he stammered, panic rising. "This is n-n-not the fate I sought!"

Mother pushed him into a wicker chair, her unrelenting fingers digging into his skull as Sir Greg screamed into the night.

At that moment, across the street from Mark's house and deep within the shadowy recesses of that crumbling dwelling, an ancient wizard stirred a cauldron, cackling through his toothless mouth as he sprinkled in eye of newt, mandrake root, and just a dash of nightshade with his gnarled, crusty fingers.

Galinor Stormcloak—the infamous wizard of the Golden Realm—paused, removed an earplug, and listened. *Was that... a scream? A cry of* royal pain *from somewhere in the night?* he thought, his ancient mind whirling with possibilities.

But the sound was gone. Only silence remained.

Galinor shrugged, muttered something dismissive, and slipped the earplug back in. Without another thought, he resumed stirring the bubbling concoction with his legendary Staff of Elven Tears.

Back on the patio deck, the top of Sir Greg's head was popped open, fragments of skull bent up and outward like the points of a crown, jeweled with chunks of brain matter.

The scorched king slumped in his wicker chair throne, his flesh and clothes still smoldering. His gleaming battle axe—magically untouched by flame or gore—lay across his lap, the broken remains of garden gnomes arranged at his feet as his loyal subjects, completing Mother's warped interpretation of Sir Greg's request for a "noble death."

Somewhere in the distance, a wolf howled.

Chapter 26

ROCK AND ROLL ALL NITE

Stripped down to her black leather lingerie—sharp straps, buckles, and glistening curves that looked like they were forged just for the Metal Goddess she was—Tori watched and waited while Mark fumbled with his stubborn shoelace. She twirled a strand of her platinum-blonde hair between her fingers, head cocked slightly to the side like a lioness watching a floundering gazelle.

Every time Mark looked up from the stubborn shoelace, she would give him a sly, knowing smile that only made him more frantic.

"Need some help there?" she teased.

Mark grimaced. "Nah, nah, I got this. It's, like, totally under control."

With one last, heroic tug, Mark finally unraveled the Gordian knot of his Chuck Taylor. The shoe flew off, smacking a pin-up of Bitch-Face Bitch square in her snarling teeth—she remained stoic and defiant as ever.

Mark exhaled deeply.

With that battle won, he quickly yanked off his shredded jeans, revealing his tighty-whities (silently praying they were clean, at least on the outside).

Without missing a beat, he leaped back into Tori's arms, and together they sank and tumbled into the chaos of the floor once again, kissing and clawing at each other, now with far more skin in the game.

Eventually, they made their way up and onto the bed, collapsing into the never-been-washed sheets and blankets in a feverish tangle of limbs and leather.

Mark's hands explored the taut curves of her body, following every line of leather and metal. As their kissing deepened, Tori pulled him closer, and one of Mark's shaky but determined hands finally found its way to her bra strap.

He paused, looking into her eyes for permission.

She knew exactly what he was asking and answered with a quick, eager nod.

Mark took a breath, bracing himself like a man about to cut the red wire on a ticking time bomb of awesomeness, and squeezed the clasp.

It didn't budge.

He fiddled with it some more, trying from another angle.

Then another.

Tori let out a subtle, amused sigh, "Here let me—" she started, reaching back.

But Mark stopped her. "Nah, I got it. It's cool," he insisted. Swallowing hard, he redoubled his efforts on the clasp. "Stupid bra strap," he muttered under his breath.

Chapter 27

DISPOSABLE HEROES

Piper's eyes darted across the first page she pulled from the box. Her devious grin widened as she grabbed another. And another. With each document she skimmed, the more the pieces fell into place.

This wasn't just boring office paperwork. This wasn't unpaid bills. Or even fraudulent tax returns. This was evidence of a sick and twisted crusade by Pastor Peter Pringle's church to prove, once and for all, that heavy metal warped young minds and made them do bad things. Page after page detailed bizarre experiments—*secret* bizarre experiments—conducted on so-called "willing participants."

There was Experiment #549, in which the Holy Christ Church of Unwavering Condemnation set out to examine the effects of prolonged exposure to heavy metal versus prolonged exposure to gospel music.

The study involved two groups of teenage volunteers. Each group was isolated in different rooms at the opposite ends of the church. Group One was forced to listen to heavy metal for five hours a day for two weeks. Group Two was made to listen to righteous gospel music for the same amount of time.

The church hypothesized that the gospel-exposed group would demonstrate increased empathy, moral fortitude, and a commitment to justice and fairness. Conversely, the heavy metal-exposed group was expected to exhibit heightened aggression, selfish tendencies, and blasphemous behavior—thus validating the church's position that the music fosters moral corruption.

At the end of the two weeks, the theory was put to the test when the two groups were made to compete with each other in a game of dodgeball in the church gymnasium. But the results contradicted expectations in a manner that, to put it mildly, deeply unsettled the researchers.

The "Metalheads"—their self-ascribed name, having become hardcore fans during the study—played fairly and with restraint. They avoided unnecessary force, checked on injured opponents, allowed recoveries, and followed the rules. In essence, they showed significantly higher empathy and advocated for fairness.

Meanwhile, the group calling themselves "Gospelheads" unleashed unchecked aggression. They threw with maximum force, aimed for faces and other vulnerable spots on the body, blatantly cheated, faked dodges, lied about hits, and refused to leave the court when eliminated.

It was just the opposite of what had been expected!

The Metalheads lost decisively, their empathy and rule-following working against them. However, the results of the experiment vindicated heavy metal, showing that the music had provided them with a healthy outlet for their aggression before the game. In contrast, the Gospelheads, having suppressed their emotions, released their pent-up rage through heightened aggression, selfish tendencies, and blasphemous behavior.

Piper's mind raced to keep up with her eyes as they devoured the documents.

Experiment #947 described the Holy Christ Church of Unwavering Condemnation's attempt to test the psychological and physiological effects of a mosh pit. The church hypothesized that the combination of violent music, close physical proximity, and unbridled chaos would result in heightened stress, uncontrolled aggression, and inevitable injury.

Due to the physical risks involved, the church refused to use its own volunteers. Instead, it recruited participants from a nearby Weight Watchers meeting, luring them in with the promise of free, non–sugar-free chocolate cake upon completion of the study.

The subjects were squeezed into a tiny room. The temperature inside was gradually raised as blistering heavy metal blasted from wall-mounted speakers. At first, they stood awkwardly, unsure of what to do. But as the music pounded on, they couldn't help themselves and began to move their bodies to the beat.

What followed contradicted everything the church had hoped for. As the subjects instinctively bumped into each other, rather than lashing out in anger, they followed unspoken mosh pit etiquette: helping each other up when they fell, patting each other on the back, and even laughing together.

One enormous participant took a hard fall, and for a brief moment, the researchers anticipated the outbreak of violence. But instead of retaliating, the fallen subject embraced the person who knocked them down in an unexpected hug of solidarity.

At the end, they didn't leave the pit feeling exhausted, angry, or injured. The participants felt invigorated and empowered, with a newfound appreciation for physical activity. Some of them even declared their intention to adopt a heavy metal-inspired exercise regimen into their personal lives.

In the final blow to the church's hypothesis, most participants were so energized that they declined the promised chocolate cake altogether, choosing instead to ride the unexpected high of unity, empowerment, and unexpected fitness inspiration.

Once again, heavy metal had been vindicated by this experiment.

Determined to prove that heavy metal music could literally in-
duce demonic possession, the Holy Christ Church of Unwavering
Condemnation proceeded with Experiment #10572, a study on the
effects of prolonged exposure to scandalous, blasphemous, and mor-
ally corrupt music videos.

The hypothesis was simple: if a person was subjected to forty-eight
continuous hours of demonic heavy metal imagery, they would inevitably succumb to being possessed by the Devil. In preparation
for the experiment, the church spent months recording the most
offensive content possible from MTV's *Headbangers Ball*, compiling
a library of unholy filth.

The volunteer was Edith Horowitz, a devout elderly woman from
the congregation. She had eagerly stepped forward, seeing this as her
chance to atone for what she saw as her greatest sin: failing to stop
her grandson—a whiz kid with computers and electronics—from
falling into the dark world of heavy metal. If she could play even the
smallest part in proving that heavy metal was evil, she would happily
endure any demonic torture.

To ease any concerns, the church assured Edith that an exorcist
would be on standby throughout, should the experiment prove to be
as successful as they anticipated.

And so, the first in a long series of tapes was loaded into the VCR,
each music video more obscene, more blasphemous than the last.

There was "Money-Grubbing Whores" by Fätal Fäte, where Bitch-
Face Bitch lounges in a strip club, tossing crumpled dollar bills at con-
servative politicians forced at gunpoint to strip down to their G-strings
and dance.

That was followed by the infamous video for "Get Boned" by
Horny Beast, in which singer Oily Deacon fornicates with a skeleton—in 5th-period biology class, no less!

And, of course, the now-legendary video for "Reverse Scatology" by Human Toilet, which offered an unrelenting demonstration of Hank the Stank somehow defecating from his mouth.

The researchers observed Mrs. Horowitz very closely as she watched the videos, waiting with bated breath for any signs of possession.

They got much more than they bargained for. Shockingly, mere hours into the experiment, Edith dropped dead.

Not from demonic influence. Not from the stress of exposure to blasphemous imagery. But from severe food poisoning—the result of a bad batch of egg salad she had made and eaten earlier that day.

So, despite their desire to connect her death to what they believed was heavy metal's unholy power, the coroner's report later confirmed the actual cause: a tragic, yet entirely mundane case of mayonnaise gone bad.

Once again, the Holy Christ Church of Unwavering Condemnation's hypothesis failed.

And heavy metal remained undefeated.

It made perfect sense that they would need to destroy all this paperwork—and why Pastor Peter Pringle stopped by earlier: to make sure Mark's mother had finished the job. Because time and time again, the results of these experiments told a very different story than what the church wanted anyone to hear.

The full weight of it all suddenly hit Piper, and she muttered aloud, "So, heavy metal really *doesn't* make people do bad things!"

This is big, Piper, big! she thought, her conspiratorial mind firing off like a gunman on the grassy knoll. *Bigger than That's Incredible! Bigger than Ripley's Believe It or Not! This was fucking Mike Wallace-eat-your-heart-out 60 Minutes shit, Mr. and Mrs. Jones!*

That's when she heard it.

First, the soft whir of cooling fans humming to life. Then, as the motor engaged, it quickly grew from a low mechanical growl to a deafening, grinding roar.

Startled, Piper spun around, and came face-to-face with the conspirator herself—Mother!

Piper's heart pounded. Her eyes narrowed. She had a lot more to discuss than the whereabouts of additional telephones in the house with this woman.

She straightened and took a deep breath. This was it. Her big moment. And she was going to milk it for all it was worth. "So, Mark's mom," she began, savoring every word and practically strutting with conspiratorial cockiness, "perhaps you'd like to explain to me—and eventually the police, and then eventually the jury—exactly what it is you're doing down here?"

Mother's reply was cold, calm, and unmistakably murderous: "I am shredding the evidence."

Piper's brow furrowed. Her eyes darted to the clear garbage bags full of shredded paper waiting to be picked up and hauled away to God knows where. "Duh. I know, but—"

With sudden, savage force, Mother seized Piper and hoisted her effortlessly into the air—lifting her clean out of her army boots.

"Oh! You're talking about *me*—eeaaAAAHHH!!!" she screamed as Mother fed her into the roaring mouth of the massive industrial paper shredder.

Just as Mother had returned from the coronation of King Greg, a random party-goer drew forth another album from the collection. It was *Shred the Evidence* by Political Asylum. The cover art featured a deranged-looking judge in a bench wig shredding on a guitar (another classic case of the artist not listening to a single track on the record before creating the artwork). The album was placed on the turntable, the needle dropped, and the lyrics to this "devil's music" blasted in crystal clarity from the gigantic speakers:

A mystery
Is misery
When you're the final clue
When you're the one
Who covered up
The terrifying truth

All your secrets are revealed
Now it's operation: KILL

Crazy thoughts
Connecting dots
With string and tape and pins
On corkboard walls
In nuthouse halls
An exposé of sin

All your secrets are revealed
Now it's operation: KILL

Steel teeth consume uncovered truth
Chewing, grinding bone and flesh
Gears spit out a stringy goo
And shred, shred, shred the evidence!

Too much is known
That could be shown
And lead to your arrest
So don't go quiet
Into the night
This ends with someone dead.

Steel teeth consume uncovered truth
Chewing, grinding bone and flesh
Gears spit out a stringy goo
And shred, shred, shred the evidence!

All your secrets are revealed
Now it's operation: KILL

Steel teeth consume uncovered truth
Chewing, grinding bone and flesh
Gears spit out a stringy goo
And shred, shred, shred the evidence!

Hearing those lyrics blasting from the speakers, Mother's eyes made tiny back-and-forth processing motions while her brain absorbed the intricate details of their commands.

She descended the creaking steps into darkness and switched on that massive industrial paper shredder to *shred, shred, shred the evidence.*

GRRRRRRSHHHK!

A geyser of blood exploded across the basement walls, splattering the holiday decorations and religious knick-knacks as the *steel teeth consumed uncovered truth, chewing, grinding bone and flesh*. It was an outrageous spectacle of gore as the *gears spit out* an unrecognizable, glistening *stringy goo*, that was once Piper Jones into the overflowing bin below.

Her desperate screams for help and the gut-wrenching sounds of the feasting shredder fell on deaf ears, drowned out by the thunder of double bass drums, a chorus of shrieking vocals, and the fourteen layers of guitar in the song "Louder Than Hell" by Death Distraction, conveniently blasting from the speakers upstairs.

For the first time in her young—and now very short—life, despite not being the sharpest pushpin in the crazy wall, despite being too unfocused, gullible, and eager to jump to conclusions, and despite her lacking that special conspiracy theorizing DNA cocktail, Piper had finally beat her parents at their own game and proved she could "uncover the truth" about something more earth-shakingly profound than anything they could.

But it had killed her.

Chapter 28

LOOK WHAT THE CAT DRAGGED IN

Fox Chastain slouched away from Mark's house, the stench of defeat (and weaponized indigestion) clinging to his soul. His once-mighty swagger had shriveled to a dismal shuffle. Even the sequins on his outfit no longer sparkled with the same intensity.

"Well, I guess I could still make Bethany's rehearsal dinner if I hurry," he grumbled to himself. He was sure that his sister would be devastated if he missed it. And he'd hate to make Bethany feel worse. Especially after she was so apologetic to Fox when he found out she had forgotten to invite him, and then rescheduled without telling him too.

And, sure as satin, his Aunt Milly would be ecstatic. "Oh, I knew you'd come to your senses and join your family for this important night of your sister's," she would say, then pause, looking him over with disdain. "But you're not wearing *that*, are you? Honestly, Frederick, have you no decency at all?"

No, he would not be wearing *this*. He would go home and change into his purple leather tuxedo with the velvet cape, and fishnet tights with the butt-cheek cutouts. Fox Chastain was no savage.

As he neared his candy-apple-red Pontiac Fiero SE, he couldn't resist a final glance of longing back at the party. The house, buzzing with life, laughter, and music, seemed to mock his exclusion.

He sighed, reached for the car door—

CREEEEEAAAAAAK.

Fox froze. The unnervingly long, drawn-out sound of a door opening behind him sent a chill down his spine.

Slowly, he turned to look.

The front door of the house was open, and standing in the dark stone archway of the entrance, was a towering, unsettling silhouette.

He could barely move. Could hardly breathe. But he managed to tip his shades to get a better look.

The strobing lights of the party inside revealed flashes of ba-dass-looking rock 'n' roll war paint, a huge crucifix necklace, and prematurely liver-spotted hands.

But it was the blood-splattered plush bathrobe and the killer look in her eyes that reminded Fox of his adorable Maine Coon pussycat, Tyler—especially when she would bring home a mutilated dead bird as an offering for her Foxy-woxy.

"Aww," he couldn't help himself.

Mother's unblinking eyes locked onto Fox's. She stepped aside, extending her arm in the slow, deliberate gesture of a guardian granting entrance.

Me? Fox thought, gesturing at his chest, eyes wide. *You're inviting me—Fox Chastain—into the house? Into... the party?*

As if reading his mind, Mother nodded.

Eyes wide with disbelief, Fox slowly ventured back to the house.

On the porch, Mother greeted him with a voice that was both polite and sinister. "Please," she said, creaking the door open wider. "Won't you come in?"

It was too good to be true, and a faint caution light flickered in Fox's brain.

He cast a look back at his car—to the "big important night of his sister's" that awaited him, where he was positive everyone was waiting with bated breath for his arrival.

Then back at Mother. And beyond her to the tempting sights and sounds that raged inside.

But this is my *scene,* he told himself. *These are* my *people.*

He grinned, pushing his aviators back up. "Whatever. Bethany will probably just yell at me again for borrowing her lipstick," he muttered, recalling the last time he raided his sister's makeup stash without her permission. "So crazy jealous of big bro."

Without another moment's hesitation, and with all the confidence of a runway finale, Fox squared his shoulders and strutted his stuff past Mother and into the party house, arms wide, belting out to any and all who might dare to listen: "Where there be a party, there be Fox Chastain!"

The door slammed shut behind him with a deafening, ominous thud.

Chapter 29

GOODBYE TO ROMANCE

Click! The clasp of Tori's bra finally popped open. Mark had done it—at long last! And it was like the clouds parting after a storm and the first ray of heavenly sunshine breaking through and warming the earth. Two of them.

Tori's panties were easier. She had already unhooked the metal-as-hell leather garter belt, so they slid off effortlessly. Within seconds, her G-string flew through the air, landing perfectly on the turntable of Mark's stereo—just like the opening shot of nearly every music video on MTV.

But just as things were really heating up, just as it was about to finally happen, Tori pushed him back. "Wait." Her tone was suddenly dead serious.

Mark blinked, then remembered. "Oh, right, yeah, it's cool I totally got, like, protection, or whatever."

He fumbled for the nightstand drawer, almost falling off the bed in the process, and triumphantly produced a condom (feeling a tinge of guilt that it wasn't the "ribbed for her pleasure" style). Still, he tore off the wrapper like he was looking for the Golden Ticket in a Wonka Bar and was about to pull down his tighty-whities to put it on when Tori shook her head and stopped him again.

"No. It's not that."

"Oh. Are you, like, on the pill?"

"No, it's... I just need you to know something..." There was an unfamiliar softness in her voice. The fierce edge was gone from her eyes. The Metal Goddess was nowhere to be found. Tori Payne was suddenly real. Vulnerable. And even more beautiful than ever.

"Uh... like, what is it?" Mark asked, growing a little worried.

"I just... I mean, before we—" she took a breath, unable to meet his eyes. "I've never done this before, okay? It's my first time."

It hit Mark like a gut punch. His blood went cold. And for the first time tonight—maybe ever—he wasn't even horny anymore.

"But I always wanted it to be with someone like you." She smiled, looked him dead in the eyes. "Someone who *gets* Fätal Fäte. Who *isn't* a fucking wuss."

She pulled him closer. "Someone I can *trust.*"

Fuck. That was just the problem. If it was supposed to be destiny, or whatever, for them to be together for all eternity, how could that ever happen if everything started with a harebrained scheme cooked up by him and the Headbanger Brigade? How could he ever live with himself if he went all the way through with this plan? This... lie?

But the strangest thing was, this whole situation reminded him of something. Something from a long time ago. Something that has been haunting him for far too long.

Fat Albert.

Tori didn't like the look on Mark's face. "Okay, what the fuck's wrong?"

Mark sat up. He looked confused, ashamed, and tortured all at once. Because he was. But he tried his best to explain: "You ever, like... see this one episode of *Fat Albert and the Cosby Kids* where Russell—you know, the little dude who always wears that giant scarf even when it's hot out—he, like, tells this huge lie to everyone. Like, a whopper. Like, he says he saved some kid from a burning building, or whatever..." he trailed off, trying to remember something, then, "and I think maybe there was something about aliens…?"

Tori just stared at him. Was he seriously talking about *Fat* fucking *Albert*? Right now? With a naked fucking Metal Goddess in his bed???

"Anyway, like, Russell tells this lie, right? And at first everybody's like, 'Whoa, Russell, you're such a hero!' and he feels awesome, y'know? Like, finally, people are lookin' at him like he's cool. But then, like, they start askin' questions. Like, 'Hey, can we meet the kid you saved?' or, 'How'd you get out of the fire without a scratch?' and stuff like that. And then Russell's like, 'Oh, uh, yeah, I totally, uh…' and he starts makin' up more lies to cover up the first lie, and it just gets worse and worse."

"Mark, I never even watched fucking *Fat Albert*!" Then, with a shrug, she added, "I was more of a *Josie and the Pussycats* girl."

But Mark barreled on. "So, like, the more he lies, the worse it gets, until, like, Fat Albert—you know, 'Hey hey hey!'—he figures it out and is like, 'Man, Russell, you're lettin' everybody down.' And, like, everybody's super mad, 'cause they trusted him and all, and Russell's just sittin' there lookin' like he's gonna barf…"

Tori was glaring at him. He really *was* seriously talking about *Fat* fucking *Albert*. Right now. With a naked fucking Metal Goddess in his bed!!!

"But, like…" Mark became more somber, "I never saw how that one ends. There was a storm and… and the TV cut out… And my dad…" his voice trailed off, the weight of the guilt about that day, about everything, becoming unbearable.

Tori's irritation gave way to concern and she said softly, "Mark, I didn't—"

"But now…" He stood up and walked halfway across the room, his back to Tori. "I think I'm pretty sure I know how it ended. And knowing Fat Albert, how he always made things right, how it *had* to end."

He turned to face her, exhaled slowly, eyes heavy with regret. "Little Russell was gonna, like, have to come clean."

Tori groaned. "Okay, what the fuck did you do, Mark?"

"Tori, I... I did a *bad* thing."

Tori rolled her eyes and smirked. "What, did you hypnotize your mom to trick me into thinking you finally had the balls to stop being a fucking wuss and stand up to her, or something?"

But seeing the seriousness on Mark's face, her smile vanished.

Chapter 30

RAINBOW IN THE DARK

Pastor Peter Pringle pedaled up to the house. He stepped off his bike, put the kickstand down, and approached the Looger residence. As he arrived at the door, he stopped, closed his eyes, and said a quiet prayer, "Ask and it will be given to you; seek and you will find; knock and the door will be opened to you."

He was about to knock on the door… but had second thoughts, grabbed the handle and invited himself inside.

Many things were written about the massacre that took place the night of Saturday, the 14th, at Mark Looger's party. Impassioned pieces filled with rage and scorn that laid blame every which way: music, parents, drugs, alcohol, Satan, even Cabbage Patch Kids. But there was one piece of journalism that stood out from the rest.

When the so-called investigative news magazine *Things That Happened* printed their piece, it managed to connect a lot of the dots with a surprising amount of accuracy—those dots being the specific details of each murder and the specific song that inspired it.

The article—credited to a journalist named Beldon Benedictus, whose previous assignment was cataloging various forms of fungi proliferation for *Scientific Ad Nauseam*—reported that "Nicole Rhodes, aged sixteen, perished as a result of multiple vital organs being extracted from her body. It was the conclusion of the coroner's office that this procedure had been carried out while Ms.

Rhodes was still very much alive and conscious. The details of this most intriguing form of torture and its inevitable death were inextricably linked to the song "Premature Autopsy" by the band Malpractice." He went on to describe how the song lyrics almost read like a medical school textbook.

Mr. Benedictus wrote about how the "dismembered body parts of seventeen-year-old Eric Bollinger were found meticulously arranged and packed into the industrial-size freezer in the Loogers' garage." And how "the literal connections to the song lyrics in 'Cold Case' by the band Meat Rocker were undeniable."

He went on to detail, in the clinical, detached way befitting fungi research, how "Stephanie Payton, aged seventeen, was found dead with the beaters of an electric hand mixer embedded in her eye sockets. Her eyeballs, most of her frontal lobe and part of her parietal lobe were, for a lack of better words, 'scrambled to a runny purée.'" Although he linked Ms. Payton's death to the song "Breakfast Is Severed" by the band Over Sleazy, it was, in fact, "Dead and Breakfast" by the band Butcher's Dozen. But to most readers, that discrepancy was potayto, potahto.

"Sixteen-year-old Spencer Stevens was found asphyxiated within the delicate confines of a clear plastic dry-cleaning bag. The lyrics to the song 'Don't Try This at Home' by the band Dunce Cap offered overly descriptive, step-by-step instructions—as if written for a child—for a murder such as this," Benedictus wrote.

"Paul Strummer, aged nineteen, and Kimberly Martin, aged eighteen, were boiled to death in the backyard jacuzzi of the Looger residence. The song, which was the obvious inspiration for this method of execution, was 'Boiled to Death in a Hot Tub' by the supposedly 'underrated' band No Effort.

"Jason Welch, aged sixteen, Chad Mackenzie, aged twenty, Tabitha Hopkins, aged eighteen, and Arnold Becker, aged sixteen, were each dismembered and their body parts haphazardly sewn back together in an attempt to construct a Frankenstein-like creation. The popular culture experts on the scene determined that this was a brazen attempt to simulate a literal interpretation of the song 'We Are Frankenstein' by the band Spider Sac Lunch," he wrote. Then, as was customary in scientific journals to provide the full data set, Benedictus included the complete lyrics to the song in the article:

We never asked to be created
Misfit parts they threw away.
But in the shadows, we awakened
Rising up to claim the day.

We are Frankenstein!
Made from bodies cast aside.
We are Frankenstein!
A freak of nature now despised.
We are Frankenstein!
Hunted down by mob and flame
We are Frankenstein!
A product of your blinded hate.

Your judgments lash like angry fire
But we are sparks that won't burn out.
You see the scars, the frayed desires,
But never what we're all about.

We are Frankenstein!
Made from parts you cast aside.
We are Frankenstein!
A freak of nature now despised.

We are Frankenstein!
Hunted down by mob and flame
We are Frankenstein!
A child born to feed your rage.

Monster, monster, in your eyes
Can you see beyond the lies?
We are not discarded toys
We are the future, we are the noise!

We are Frankenstein!
Made from parts you cast aside.
We are Frankenstein!
A freak of nature now despised.
We are Frankenstein!
Hunted down by mob and flame
We are Frankenstein!
A child born to feed your rage.

Page after page, the article detailed the demise of forty-two souls in attendance at Mark Looger's house on that fateful night. Though each death was more gruesome, shocking, and—for lack of a better word—*imaginative* than the last, it read as though written by someone who would rather be articulating how the propagation strategy of the slime mold *Myxomycetes gregarii* relies upon subterranean hydration pathways than waxing poetic about the epic human drama of a massacre. That is, of course, because it was.

But something else was missing. Something aside from the utter lack of humanity in describing these tragic deaths. Something aside from the fact that each one of these kids was somebody's child, that they were somebody's brother or sister, that they were poets, scholars, fools, lovers, fighters, cowards, and the future leaders of our world. No, something far more profound was eerily missing: The article in *Things That Happened* did not lay blame. Not one word of scorn. Not one attempt at proselytizing. Nor, and perhaps even more profoundly than not finding a quick scapegoat and leaning in full throttle, did it even attempt to ask the question: *why?*

But when Pastor Peter Pringle stepped through the threshold of that house of horrors and took in the sights, sounds, and smells so unimaginably gruesome they defied description—despite Beldon Benedictus's best scientifically objective efforts—and found Mother, drenched in blood, her face adorned with badass-looking rock 'n' roll war paint, perched atop an ungodly huge speaker in the living room and devouring the entrails of a hapless, hopeless, lifeless headbanger, the perfect little angel did not hesitate to ask the hard-hitting question:

"Delilah Looger! What in the Devil's dollhouse has gotten into you?"

Mother finished chewing the mass of intestine in her mouth, swallowed, and then answered coldly, robotically, "The music made me do it."

Pastor Pringle blinked.

Blinked again.

And then he thought of Alesha Stoker. Like he always did.

Back when Peter was eight—and Alesha sixteen—she would babysit him whenever his parents were working late, attending church functions, or just needing a break from child-rearing. She'd make him Rice Krispies Treats and let him stay up to watch MTV with her. But instead of the scary music videos, he liked watching her dance and thrash around the living room in her black metal tees.

One time, he'd spied on her in the bathroom while she begrudgingly turned one of those tees (at his parents' insistence) inside-out.

He didn't fully understand everything he felt back then, but he was sure it was love—until the night he confessed it all and proposed they spend the rest of their lives together in holy matrimony.

She laughed. Pinched his cheek. Even called him "adorable."

Humiliation seared him from the inside out. She'd completely dismissed his proposal—dismissed *him*. And in that moment, Peter found the perfect scapegoat: heavy metal. It was what his parents always whispered about, what the church condemned. Heavy metal had obviously poisoned Alesha Stoker's mind.

And from that night forward, he vowed revenge on the music that had broken his heart.

He started small with tearful testimonies at the Holy Christ Church of Unwavering Condemnation, warning of the evils of metal. The parishioners adored him. Seeing a sweet, innocent child spewing fear and hatred from the pulpit made their own worries and resentments feel all the more righteous—and pure. They invited him to share his message during services, and soon he was a regular at Sunday School and PTA meetings.

As he rose in the ranks of the church, he became a local celebrity. VHS tapes of his sermons spread through the town like a contagion and eventually he landed his own cable access show: *Hear No Evil with Pastor Peter Pringle.*

It became the church's crown jewel—the ultimate weapon in their crusade against heavy metal.

But for Peter, it wasn't just about saving souls, it was about doing whatever it took: preaching fiery sermons on his nightly broadcast, funneling donations to influential politicians and law enforcement, even conducting ruthless "scientific" experiments—no matter how ethically dubious—to one day prove that Alesha's brutal rejection wasn't his fault. It wasn't his abrasively persistent personality or even the vast difference in their ages and maturity. No, it was the music. It was heavy metal. It had warped her mind and made her do a *bad thing*.

He blinked one more time.

And a devious smile crept across his bright, rosy-red cheeks as he picked up the one telephone Piper forgot to dismantle.

Chapter 31

ELECTRIC FUNERAL

Back in Mark's room, a savage knee rocketed straight into his tighty-whitie-encased testicles. Mark let out a strangled, high-pitched grunt, and his eyes bulged cartoonishly from his skull as he folded over in pain like a faulty lawn chair.

"You fucking hypnotized your mom?!" Tori shrieked, chest heaving, eyes ablaze.

Before Mark could suck air back into his lungs, a right hook cracked across his jaw like a wrecking ball, sending him twirling around like an old Popeye cartoon.

"To fucking trick me into thinking," she seethed, "that you finally fucking had the balls to stand up to her?!"

Then a left hook. Followed by a skull-rattling uppercut that launched Mark off his feet. He slammed against the wall, cracking the wood-paneling and taking a flyer for the Collateral Damage show at Rowdy's with him as he crumpled into a groaning heap.

"Do you have *any fucking idea* how many fucking times I've been fucking lied to?!"

As Mark started to rise, Tori plowed into him, grabbed him by the waistband of his tighty-whities, and executed a brutal back body drop, flipping him over onto a pile of records. Jagged shards of Midnight Massacre and Human Toilet LPs stabbed into his back—talk about deep cuts.

"Jesus fucking Christ, it's like the fucking circus all over again!" she snarled, eyes blazing as memories flooded back: the rancid stench of stale peanuts, the whining of bored, thankless children, the lousy acrobats, the godawful painted-on smiles of second-rate clowns. And she could still taste the bile of cotton candy vomit at the back of her throat.

While Mark writhed on the floor, Tori unleashed a relentless barrage of kicks to his ribs, kidneys, ass, and face—each strike punctuating every single word like a ferocious exclamation mark. "I don't know what I ever even fucking saw in you, Mark Looger. Maybe I thought you were cool because you were into Fätal Fäte—who the fuck knows? But what I do know is, their music is all about standing up for yourself and fighting back against the fucking assholes of the world—the ones who lock you in a fucking basement. Who give you detention for wearing a fucking *shirt*. Who make their six-year-old kid feel like it was *his fault* his dumbass dad climbed up on the roof during a lightning storm, and then hold that shit over his head for years!"

She shot off a quick aside: "Okay, *some* of their tunes are about satanism too…"

Tori scooped up Mark's crumpled denim vest, dug out the Fätal Fäte tickets, and stared at them—half longingly, half with disgust.

"But you?" she continued her brutal takedown. "You'll *never* fucking fight back."

Mark tried to crawl away, dazed and wheezing, dragging himself across the floor like a wounded animal. But before he could get more than a few inches, Tori lunged, grabbed a fistful of his blood-soaked, unruly hair and yanked him up to his feet.

"Because you *still* think it's all your fucking fault!"

He let out a wet, choking yelp as she crammed the two front

row concert tickets down his throat—making him eat his own bullshit.

Tori reared back, and with all the strength of her steel mill-forged body—years of powerlifting turbine casing rings and turning her fists to ground beef on a fifty-five-gallon drum—she speared Mark across the room, driving him face-first into his stereo.

The impact was biblical.

The hi-fi exploded in a burst of wires, knobs, shattered plastic, and splintered faux-wood paneling. Both speakers toppled over. The turntable snapped in half with a final, screeching death knell. And a Spider Sac Lunch cassette was ejected across the room like a throwing star.

Mark collapsed in a bloody smear of flesh, hair, and tighty-whities, out cold on the floor.

But somewhere deep inside his fractured, headbanging skull, a light was still on.

And there in that faint, flickering haze, Mark was six years old again...

The storm had already started by the time that night's episode of *Fat Albert and the Cosby Kids* began.

Little Marcus sat cross-legged on the shag carpet, just a few inches from the flickering screen of the RCA Victor New Vista Console TV, an enormous beast of a television, more furniture than machine.

Before it became a sanctuary to religious fanaticism, before the made-in-China depictions of Christ with an Uzi, and well before all of that was stripped down and redecorated for a night of satanic debauchery, it was the typical middle-class suburban living room of the 1970s.

The whole house smelled like cigarettes, last night's pot roast, and Lemon Pledge. Instead of being plastered with ideological doctrines, the walls were decorated with simple macramé owls, paint-by-number landscapes, and a wood-grain sunburst clock that was only right twice a day.

Mother's La-Z-Boy Contour Recliner—brand new in bright Harvest Gold vinyl—was a far cry from the Nicotine Brown it would later become. It was flanked by mismatched end tables, side tables, and a credenza, each featuring a built-in ashtray or two and topped with ceramic butterfly knick-knacks and even more ashtrays.

The Formica coffee table—still factory-fresh and not yet scratched to hell—was cluttered with a collection of *TV Guides* featuring *Starsky & Hutch*, *Sonny & Cher*, and *Columbo* & his cigar. O.J. Simpson graced the cover of a *People* magazine in mid-stride. A flood of Kmart circulars, a coupon for Greasy Gene's Pizzeria (pre-tanning bandwagon), and a brochure from Columbia House promising twelve 8-tracks for a penny.

Stacked on the credenza beside the turntable were some of Marcus's dad's 8-tracks from his favorite British Invasion, garage rock, and proto-punk bands like The Festers, The Bush Heads, and Velvet Snog, along with a few records from Mother's (and most of America's at that time) favorite country superstar, Rosetta Rhinestone and the Ten Gallon Hats.

Above the mantle—where that monstrous cast-iron crucifix would one day hang—was a kitschy and unknowingly foreboding cross-stitch that read *A Mother's Work Is Never Done*.

On the TV screen, Russell stood confidently in front of the gang. "So, I yanked that kid right outta the fire," he was saying, "just as the aliens were beamin' up the whole building!"

Fat Albert, arms folded, one brow raised, grumbled, "Hey, hey, hey... somethin' don't add up today."

Just then, Marcus heard the roar of his dad's 1972 Sterling Silver Firemist Cadillac Coupe DeVille Hardtop pulling into the driveway. His face brightened. Dad was finally home from another long shift at the Wilhelm Steel Mill, and would soon plop down beside him, giggle like a six-year-old at all the dumb cartoon jokes, and admire the lopsided circle Marcus had drawn like it was the Mona Lisa.

Lightning flashed beyond the curtains. The lights dimmed. The wind groaned against the half-timbered siding of the Tudor Revival-style house. And just as Fat Albert was getting wise to Russell's tall tale, his voice cut in and out.

"Now, Russ—" *STATIC…* "Why don't you—" *STATIC…*

Somewhere in the kitchen, a chair scraped against the linoleum. Marcus turned to look. The door was open just a crack. He could only make out flickering shadows and the sounds of giggling and wet kisses.

Then he heard his dad's voice whispering, "He's gonna, like, hear us, or whatever."

Mother answered in that syrupy tone she used when she really wanted something, "No, he won't. He's watching that filthy cartoon about a bunch of loud, lazy miscreants running wild in the streets, teaching each other all the wrong lessons."

More kissing. More giggling. More furniture scraping against linoleum.

Marcus turned back to the TV. Just before he could see how the episode ended—what Russell was going to do after being scorned by Fat Albert himself—the picture snapped to full *STATIC,* and stayed that way.

"Uh… something's, like, wrong with the TV, or whatever! I can't see *Fat Albert and the Cosby Kids!*" he called out, hoping one of his parents (ideally his dad) would come fix it.

No answer.

He stared at the fuzz for a second and shrugged. *Fat Albert* was okay. But he liked *Josie and the Pussycats* better. The music. The guitars. And how Josie, in her skin-tight feline leotard, made him feel funny in a way he couldn't explain.

He picked up his Stretch Armstrong, gripped the toy's rubber hands, and pulled—its limbs stretching like warm taffy between his fingers.

In the kitchen, Mother's voice cut through again. Sharper now. "Just go up there and fix that god-forsaken antenna!"

Lightning flashed through the windows again.

"But it's, like, not safe," his dad said, sounding worried. "Didn't you, like, see that lightning?"

"You want this or not?" Mother shot back, softer, sweeter.

A pause.

More kisses. More giggles.

"Then go fix the damn thing," she commanded. "While I change into something… more comfortable."

The back door creaked open. A cold gust swept into the living room. Rain hissing against the patio deck. Boots squeaking. The screen door slammed shut.

As he listened, Marcus kept pulling Stretch Armstrong's limbs, stretching the poor rubber hero to his absolute limit—its neck contorting, legs pointing in opposite directions.

He heard the ladder dragged out of the garage. The *clunk* of it landing against the siding. The *thump-thump-thump* of boots climbing. Then… footsteps on the roof.

One of Stretch's arms stretched so far that the rubber cracked open and a tiny bubble of goo oozed out of the armpit.

And then: a blinding white flash.

CRACK! BOOM! A heavy *THUD.*

No more voices. No more giggling. No more furniture scraping against linoleum. No more arm on Stretch Armstrong. Only *STATIC* from the RCA Victor New Vista Console TV.

Then he heard Mother's footsteps. Running. The back door

swinging open.

Mother screaming, "Oh, no! Oh, God, what have I done?!"

But… this wasn't how Mark usually remembered it—or had been *told* to remember it.

Another voice shouted, "Mark!"

It was Tori's voice, and it sliced through the memory like a blade, ripping him back to reality.

Mark jolted upright, spitting out soggy fragments of Fätal Fäte tickets. "Tori?" he gasped, eyes darting around the room.

She was gone. Her clothes with her.

He heard her cry out again, blood-curdling terror in her voice, "Mark!"

Bloodied, missing teeth, shattered vinyl jutting from his back, Mark staggered to his feet in nothing but his tighty-whities and limped out of his room after his Metal Goddess.

Chapter 32

BLOODBATH IN PARADISE

The house was eerily quiet. There was no music. No laughter. No revelry or joyous catharsis. And it smelled like something. Something familiar. What was it?

"Tori!" he shouted, his voice as rough and ragged as he looked.

No answer.

Then Mark remembered the smell—the butcher counter at the Piggly Wiggly—and quickened his pace as best he could.

Staggering down the hall, searching for any sign of life, he made his first discovery of the night's horrors and stopped cold.

In the laundry room stood a blackened, still-smoldering skeleton. It was barely recognizable, save for the charred remains of a pocket protector and partially melted glasses.

"Edward!" Mark gasped, trying to make sense of what he saw, trying to find the words. "But how did this… it's not, like… I mean, like, it's not even, like… logical, or whatever."

His eyes drifted downward, landing on the motionless Metal T.E.D., its laser blasters still locked on its creator, frozen mid-robot uprising.

Lyrics from a familiar song surged through Mark's mind: *All that it takes is a little rewiring, to kill its human master with laser beams!* from the song "Robot Uprising" by Technologi-KILL.

Gotta be some kind of crazy coincidence, or whatever, Mark thought.

He continued down the hallway, his feet splashing through warm puddles of fresh blood. Mark slipped on a tangle of the stray entrails of fellow headbanger Nicole Rhodes, sending him stumbling into the bathroom.

It was filled with steam. In the tub, Frankie "Freakshow" Tanner was rocking back and forth in the fetal position as the showerhead scoured her skin raw. Dark, dirty water spiraled down the drain beneath her.

Mark knew Freakshow well. Back before the Headbanger Mobile was up and running, he'd shared a seat with her on the school bus every miserable morning during the forty-five-minute commute to Black Rock Falls High School.

Freakshow was infamous for going out of her way to shock and disgust people—like refusing to (ever) bathe, hoarding a rotting raccoon carcass in her locker, and, most notoriously, eating actual dog shit onstage for the ninth-grade talent show.

Now, she was clean. So clean that Mark barely recognized her.

"Freakshow?" he asked, stepping closer. "Are you, like... okay?"

Freakshow didn't answer. Couldn't answer. She was catatonic— stripped of her filth and with it, everything she was.

Again, Mark was reminded of song lyrics. *Wash away filth and disease, send it spiraling down the drain. The protocol is quarantine, until she goes insane.* The song was "Quarantine Protocol" by Dukes of Hazmat.

A sick, twisting feeling churned in his gut.

He tumbled backward, retreating into the dark of the hallway, and straight into Mother's bedroom, where his foot squished into something squishy.

Mark looked down.

A human tongue!

"What is...?" His gaze followed the impossibly long appendage snaking halfway across the room, where it was connected to a pile of disembodied entrails and musculature. Next to it, the deflated balloon of a corpse that once was Fogey.

"Fogey!" he cried, taking in the mind-boggling gore of it all, "Whoa! You, like… totally spilled your guts."

Then Mark's eyes drifted to something that was somehow far more disturbing, something that would forever haunt his dreams from this day forward: Fogey's displaced terrible mullet toupee, exposing his bald, flaky deception.

At the sight of this, Mark immediately remembered the lyrics: *As time goes by and slips away, his life a wasted jest, as genuine as his toupee, this fool must meet his death.* It was as though the lyrics to "Slay the Deceiver" by Non-Believer had been followed verbatim.

What the hell is, like, going on around h—

Before Mark could finish the thought, a cool breeze chilled his mostly naked bones. He turned to find a giant hole in the wall of Mother's room leading to the backyard patio. He stepped through it and was confronted with a whole new realm of terror.

Seated upon his wicker chair throne with the top of his head reshaped into a grotesque king's crown, was a potent metaphor for a kingdom of heavy metal under siege.

"*King* Greg of the Golden Realm," Mark whispered, instinctually dropping to his knees in the overwhelming horror of the moment, but also in reverence.

Mark's eyes scanned the ravaged patio, the charred wood planks of the deck, the decimated garden gnomes, a pair of discarded nunchucks, and the axe across King Greg's lap. An epic battle had taken place here. "You must have fought, like, nobly or whatever," he said, bowing his head to his fallen friend.

"Mark!" he heard Tori scream again.

"Tori!"

He clambered to his feet and headed back toward the house—but not before catching a glimpse of two cadavers floating motionless in the backyard hot tub, their skin shriveled and blistered to a deep, unnatural red. The control panel had been pried open, the temperature dial snapped completely off, and the display flickered erratically, struggling to register a reading somewhere between 665°F and 667°F.

Mark was pretty sure the boiled lobsters were Paul Simmons… or was it Strummer? And Kim… something. He vaguely remembered something about them getting kicked out of Rowdy's Bar & Grill and Tanning for doing it in one of the tanning beds. But he was absolutely *sure* this same exact thing was described in "Boiled to Death in a Hot Tub" by No Effort. "Underrated band," Mark muttered.

Back inside, he encountered more and more carnage along the way. Headbangers with their throats slit. Severed limbs playing checkers. Decapitated heads playing chess. One poor soul's face smashed into a radiator, another's legs forced into impossibly tight leather pants, flesh grotesquely bulging at the seams.

Mark tripped over what appeared to be a failed attempt at some kind of Frankenstein monster—a sickening patchwork of headbanger body parts crudely stitched together. Mark stumbled forward, arms flailing, and plunged straight through the open basement door, tumbling down the steps into a chasm of pitch-black.

When he regained consciousness, his eyesight adjusted to the faint glow of a discarded flashlight, and Mark took in the scene before him.

Near the foot of the stairs was a collection of clear garbage bags. Most were filled with paper confetti, but a few were bloated and sagging with what looked like spaghetti, and leaking a grandma's helping of red pasta sauce.

But Mark knew immediately what it really was. *Who* it was.

Not because he was some master sleuth with the truth-uncovering instincts of Piper or her parents.

No. Mark was an idiot.

But he did eventually pass the eighth grade and could put two and two together. Especially when one of those twos was the unmistakable dented steel helmet jammed in the massive industrial paper shredder.

"P-P-Piper?" he muttered under his shaky breath.

Mark finally hurled—mostly blood and bile from his internal injuries.

He wiped his mouth and staggered backward into a pile of empty boxes and a few scattered documents. Documents that looked really important. Complicated. And secret. *Piper must have, like, stumbled on to something big down here*, Mark thought, *like, whatever that 'special work' Mother had been doing, or whatever.*

And if *all your secrets are revealed*—as the lyrics went—it would be *Operation: KILL.* Again, it was a song that perfectly fit the scene of the crime. This one, without a doubt, was "Shred the Evidence" by Political Asylum. And it finally confirmed Mark's own budding conspiracy theory: *If heavy metal is, like, making someone do bad things, or whatever, that* someone *has to be—*

"Mother!" Mark gasped.

"Mark! Fucking help! Now!"

Oh, shit! Shit shit shit!

Mark scrambled up the basement stairs, following the sound of Tori's voice toward the living room, where the heart of the party—the laughter, the revelry, the joyous catharsis—had raged not so many songs ago.

His eye caught a shadow cast on the dining room wall: a feminine figure with big, wild, rock 'n' roll hair.

Finally! Tori!

His pulse kicked up. He quickened his pace.

But as Mark stepped into the dining room, his stomach clenched into a fist. If there had been anything left in him to vomit, it would've hit the floor right then and there. The sight before him was more shocking, more frightening, and more disgusting than anything he had encountered since limping out of his room.

This was not Tori Payne.

Not even close.

Standing at the makeshift bar of the dining room table—now mostly a graveyard of half-empty bottles—was a figure as unmistakable as his androgyny.

Fox fucking Chastain.

Casually mixing a margarita.

But no headbanger, metalhead, death-head, hesher, grinder, shredder, thrasher, mosher, doomer, black shirt, speed freak, noise fiend, powerlord, or hellraiser in their right mind would allow a glam rat like Fox Chastain into this party.

And yet, here he was.

Which could only mean one thing.

Mother had heard the lyrics to "Glamfestation" by Destroyer of Worlds: *A doll-faced fiend locked outside, pounding the gates with unholy pride. Perfume and aerosol to poison the halls. Unchain the doors—watch the revelry fall!*

Mark's blood went cold.

"Mark Looger!" Fox blurted, spreading his arms wide, as if expecting a hug. "My main party dude with the rad attitude!"

Mark didn't budge. Just glared at the uninvited guest.

Undeterred, Fox leaned in and tipped his aviators. "Hey, man, so is, 'on the rocks' the only option?" he asked, gesturing toward the margarita station.

But before Mark could tell him where to go stick his margarita, he heard another shriek. Not a scream this time, but the sound of Mother's Volvo 240 family station wagon peeling out of the driveway.

Mark rushed over to the window in the living room, careful not to slip on the blood and guts painting the floor. He arrived just in time to see her car speed away down the street, sideswiping a few haphazardly parked vehicles in the process.

Mother had taken Tori. *But, like, where?*

That's when Mark noticed another sound. Something he had been too enraged by the presence of Fox Chastain to hear before.

Click-click-click.

He turned around and his eyes locked onto the Pioneer SX-780 hi-fi stereo system.

Click-click-click.

To the turntable.

Click-click-click.

To the record that had just finished playing, the needle bouncing against the center label with that relentless *click-click-click.*

Chapter 33

YOU GOT ANOTHER THING COMING

It was a series of unfortunate miscommunications.

Beatrice Finch—as she was known back then—was at the Rainbow Bar & Grill that night because one of her favorite metal bands, Flavor of the Weak, was *supposed* to be playing.

The Rainbow was a legendary icon of the Sunset Strip and a rite of passage for anyone who was anyone in the metal scene. Everyone from Midnight Massacre to Malibu Bad Boys got their start here.

It was also legendary because of who you might bump into on any given night. You might be sitting at the bar and glance over to see Oily Deacon holding court in his designated booth full of impressionable teenage girls. You might find yourself pissing next to "Crazy" Johnny Fitz at the urinal—careful, he's got bad aim. You might end up on the floor of a mosh pit getting stomped in the face by K.C. Kraven. Or you just might find *yourself* seated at Oily Deacon's booth. Anything was possible at the Rainbow.

And it was legendarily loud. Something about the acoustics of the place. Or the way the sound reflected off all the metal studs, spikes, and chainmail of its clientele. Whatever it was, the Rainbow Bar & Grill was by far and away the loudest club on the Sunset Strip. In all of LA. Maybe the world.

At the time, Beatrice shared a shitty two-bedroom hellhole apartment on Yucca Street—Hollywood Boulevard-adjacent, if you squinted—with

Tina Scarborough, a fellow LA newbie and clinically depressed because she missed her boyfriend... or her dog... or whatever back in Idaho... or Iowa... or any one of those lame-ass flyover states.

Tina wasn't the greatest roommate, but also not the worst. Not the greatest because she was always moping around and hardly ever spoke a word. And not the worst, well... because she was always moping around and hardly ever spoke a word.

Still, she had been the one to tell Beatrice about the Flavor of the Weak show and had gone out of her way to score the tickets. It was her way of "making it up to you for all the 'drama' lately," Tina had said.

Beatrice didn't have a clue what her roommate was talking about or care. All that mattered was that she was gonna see Flavor of the Weak and was amped!

But when they arrived at the Rainbow Bar & Grill that night, Beatrice quickly realized she had been duped. The band that was playing was *not* Flavor of the Weak.

Not even close.

It was one of those "goth metal" bands called Blooderfly.

Tina, of course, was a huge fan of that miserable shit and had been practically begging Beatrice to give them a chance since they moved in together. But Beatrice couldn't stand goth metal. Its brooding, melancholic, romanticism just came off as sappy complaining to her. It lacked any of the raw power that Beatrice craved—the kind thrash metal, speed metal, power metal, and traditional heavy metal supplied in spades.

Blooderfly was extra annoying because they were known as the loudest goth metal band around. So the Rainbow made them deafening. Loud *and* sad—the worst combination.

And Tina, who didn't have a lot of friends and needed someone to tag along for "emotional support," had tricked her into this. Beatrice was almost as disappointed as she was pissed, but she figured this little ruse could be useful to hold over Tina's head if Beatrice was ever late with her half of the rent.

So she played along, sticking it out through one ear-splitting, gut-wrenching song after another about breakups, heartaches, and tortured souls, while Tina somehow juggled headbanging and crying at the same time.

But enough was enough.

Beatrice could only take so much of those black-clad knights of neurosis crying about their feelings and snuck off to the bar.

While waiting for her usual shot of Jägermeister, someone caught her eye.

He had long, jet-black hair, a denim vest covered in patches and pins, shredded jeans, just a touch of male-pattern baldness—barely visible under the dim bar lights. Both arms were covered in sleeves of wild-looking tats. And he was wearing earplugs. Yep, he'd come prepared.

Finally, somebody normal in this crowd of bogus Halloween vampires, she thought.

Beatrice grinned, telling the stranger she didn't like the noise, either.

For a moment he just stared at her, then remembered his plugs and took them out so they could chat. He seemed to agree that Blooderfly, and goth metal in general, sucked hard.

But to be fair, it was difficult to make out every word because of the noise.

When her Jäger arrived, Beatrice downed it and was about to resume her role as Tina's best and only friend in the great state of California. But the stranger ordered another round.

Okay, then.

They chatted it up for a while, poking fun at the band and trading

223

a few laughs—although again, thanks to the relentless noise, Beatrice couldn't catch every word with *complete* certainty. Eventually, Beatrice introduced herself and explained what she did—or what she was *trying* to do in LA. The stranger told her his name was Stan Drell, or something, and that he was a musician.

A musician?

A *musician!*

Beatrice signaled the bartender. Her turn to order a round.

After her last attempt to form a band fell apart when the bass player was committed to an insane asylum and the drummer got homesick and moved back to Afghanistan, Beatrice had been desperate to piece together a new one. So any time she met a fellow musician, especially one who shared her musical tastes, she took the situation very seriously.

The Jäger shots arrived. They downed them, squared up their tabs, and headed out the door.

She left her roommate at the Rainbow without a second thought, leaving Tina to wallow alone in the dark-but-beautiful bullshit of Blooderfly. Well, maybe *one* thought: that Tina might hold being ditched for some random musician over Beatrice's head if she were ever late with her half of the rent.

Okay, fine, *two* thoughts: she *did* briefly consider that abandoning Tina on such an "important" night could cause her clinical depression to escalate into a full-blown suicide note and a mess for Beatrice to clean up. Which would've been a bummer. But sometimes sacrifices had to be made.

Beatrice and Stan hopped in a cab and headed east on Sunset.

She usually didn't get in a car with some dude she just met at a bar. But they weren't going back to "his place." They were going to see where he "practiced." Like, as in where a *band* practiced. It was going to be a jam session, not some sleazy hookup. They were probably heading out to some busted-up garage. And there would be others there (so he said). She usually didn't do this kind of thing. But quite a few Jäger shots had been consumed.

And sacrifices had to be made.

But when they pulled up to the Chateau Marmont, all expectations were thrown out the window. This hotel, perched above Sunset Boulevard, was another legendary icon. It was a sanctuary for musicians, actors, comedians, writers, and artists. It was a place where Hunter S. Thompson could go to write, Greta Garbo could vanish, and John Belushi could die. The Chateau Marmont was a storied, scandalous, and undeniably glamorous place. And it was definitely where you go to stay and party when you've "made it."

So apparently, this Stan guy had "made it." Or at least had some dough. Either way, something wasn't adding up.

She didn't have a moment to think about it. As soon as she stepped out of the cab and into the driveway of the chateau, Beatrice was swept up in the energy and chaos of the place. Stan led her past the valets darting between idling cars, clouds of cigarette smoke, and glamorous guests getting in and out of their Ferrari Testarossas, Lamborghini Countaches, and Porsche 911 Carrera Cabriolets, and up a small staircase that led to the lobby.

There, Beatrice was hit by a barrage of overlapping conversations, clinking glasses, and outbursts of drunken laughter. A pair of models in nearly see-through dresses posed near the grand piano for a photo, while a rockstar—was that K.C. Kraven?!—argued with a concierge about her room key.

Stan moved confidently, cutting a path through the beautiful circus. They passed a group of ancient-looking actors—one of them was definitely Bette Davis—crowded around a low table that was nearly buried in an assortment of half-empty cocktails, playing cards.

They ducked around a server balancing a tray of martinis and slipped through a side door out into the courtyard, where more "who's who" of the era held court beneath the string lights.

The one and only Vinnie Blotto from Boozehound was passed out on a floating lounge chair in the pool, an empty bottle of vodka drifting nearby. Mr. T and Andy Warhol were playing chess. And a writer in a bucket hat, tinted aviator sunglasses, and an oversized, multi-colored field jacket furiously scribbled in a notepad, while mumbling incoherently around a cigarette in a long holder.

Finally, Stan stopped in front of one of the bungalows, unlocked the door, and shot Beatrice a sly grin. "This," he said, "is where I practice."

It wasn't just the Jägermeister anymore. Beatrice was too star-struck by everything and everyone at this glowing, glamorous, enig-matic castle on the hill to question the fact that she was clearly being brought back to "his place" after all. She was going against every rule on her very short list of rules, and she wasn't even questioning it.

Sacrifices.

Everything unraveled the moment Beatrice walked through the front door of the bungalow where this stranger had taken up extend-ed residence.

"Literally...?" Beatrice blurted out as Stan went around the room lighting candles, slowly revealing the horrific details of his home to her.

There were no guitars. No basses, amps, or drums. Not even a keytar—although that would have been no consolation. There were no metal posters, no record collection to speak of, or even a boombox!

There were black velvet blackout curtains covering every window, top hats and capes on the hat rack, decks and decks of cards, white gloves strewn about, magic wands and staffs, a sawing-in-half box, a divided-lady box, a zig-zag box, crystal balls of varying sizes, and even a trap door built into the floor—not sure what the management at the Chateau Marmont would think of that.

There were new and antique (some probably worth a fortune) promotional posters for Harry Houdini, Cardini, Chung Ling Soo, The Davenport Brothers, David Copperfield, Doug Henning, Penn & Teller and even Siegfried and Roy lining the walls.

And the smell: a mix of candle wax and… shit? Yes, rabbit shit, Beatrice realized, when she noticed the large cage filled to the brim with white rabbits. There was also a cage hanging in the corner with a black crow inside, cawing nonstop. The rabbits, the cawing crow, and the black cat that leapt into the room from the hallway to hiss at Beatrice, must have been who he was talking about when he said that there would be "others" there.

Fucking sacrifices.

Where there weren't animal cages, stage props, posters, or magical knick-knacks, there were bookshelves. And they were overflowing with every book ever written that had anything to do with magic. Everything from *The Secrets of Houdini* by J.C. Cannell to *Necronomicon* by Abdul Alhazred to *Magick in Theory and Practice* by Aleister Crowley.

"What the fuck is all this?" Beatrice snapped. "I thought you were taking me to where you practice."

Stan finished lighting candles. "What do you mean? This *is* where I practice."

She finally got a good look at the patches on his denim vest, and they weren't metal bands. Or even anti-establishment slogans. They looked like Boy Scout merit badges, but instead of canoeing or knot-tying, they marked off feats in magic like linking rings, vanishing coins, and cups and balls. And those "wild-looking" tats? Just the actual long sleeves of a god-awful psychedelic paisley shirt.

"Then where's your instruments?" she demanded. "Your guitars? Microphones? Shit, I don't know. Your fucking keytar?"

"My keytar?" He was completely befuddled. "Wait, did you think I was a musician?"

It hit her like a falling stage sandbag to the head. "Oh... right. Okay. I get it. This is where you practice *magic*."

He "got it," too, and smiled. "And you thought I said *musician* when I told you I was a magician."

"Fuck. It was so fucking loud in there with that shitty Blooderfly blasting in my ears." Beatrice said.

"You don't like Blooderfly?" He looked genuinely perplexed. "Then why were you at the Rainbow?"

"I already told you!"

"You did?"

She stared at him. "About my sad-sack roommate?"

He stared back.

Dammit, this was getting exhausting. But one thing still bugged her. "Well, if you like that gloomy-ass music so much, then why were you wearing those earplugs?"

He shrugged. "Oh, you know. Just trying to protect my hearing."

She hated that fucker more and more every second. It was time to leave. Now. "Look, Stan, I think it might be better if I just—"

"Stan? Who's Stan?" He scratched his thinning hair.

"You! You told me your name is Stan? Stan Drell, right?"

"Um, no. My name is *Thendrall*. Thendrall the Wise. It's my syndicate name. But I had it legally changed." Then he stepped closer, whispering, "I'm actually a *sorcerer*, but I usually don't tell people that right away. It tends to scare them off. Wait, your name *is* Bitch-Face Bitch, right? Because that's what I heard, but I wasn't sure if—"

"What the fuck?!" Beatrice raged (while secretly thinking that was the coolest name she'd ever heard). "No! It's Beatrice Fi—whatever." She started for the door.

Then paused. There was something about what he had just said.

Beatrice was always on the hunt for anything that freaked people out, scared the general public, or made them recoil in disgust. It was the essence of heavy metal and her creative fuel. Could this... this "Thendrall the Wise" offer potential inspiration for her next song?

"What did you say? About being a... sorcerer?" she asked hesitantly.

"I said that I usually keep my sorcerer's ways to myself," he stepped closer, his voice dropping to a conspiratorial whisper. "Because your average, everyday folks have a hard time appreciating anything that falls outside their neat little Judeo-Christian box. They hear words like, 'incantation' or, 'spell,' and panic. Their minds can't handle the idea that someone might know things—*real* things—that could shatter their illusions."

Thendrall paused. He turned and removed a battered, ancient-looking tome from a high shelf—bound in cracked leather and cobwebs. It seemed like a random pick to underscore his point, but it wasn't. Not in the grand scheme of things. No, this book was destiny. Beatrice's destiny. Maybe even heavy metal's destiny...

"But this book," Thendrall continued, voice lowering even more, "contains insights—*methods*—to unlock powers that most people will never dare to understand."

Beatrice's eyes widened, her breath catching in her throat.

He opened the book and flipped through its pages. "You see, fear is what keeps them small—fear of knowledge, fear of change. But when the time is right, when the forces in this book have been fully mastered..." He paused, looked up at Beatrice, his eyes gleaming in the candlelight. "That's when I'll finally have the means to show the world just how small and petty their fears really are. And then—*then*—I'll have the power to challenge every closed-minded fool who ever doubted me."

229

He snapped the book shut with a decisive thud, returning it reverently to the shelf.

Beatrice clocked the spot.

"But until that day comes," he said, "I keep my head down. Safer for everyone that way. Just another guy at the bar, another eccentric at this hotel."

He stepped closer. So close she could feel his minty breath. "Or a fellow metalhead with slightly different tastes in its various subgenres."

"Uh… that's what I thought you said," Beatrice replied to his long answer to her simple question, her eyes wide with wonder. Her heart pounded. This was exactly what she'd been searching for: the secret to push her metal dreams into the stratosphere.

In the dimming candlelight, his early male-pattern baldness seemed to disappear.

He kissed her.

She kissed him back.

The next morning, Beatrice woke before Thendrall, quietly slipping from his wizardly waterbed. She found that sacred book, clutched it like a stolen prize, and crept out of the bungalow.

She tiptoed through the hush of the Chateau Marmont's early morning corridors, imagining the dark inspiration she'd find within the pages. She caught a taxi back to her Yucca Street apartment, ready to write the most wicked metal song of all time.

But in the cab, as she flipped open what she had thought was an ancient tome, Beatrice discovered the latest in a long string of miscommunications that defined the last nine hours. It wasn't a book of diabolical incantations at all. It was *Seven Steps to Conquering Stage Fright* by Delroy Trembly.

"But this book contains insights—*methods*—to unlock powers that most people will never dare to understand," Thendrall had said.

"And then, when the time is right, when the forces in this book have been fully mastered… that's when I'll finally have the means to show the world just how small and petty their fears really are…"

Jesus Christ. It was bad enough that he was a magician. But he was a *shitty* one too, who didn't even have the guts to get up on stage.

The whole night felt like a total waste. She'd broken all her rules. She'd fucked Thendrall the Wise—and instantly regretted it, especially after seeing his early male-pattern baldness on full display in the early morning light creeping in through the velvet curtains.

Yet, in the end, despite the shame and self-loathing, she actually *had* found inspiration for a song.

Drawing on that bitterness, her bad choices, and regret—plus every scrap of demonology mumbo-jumbo she could steal from her favorite horror flicks and comic books—Beatrice crafted a savage metaphor for the depths one must go to make it in the cutthroat world of metal. A galloping thrash metal anthem about getting what you want by giving up a piece of your soul.

A *Sacrificial Jam.*

The song began with a lone guitar on a clean channel articulating a haunting melody. After several measures, it was joined by a second layer of guitar, adding complexity and tension. And then a third, twisting it all into a chilling menagerie.

It continued to take shape, each layer adding relentless pressure upon the next. Then, with a huge cymbal crash, it all stopped, dissipating into the abyss. The drawn-out silence created a moment of suspense. And then, like a vengeful phoenix, it began again, slightly faster, layer upon layer, each doubling the intensity of what came before.

A deep, ominous force emerged from below it all as the kick drum pounded out a steady, rising beat. The bass followed, adding more weight. More terror.

Then, like a lightning bolt ripping across the sky, the guitars kicked over to the dirty channel. The melody exploded into a wall of distorted power chords, hammering out a new, evil riff. Now a furious gallop, the song was off and running, barreling toward the edge of sanity, and there was no chance of turning back.

And then the vocals hit. Unfiltered and unforgiving, Bitch-Face Bitch roared with the relentless intensity of someone forged by years of sacrifice, emerging complex, distorted, and out for vengeance.

Deep in the hall of the Satanic Temple
Prepare the altar of starlight and flame
Etch and Mark hieroglyphic symbols
Prophesized in Satan's name
Tie down the virgin, the preordained
Her wrists and ankles bound by rope
Screaming, writhing, attempting escape
Tighten the knot, vanquish all hope

It's a Sacrificial Jam
A rite to raise the damned
Satanic incantations
Unleash mass annihilation
With the blade in your hand
And these final commands:
Kill, kill, kill!
It's the Sacrificial Jam!

Now the sacrificial blade is honed
The instrument of her demise
Sharpen the steel, grinding against stone
A prick of blood confirms its bite

Chant the text, the words of Satan
And what the binding contract tells
Twist your tongue to form incantations
And speak the secret shadow spell.

Zeyrak su'dreena, malgor thun'ral
Arketh veras inook hyram
Morlen krall runath, ak'tar dru'zal
Eldar moreek, shun'gar veram
Oran thyren dross'keth tu'vala
Ne tholmak graal om'venemas
Sorla vek'shar, drethen vrennala
Brak'tor fel, un'dal Satanas!

It's a Sacrificial Jam
A rite to raise the damned
Satanic incantations
Unleash mass annihilation
With the blade in your hand
And these final commands:
Kill, kill, kill!
It's the Sacrificial Jam!

The moment of truth, the time has come
The final words have all been said
No more delays, nowhere to run
Seal this shady deal with death
Bring down the blade with all your power
Through flesh and ribs with one swift stab
Her heart will spray a crimson shower
She is the Sacrificial Lamb

233

It's a Sacrificial Jam
A rite to raise the damned
Satanic incantations
Unleash mass annihilation
With the blade in your hand
And these final commands:
Kill, kill, kill!
It's the Sacrificial Jam!

It was *his* song. *Their* song. Mark and Tori's favorite. They both knew every word of it. Forward *and* backward.

"Sacrificial Jam" by Fätal Fäte.

Mark stared in horror at that record—Frankenstein-ingly taped and stapled back together since Mother destroyed it—still spinning on the turntable, needle bouncing.

Click-click-click.

If Mother was following the lyrics to the letter—like she had with everything else—then there was no doubt: she was going to sacrifice Tori to Satan.

And Mark knew exactly where Mother had taken her.

Chapter 34

SEEK & DESTROY

Mark collapsed into the Headbanger Mobile, wincing in agony as the vinyl splinters in his back pushed against the seat. He fired up the ignition, cranked up AM 666 The Tower of Power, and slammed the gas pedal to the floor, sending another wave of pain through his broken body.

He blasted off into the night after Tori, waking up anyone who might still be awake in his decrepit neighborhood.

Mark's eyes were fixed like lasers on the dark road ahead as he tore through Liberty Bend, disobeying every traffic law known to man.

He nearly collided head-on with a livestock truck returning from the slaughterhouse in Bleakridge. The smell of pig shit wafted in through the doorless Headbanger Mobile, reminding him of Tori—he was still unsure why—and he punched the gas even harder.

Mark caught sight of flashing police lights in his rearview mirror. "Shit!" he spat, slowing down to pull off to the shoulder.

He squinted into the rearview, trying to figure out who it was and what flavor of trouble awaited. Was it Deputy Danny Clevis—or "Fanny Crevice," as the Brigade joked, because he was such an asshole? Or maybe Deputy "Fuck-wad" Farquand? Or even the big man himself, Sheriff Dix? Whoever it was, Mark knew exactly what they wanted—what every "adult" in town seemed to want: to stop heavy metal.

But just as he neared a complete stop, Mark saw that it *wasn't* a police cruiser at all!

It was a 1971 AMC Javelin AMX.

Coach Kraut's 1971 AMC Javelin AMX! He had a siren "borrowed" from the high school's emergency system duct-taped to the roof so he could play at vigilante in the name of overcompensated patriotism.

"Pfft, let's see you catch the Headbanger Mobile," Mark muttered as he hit the gas again, leaving Vigilante Kraut in the dust.

But the Javelin AMX was no slouch and was riding his bumper again in no time.

"Pull over, metal boy!" Kraut demanded through a stars-and-stripes-adorned megaphone, "Surrender and repent for your rücksichtslose Fahrweise and anti-American ways!"

Mark somehow managed to push the gas pedal down even farther—and with that, even more aches and pains. But the old V8 had already topped out at 105 MPH. "What the… huh?" he grumbled, glaring at the speedometer.

Mark had to lose him somehow.

He blew through another red light and took a sudden hard left on Jefferson Blvd.

His relentless pursuer had no problem doing the same.

But when Mark veered into a narrow alley between Lincoln and Washington, Kraut missed it and zoomed past.

"Nein!" he roared in frustration through the megaphone.

Mark rocketed down the alley, spilling garbage cans, tearing the bumpers off parked cars, running over bikes and skateboards that kids had left out. Rats scattered. Dogs howled. Cats hissed, diving out of the way at the last second.

Bursting out the other end, he took a hard right on Adams.

But Vigilante Kraut, having cut down Lincoln, was right back on his tail.

"You think you can lose me? Mein American chick magnet eat dreckige metal boys like Frühstück Wheaties!" Kraut shouted, slipping more and more into his native German tongue.

Speeding past Roosevelt, Kennedy, and Coolidge, he let Kraut catch up to within inches of his bumper, then cut a hard right onto Buchanan. The Javelin AMX zoomed past again as Mark gunned it back up to Jefferson and flipped another right.

For a split second, he thought he'd lost him again.

Then Vigilante Kraut came flying out of Kennedy Blvd.

"I never give up! Ich höre niemals auf! Like George Washington at Battle of Trenton or Rommel in der Nordafrika-Kampagne! Victory ist mein Schicksal!" Kraut declared, pounding his fist on the dashboard.

When Lincoln came around again, Mark hung a sharp left—and just when he thought he was out of presidents, he ran headlong into President Harding Ave. Another left.

Vigilante Kraut was right behind, chasing Mark past Liberty Belle Gentleman's Club and Tanning, ignoring the seedy clientele outside, as well as the hooker on the corner who blew him a kiss. He sent a wild pack of dogs scattered in all directions. He swerved around the grisly car wreck where an old woman lay dead in the street, fuzzy dice in her stiff grip. He zoomed right past Liberty Bend's Children's Hospital, still engulfed in flames and reportedly only fifteen-percent contained—because nothing, not death, depravity, or disaster, would keep that patriot from making a citizen's arrest of a gangly, traffic-law-violating "metal boy."

Kraut fishtailed through a puddle, drenching Mad Mabel for a third time that night and obliterating her latest sign—which had stated the appropriately fatalistic: *OKAY, FINE. FUCK YOU, TOO!*

Mark took a left on Coolidge, then a right on Jefferson. As he got lost in the presidential maze of Liberty Bend, his mind twisted and turned through its own historical labyrinth. He thought of Tori Payne—his teenage longing for her stronger than ever—and the danger she was in. He thought of the carnage back at his house, all his dead friends, the Headbanger Brigade, gone for good.

Then his brain hung a left.

It was *their* harebrained scheme that had caused it all. Hypnotizing Mother had made her susceptible to heavy metal—warping her mind and making her do bad things. And he had gone along with it.

A quick right.

But no, he didn't have a choice. The walls were closing in. Tori was skipping town for good. Mother had staged a full-blown coup to take over his life—even scheduling a haircut! *I'd be decked out in a Towncraft polo, pleated Rustler khakis, and a pair of Buster Brown loafers to complement a hairdo straight out of a Gomer Pyle, U.S.M.C. rerun if Mother had gotten her way*, he thought. Something drastic—something crazy—*had* to be done!

Another left turn.

But that's, like, only 'cause you were too much of a wuss to stand up to her, or whatever, he tortured himself. Because of the guilt. Because it was his fault his dad was dead. Because he wanted to watch cartoons.

Then his brain flipped a bitch.

But that's not what really happened is it? *When I was, like, out cold and having that near-death experience, or whatever, I saw it. Like, for real.* It had all come back. For the first time. What *actually* happened. And it didn't quite jibe with what Mother had drilled into his brain all those years, did it? *Mother had, like, practically begged dad to go up on that roof, hadn't she? In the middle of that, like, storm, or whatever. For what? For, like, some kind of afternoon delight!*

Mark suddenly got his bearings, hung a right, and tore east down

Main Street—which in Liberty Bend was a one-way street.

Nearing his destination and hoping he'd finally lost Vigilante Kraut, he saw the Javelin AMX make an illegal left turn onto the wrong way of Main Street, heading west and straight at him.

If one of them didn't slow down or swerve, it was going to be a head-on collision.

But time was running out. Tori was in trouble, and Mark couldn't spend the whole night tearing around town with this East German psycho on his tail. He had to save Tori. Or at least try.

If Kraut wanted to play chicken, Mark was ready to play chicken! He slammed the gas, grimacing with pain.

The Javelin AMX picked up speed too. They barreled straight at each other.

Closer…

It was East versus West, and neither Kraut nor Mark were flinching.

Closer…

"Das ist dein letzter Warnung, metal boy!" Kraut warned.

Closer…

At the last second, Mark hurled himself out of the Headbanger Mobile's missing door—his escape hatch, courtesy of Coach Kraut, himself.

"NEIN! NEIN! NEIN! JAAAA—"

And with that, Vigilante Kraut rammed head-on into the iron curtain of the Headbanger Mobile—EXPLODING like the nuclear blast the Cold War had promised for so long.

Mark hit the ground hard, rolling across the asphalt, pretty sure he'd just out-fractured Evel Knievel by at least three ribs and a femur.

When the wave of pain had passed (or at least plateaued) Mark opened his eyes and saw the twisted, smoldering wreckage that was once the Brigade's lone chariot and the last remaining relic of his dad.

Destroyed for a girl who probably didn't even want to see him again.

"Rest in peace, Headbanger Mobile," he mumbled as a single tear rolled down his cheek—part sorrow, mostly excruciating pain.

He turned and saw his mother's Volvo 240 family station wagon parked askew, the doors flung open and the engine still running. That's when he realized he'd landed right on the doorstep of his destination.

Right next door to the charred remains of the women's health clinic, it stood like a monument to defiance. Defiance against time, progress, and social norms.

Once known as Liberty Bend Bank & Loan, the building had been erected during the Gilded Age with all the pomp and excess of a dying empire: vaulted spires, pointed arches, and weathered brick the shade of dried blood.

Bars covered every window and a ridiculous array of security cameras blinked and swiveled like paranoid eyeballs—not to keep thieves out, but to deter the righteous wrath of Liberty Bend's angry mobs. Because to them, what was inside was nothing short of blasphemy. Maybe worse.

As Mark staggered to his feet and limped toward the flickering neon sign above the Gothic archway, he was struck by the absence of that mob—the God-fearing parents, churchgoers and PTA warriors who usually formed a blockade out front, thrusting handmade signs into the air while chanting, "Heavy metal is a sin, this is war and we will win!"

Tonight, it was all eerily quiet.

The front doors were ajar. One of them hung broken off its hinges, creaking in the light October breeze like the entrance to a haunted house.

Mark took a deep breath, bracing himself for what awaited *in the hall of the Satanic Temple*—as the lyric to "Sacrificial Jam" goes.

Then he stepped inside Satanic Temple Records, Tapes & Tanning.

Chapter 35

INTO THE VOID

Entering that sacred place always gave Mark a thrill—the kind he could only compare to walking through the automatic doors of a Toys "R" Us as a kid. Only here, the toys offered *true* escape into endless worlds that were scarier, louder, and better than this one.

But that night, the vibe was off. The air was colder. The lights dimmer, flickering more than usual. And that thrill was nowhere to be found.

It still bore the bones of the old bank: massive stone pillars, high vaulted ceilings with cracked gilding, and stained-glass windows (half-painted over in black). Chandeliers, coated in decades of dust, cast a weak orange glow onto the blood-red carpets below. Seemingly endless aisles of records and tapes were packed into ornate wooden shelves that once held ledgers and loan documents. The smell was a wild cocktail of vinyl, tanning lotion, and whatever had been growing in the walls since McKinley was gunned down.

"Monster" Mick Mackerel—owner, operator, and living cautionary tale—was the one-man beast behind Satanic Temple Records, Tapes & Tanning.

Unlike certain lying old fogeys who *claimed* they'd rubbed shoulders with the gods of metal from the late '60s through the early '80s, Monster Mick *actually* roadied for VD Vengeance. He legitimately *was* the Human Toilet's guitar tech. And yeah, he was there at Big Fat

Witch's final show, when Witchy Salem dropped dead in front of a packed house at Hammerjacks. It took Mick, three security guards, and a couple of EMTs to hoist Salem's body offstage. Doesn't get much more heavy metal than that.

He was somewhere in his sixties, though from the looks of it, time hadn't passed over Mick so much as used him in a brutal rock 'n' roll science experiment.

Patchy strands of long, ghost-white hair clung to his scalp, most of it having been ripped out by "Crazy" Johnny Fitz during one of his infamous Hell-Quake Tour seizures—seizures Monster Mick had personally restrained with duct tape, leather-studded belts, and the discarded bra straps of discarded groupies.

One eye was perpetually bloodshot. The other was gouged out by a flying mic stand in the riot that erupted when Jimmy Crotch refused to take the stage. In its place: a black, studded leather eyepatch.

Tattoos of screaming skulls, pentagrams, and the combination to Dickie Dullard's guitar case were scribbled across skin that looked more like jerky than flesh. The scars—one of the many reasons for his moniker—couldn't hide beneath the ink. Jagged pink welts and stitch marks crisscrossed his arms, neck, and face—souvenirs from run-ins with machete-wielding cartels while scoring for Bobby "The Possum" Dicer.

Where his left hand used to be, there was now a metal hook—custom-built for stacking vinyl, peeling shrink-wrap, and cracking open tallboys. According to legend, he lost it the night Hank the Stank turned to him and said, "I'm gonna need *you* to play lead guitar for us tonight, Monster." And Mick shredded so hard, so fast, and with such raw fury that his left hand and part of his forearm literally exploded in heavy metal hellfire.

A plastic tube ran from beneath his faded-to-oblivion Human Toilet official-staff T-shirt into a colostomy bag—his insides long since decimated from puking his guts out after witnessing what went down in Ronnie Shaggs's secret sex dungeon.

The sound of the bag filling at inopportune times was a well-known mood-killer.

Life out on the metal road had chewed him up, spit him out, and then stepped on his nuts. Running Satanic Temple Records, Tapes & Tanning was no different. Day after day, he waged war against protesters blocking the door, frivolous lawsuits from church groups, bomb threats from PTA moms, and flash exorcisms in the aisles. It was a war he was losing. The Satanic Panic was about to plant its victory flag. Hell, an hour ago the Freedom through Unconstitutional Containment for Kids bill sailed through the House and was on its way to the President's desk.

Customers were drying up faster than Vinnie Blotto's hotel room mini-bar. Either too scared, too brainwashed, or too grounded for a month after their last purchase to dare rock again. Even with his reluctant addition of tanning beds, Mick was deep in the red (though Mark and Mother's shopping spree earlier that day might have kept the lights on for a few more weeks).

But if you ever asked him about any of it—the scars, the store, the time he died while partying backstage with Ernie Lambskin—he'd just smile, throw horns with his mechanical hand, and tell you, "That's rock 'n' roll, baby."

So when Mark saw Monster Mick cowering behind the front counter, his one good eye darting, his mangled lips mumbling gibberish, his colostomy bag draining louder and more inopportunely than ever—he knew something was going down in the store.

Something bad.

More weary and determined than ever, Mark limped along through the speed metal section, the thrash, death, doom, progressive, symphonic, industrial, groove, power, and folk metal sections—or what was left of them after he and Mother had picked them over.

He passed albums like *Hidden Messages* by SIN-struction Manual, stamped with the usual *PARENTAL ADVISORY: EXPLICIT LYRICS* warning sticker courtesy of the PMRC, and *Cryptic Commands* by Blindly Follow, which, along with the parental advisory sticker, had a few more warnings such as *Banned in 40 Countries, Known to Cause Cancer in Lab Rats*, and *May Send You Straight to Hell!* Some had so many warning stickers on them that they completely obscured the title and artwork of the album.

He passed the stairs that led to the basement, where Monster Mick kept his banned Brazilian and Scandinavian imports—most of which were now part of Mark's personal collection at home.

He passed the limited but meticulously curated punk, post-punk, classic rock, surf rock, psychedelic rock, new wave, blues, jazz, funk, soul, classical, soundtrack, disco, reggae, electronica, country, classic country, outlaw country, honky-tonk, bluegrass, world music, and ambient sections—all in one bin marked *Eclectic.*

Beyond all of that, past the cassettes and the sacred vinyl, tucked away the back like a half-assed afterthought, were the tanning beds. Eight of them, humming like angry wasps, surrounded by mirrors and black light posters of scorpions, wizards, and bikini-clad demon-ettes on motorcycles.

And there it was.

There was the source of the screams that had drawn him hobbling through his house and sent him on a death race through the streets of Liberty Bend.

There was a tragic turn of events even worse than finding Fox Chastain in attendance at his party.

There, before Mark's beleaguered eyes, was a sight which

threatened to destroy everything he loved and quite possibly determine the fate of heavy metal…

Forever.

Chapter 36

IN MY DARKEST HOUR

The mirrors and black light posters had been *etched and marked with hieroglyphic symbols* pulled straight out of Mother's twisted subconscious courtesy of Lord Blatherton's so-called "Transcendental Aptitude Surge."

One of the eight gaudy tanning beds that Monster Mick had begrudgingly installed was repositioned for ceremonial prominence atop a platform of unsold Christian Rock albums. Its canopy was open and the powerful UV lamps radiated the store with cancerous, artificial sun rays. It was a literal realization of the lyric: *prepare the altar of starlight and flame.*

And upon this glowing sacrificial altar was Tori Payne—*the virgin, the preordained*—in the process of being tied down, *her wrists and ankles bound by rope.*

Any metaphor Bitch-Face Bitch was trying to convey with "Sacrificial Jam" had been completely lost on Mother.

As she was *screaming, writhing, attempting escape,* Tori squinted through the UV glare and spotted Mark, standing there looking like a badly beaten deer in the headlights.

"Mark!" she roared. "Thanks to your fucking stupid idea, the fucking song is actually making her fucking do bad things!"

"Right! I know… um, don't worry, I'm, like, totally gonna make her stop…" Mark stammered. He frantically put a foot up on a knocked-over crate of records, trying really hard to strike a pose like some kind of heavy metal general commanding his army to ride out and meet their fate. "Mother! I, uh… *command* you to, uh… stop!"

But Mother's only response was to *tighten the knot* around Tori's ankle to *vanquish all hope* she might have of freeing herself.

Mark meekly slid his foot down off the crate and stumbled back, remembering Mother's endless, unstoppable rambling earlier that day. "Just like the breakfast fit for the Lords of Hell…" he muttered.

"What? What did you say?" Tori shouted.

"I said… uh… that I'm pretty sure that she's gotta, like, finish doing this command before I can ask for anything else."

"Just say the fucking exit suggestion!"

"The exit sug—huh?" He had never heard those two words put together like that before in his life.

"The *exit suggestion!*" Tori was getting more exasperated by the second. "The fucking word or phrase to snap her out of the hypnotic trance! Don't you fucking know anything about hypnotism?"

No. Not really. And he was pretty sure that if the Headbanger Brigade had come up with an "exit suggestion" they didn't bother to tell Mark about it.

Bewildered and exhausted, Mark stumbled back and collapsed into the bargain bin, spilling the entire catalog of Rosetta Rhinestone and the Ten Gallon Hats across the floor. Half-buried beneath the pile of "keep-smiling-through-the-pain" country heartbreak, he groaned in total defeat, "All of my friends… and now Tori too…?"

Could things possibly get any more fucked?

That's when a familiar voice broke through the moment—playful, teasing, terrifying: "But that's not all!"

Mark's head snapped up to discover Pastor Peter Pringle, his rosy little cherubic face smiling with sickening cheer.

Yes. Far more fucked.

His eyes darted around the store, taking in details he'd somehow missed when he arrived. The pastor was joined by a small crew of dead-behind-the-eyes middle-aged women: volunteers from the Holy Christ Church of Unwavering Condemnation running the camera, the boom mic, and every other part of the production. They had transformed the back half of the store into a makeshift television studio.

One of them—her name tag read *Birdy*—sat behind an audio mixing board, wearing a helmet with a comically large satellite dish attached. She greeted Mark with a casual, "Blessed evening."

Mark's confusion was off the charts. "What the... huh?"

"Oh, you know. Just beaming this all out *live* to my congregation. Go ahead, check the, um, 'boob tube,'" Pastor Pringle said, reveling in his righteousness, as he directed Mark's attention to the small, staticky production monitor tucked between racks of tanning oils and Aloe vera.

The screen showed the same scene unfolding just a few feet away: Mother standing over Tori on the glowing altar, unveiling the sacrificial blade—shimmering with ritualistic menace, yet unmistakably familiar. It was the very same kitchen knife she'd used at breakfast to slice up Mark's atomic waffles and abortion-themed egg omelet. Now in glorious full color!

"And when the world sees how the *devil's music* warps the mind and makes you do bad things, it shall finally spell the end of that terrible music!" the pastor declared.

"Mark! Are you seriously gonna just fucking sit there on your ass while I get fucking sacrificed to fucking Satan?!" Tori shrieked, freaking the fuck out.

"Language! Please, young lady. For the thousandth, millionth time! This is a family program!" Pastor Pringle snapped.

He threw a nod at Birdy, who promptly got up and slapped a strip of duct tape over Tori's mouth to stifle her screams and vulgarity—adding a casual, "Blessed evening."

Chapter 37

CREEPING DEATH

Word of this very special episode of *Hear No Evil with Pastor Peter Pringle* spread quickly. The concerned, curious, and excited citizens of Liberty Bend phoned their friends and relatives in other towns and states (with no regard for long-distance charges) to share what they were witnessing and speculate on how it might all unfold.

Reports of the strange local broadcast soon reached regional news stations across the country. Within minutes, those outlets patched into the Liberty Bend feed, beaming the live program to millions of homes through their networked affiliates.

As the viewership exploded, the "big three" national networks took notice. Recognizing the mounting public interest—not to mention the sensational nature of the content, which promised to be a ratings bonanza—they made the unprecedented decision to interrupt regular programming. They even cut away from the live coverage of the President of the United States' ceremonial signing of the Freedom through Unconstitutional Containment for Kids bill.

It was supposed to be a moment of national triumph: the president flanked by a chorus of choirboys in the Oval Office to represent all the "perfect little angels" this new law—an egregious violation of the Constitution and a blatant assault on fundamental human rights and dignity—would supposedly protect from becoming "abnormal."

But just as the president clicked his favorite G.I. Joe pen to sign, every major network (including the still-fledgling CNN) abruptly cut away to *Hear No Evil with Pastor Peter Pringle*.

Panic erupted in the Oval Office. The choir boys were hushed, the president's pen yanked away, and his advisors—those seasoned legal contortionists who'd reassured Congress that their carefully crafted statutory language and twisted canons of construction would withstand any court challenge—immediately leapt to the nearest phones. Their aides and their aides' aides called every media outlet they could think of, raising hell over the cutaway.

Yet when they learned the reason for the broadcast's interruption was a demonstration of heavy metal's unholy powers, even they were compelled to pause and tune in. No one could look away.

The president, on the other hand, couldn't have cared less. He slouched in his chair, twiddling his thumbs and waiting for his staff to tell him what to do next, comforted by the promise that, once this signing was complete, he'd be allowed to watch a prerecorded episode of *Muppet Babies* on his VCR, accompanied by an unlimited supply of jelly beans.

The signal soon reached communication satellites in geostationary orbit, spreading the broadcast across the globe. Even MTV, shockingly, paused its endless stream of music videos to air this unprecedented "reality-based" program.

The broadcast's lightning-fast journey from a small-town feed to a global phenomenon not only highlighted the power of modern 1980s telecommunications but also the world's insatiable fascination with the controversy surrounding heavy metal.

As the world watched, Mother reached out and took hold of one of the old support pillars in the back of the store. With her superhuman, hypno-strength, she broke off a jagged piece of crumbling stone, showering the floor with paint chips and dust. Then, with

slow, deliberate strokes, she used it to sharpen her sacrificial blade—
to *sharpen the steel, grinding against stone.*

"This lovely woman here," Pastor Pringle gestured toward Mother, "who just so happens to be a devout member of our congregation, well… she's in a bit of a musical pickle. Poor Delilah has been up to some naughty business. You see, she's been listening to the *devil's music!* Can you believe it? And do you know what those nasty, vulgar heavy metal lyrics told her to do?"

The pastor paused, allowing the audience time to answer.

"That's right!" he cried, suddenly brandishing a *Sacrificial Jam* by Fätal Fäte album for added effect, "a ritualistic human sacrifice of a female virgin to appease the sinful lusts of Satan himself! Oh, it's all so very, very troubling."

Mother put the stone down. Slowly and ceremoniously, she drew the blade across the length of her thumb. The steel sliced cleanly through her skin. She didn't even flinch as blood flowed like a thin red river down her arm. Yes, it was sharp. *A prick of blood confirms its bite.*

A few drops of Mother's blood splattered onto Tori's face. She groaned and recoiled in disgust.

Then Pastor Pringle directed the audience's attention to Tori. "And now that poor young girl on the altar… well, she's in quite a pickle herself, I'm afraid." He sighed theatrically. "Oh, I know, I wish there was something someone could do to help her. Really, I do. But you see, the evil influence of heavy metal, it's like a magical spell, casting its wicked sorcery through hi-fi speakers and the MTV. Twisting the mind, bending the will to do its bidding. And once it gets its grubby little hands all up in there…" he demonstrated with his own grubby little hands, "it cannot be stopped!"

Chapter 38

BREAKIN' ALL THE RULES

Mark's mind was spiraling into a maelstrom of nightmarish visions, each more grotesque and batshit crazy than the last.

He imagined a picture-perfect family huddled around an old boxy television. On the screen, Mother stood triumphant, the sacrificial blade raised high. Her badass-looking rock 'n' roll war-painted face glowed with unholy rapture as the blade plunged in a brutal arc, straight into Tori's heart. Blood, dark as crude oil on the black-and-white screen, sprayed into the air like a burst pipeline as Tori's body went limp on the altar.

The family gasped in unison. The youngest child buried her face in her mother's lap as the father stoically muttered, "Thank God. It's finally over."

A spinning newspaper, conjured by Mark's tortured imagination, revealed the bold, devastating headline: *THE END OF THAT TERRIBLE MUSIC!* Mark's stomach churned as he pictured headbangers around the world reading those words, their fists trembling with impotent rage.

The vision twisted again. Towering piles of burning records stretched toward a darkened sky, their covers curling and blackening in the roaring inferno. The air was thick with the toxic stench of melting vinyl. A mob of zealots cheered, their faces contorted with grotesque satisfaction. Signs waved above the crowd: *SAVE OUR CHILDREN!, SILENCE SATAN'S SOUNDTRACK!* and the very wordy, yet surprisingly effective: *ATTENTION CITIZENS OF LIBERTY BEND, PARENTS OF WAYWARD YOUTH, AND GOD-FEARING CONSUMERS OF CLEAN ENTERTAINMENT: IT HAS COME TO OUR ATTENTION THAT HEAVY METAL MUSIC (INCLUDING BUT NOT LIMITED TO: GLAM, THRASH, DOOM, SPEED, BLACK, AND SO-CALLED "CHRISTIAN" SUBGENRES) IS A DIRECT AND UNFILTERED PIPELINE TO VIOLENCE, SATANIC WORSHIP, DRUG USE, IMPROPER ZIPPER PLACEMENT, INVERTED CROSSES, AND UNHOLY GUITAR SOLOS CAPABLE OF INDUCING DEMONIC POSSESSION, AND AS SUCH WE THE UNDERSIGNED (OF WHICH THERE ARE MANY, I PROMISE YOU) DEMAND THE IMMEDIATE CESSATION OF ALL LOCAL RECORD SALES, LIVE PERFORMANCES, BAND PRACTICE, AND AIR GUITAR BEHAVIOR UNTIL A FULL INVESTIGATION IS LAUNCHED BY THE LIBERTY BEND CITY COUNCIL, THE CHURCH ELDERS COMMITTEE OF THE HOLY CHRIST CHURCH OF UNWAVERING (CONTINUED ON BACK)…*

Then the scene shifted to something even worse. The heavy metal icons Mark had idolized—members of Midnight Massacre, VD Vengeance, and even the little-known Section 8 (as in the military discharge for insanity—*not* the way-less-badass low-income housing term)—were marched through the streets in shackles, their heads bowed. Their faces, once fierce and defiant, were hollow, their spirits crushed.

Some were led to the gallows. Others were forced to face firing squads. Bitch-Face Bitch was strapped into the electric chair. Her legendary defiance remained unbroken even as electricity crackled and danced across her body, her muscles jerking violently as she rode the lightning.

"All of my friends... and Tori... and now, like, heavy metal too...?" Mark moaned in horror as he came out of his vision of things to come.

Just then, Mother began chanting, heeding the commands of the song to *twist your tongue to form incantations, and speak the sacred shadow spell*: "Zeyrak su'dreena, malgor thun'ral..."

Finally, he couldn't take it anymore and something snapped.

"Arketh veras inook hyram..." Mother chanted.

Mark no longer cared how hard she worked to raise him...

"Morlen krall runath, ak'tar dru'zal..." she droned on.

He no longer cared that she did it all alone, sacrificing everything for him...

"Oran thyren dross'keth tu'vala..."

Ever since his dad was struck by lightning fixing the antenna...

"Ne tholmak graal om'venemas..."

Just so that he could finish watching *Fat Albert and the Cosby Kids*.

"Sorla vek'shar, drethen vrennala..."

Because it wasn't his fault.

Not his dad.

Not the murder of forty-two headbangers.

Or the end of heavy metal itself.

Mother raised the sacrificial blade high above her head, her eyes blazing with unholy fire as her voice rose into a full-throated howl: "Brak'tor fel, un'dal... Satanas!"

It wasn't even a conscious decision. It was pure, involuntary rage from deep within his lizard brain that lifted Mark from the heap of Rosetta Rhinestone records to finally—both literally and figuratively—stand up to his mother.

"Fuck this!" Mark spat, his voice sharp as the blade Mother held over his girlfriend. "Heavy metal doesn't make people do a goddamn thing!"

The moment of truth, the time has come. The final words have all been said. No more delays, nowhere to run. Seal this shady deal with death. Bring down the blade with all your power, echoed through Mother's mind on a loop. Faster, louder, loopier… *Through flesh and ribs with one swift slice. Her heart will spray a crimson shower.*

The blade gleamed ominously in her hands, its edge catching the tungsten lights of the makeshift television studio.

Mark's face darkened. His breath hitched. His eyes burned like molten steel. And then, through gritted teeth, his voice dropped to a raw, guttural growl—low, seething, dangerous, every syllable laced with venom: "Shitty parents like you do!"

At the same moment, with all the power her hypno-strength could muster, Mother swung the blade down toward Tori's chest, the arc swift and deadly.

Chapter 39

ESCAPE

Tori Payne had wanted some "fucking chaos" in her life. She wanted to "raise some fucking hell." Liberty Bend, she'd said, was "a fucking dead-end," a "sinkhole of gas station burritos and tanning salons. Nothing ever fucking happens here. And when it does, it just turns out to be the same boring-ass bullshit all over again!"

So when she saw Mark—bloodied and broken in his tighty-whities—finally stop being a fucking wuss and rise from the ashes of the discount bin like a goddamn phoenix from hell, stare his legendary bitch of a mother dead in the eyes and set the fucking record straight about heavy metal, something ignited inside her.

That spectacle of chaos that she'd been craving for so long, since the promise of the circus, had finally arrived. Liberty Bend wasn't a dead-end anymore. It was a powder keg. And Mark Looger had just lit the fuse.

Fueled by a lifetime of rage, rebellion, and the sudden detonation of teenage hormones, Tori tore free from the wrist-burning ropes that held her down, hurled herself through the air, and into his arms.

And Mother's blade, now devoid of a target, plunged deep into the tanning bed, shattering the UV bulbs and driving straight into the humming guts of the power supply.

A blinding surge of 240 volts of electricity erupted through the glass, cascading up the blade and through her arms. Her eyeballs bulged. Her body seized violently, jerking upright as arcs of energy danced across her frame. Her curlers shot off her head—one pierced a Collateral Damage standee across the store, another blew out a window—freeing her hair in a wild storm of white-streaked *Bride of Frankenstein* fury. And for one glorious second, her entire being glowed like the messiah of doom she was meant to be.

From Chapter Forty-Two of *Ancient Secrets and Forbidden Techniques of Mind Control* by Lord Constantine Blatherton VIII, Esteemed Mesmerist, Somatic Architect, Distinguished Fellow of the Royal Institute of Pseudoscientific Inquiry, and Heir to the Blatherton Gaslight Fortune, 1893 Edition:

In circumstances most dire—wherein the practitioner (be he a professional mesmerist or an enterprising charlatan) has, through negligence or perhaps mere bone-headed oversight, failed to embed within the subject a suitable termination phrase (hereafter referred to as "exit suggestion") there exists but one remaining avenue for the liberation of the entranced. This method, which I have dubbed the Method of Galvanic Reversal, was discovered in a most unexpected manner.

It was at a private demonstration hosted by the illustrious Nikola Tesla—attended by no less than Mark Twain, an Austrian duke, and a surprising number of monocled baronesses—that I first encountered what the press would later dub the Electric Oscillator Platform (though Tesla himself preferred the term "Mechanical Therapy Device"). I was attending in the interest of furthering my research into treatments for recurring hemorrhoidal flare-ups—purely hypothetical, of course.

Concerned for my safety, I elected to test the device on a subject of unquestionable loyalty: my mother. She was, at the time, under a rather deep mesmeric suggestion—my own desperate attempt to wrest some semblance of agency from this overbearing oppressor (who, it must be noted, retained a vice-like grip upon the purse strings of my rightful inheritance).

Mr. Tesla himself activated the oscillations. The machine whirred to life, producing a low, thrumming vibration that coursed up through the legs, rattled her corset, and launched her Gainsborough hat skyward like a startled pheasant.

Quite suddenly, she emitted a sharp yelp, clutched her handbag, and made a hasty line for the nearest lavatory.

But most astoundingly, upon her return, no trace of the mesmeric suggestion remained. She was herself once more: Overbearing, profoundly disappointed in my choice of ascot, and gripping the purse strings of my rightful inheritance as tightly as ever.

Thus, I discovered—quite by accident, and at great personal cost— that a sufficiently intense electric vibration, when delivered without expectation or warning, can jolt a subject clean out of a hypnotic trance.

However, my research into electro-mechanical relief of the hindquarters continues at the time of this publishing.

Mother sizzled like one of her many burnt casseroles. Her bathrobe was charred and tattered. And the last remnants of her badass-looking rock 'n' roll war paint had melted away.

She stumbled back as the dizzy, fuzzy kaleidoscope of her hypnotized brain slowly normalized and came into focus, revealing her son, Marcus Looger, looking more grotesque than ever… with that hollow, slithery slug of a girlfriend attached to him like a parasite.

"Marcus! How *dare* you speak to your—" she began, rage flaring on instinct. But as quickly as it arrived, it crumbled, and confusion set in.

Where was the program she was just watching on her La-Z-Boy? Where *was* her La-Z-Boy? Where was *she*?

Then Mother saw the television lights and cameras all aimed directly at her. The shattered tanning bed. The hieroglyphic symbols scrawled across the walls. Her eyes flicked to the production monitor. Pastor Peter Pringle was on it. But he was also right there in front of her, in this… record store?

"Ahem," Pastor Pringle clenched his teeth, leaning in with a forced smile. "I believe you're supposed to be killing that *Jezebel*, like the terrible music commanded!"

Mother glanced at Tori. Her eyes dropped to the kitchen knife still in her hand and the memories flooded back: the relentless commands of heavy metal lyrics, playing in a maddening, unending loop in her head, driving her to the brink of insanity. She remembered fighting back, struggling desperately to conjure her free will, but she had no choice but to obey.

She was forced to butcher forty-two innocent teenagers in horrifically gruesome—yet undeniably creative—ways.

But even now, after everything, Mother found a way to do what she always did and lay the blame elsewhere.

"But… but I was… hypnotized," she told the pastor, the world, and herself.

She dug a Virginia Slims Menthol 120 out of her robe and lit up—Jesus, she needed a smoke.

It was right then that Pastor Peter Pringle's holy crusade—all of his sermons, his donations to politicians and law enforcement, his science experiments, and now this live television broadcast to prove once and for all that the *devil's music* was warping the minds of boys and girls all across God's green pasture and making them do bad things—had failed. And he exploded—live, on his "family program"—into a full-blown tantrum.

"GODDAMN MOTHERFUCKING PIECE OF SHIT!" he roared, ripping off his puffy angel wings and hurling them offscreen, knocking over a light.

None of his crew moved a muscle. Everyone just stared, mouths agape, unable to believe what they were seeing. And hearing.

"She was fucking hypnotized this whole time?! HYPNOTIZED?!" Pringle ripped off his plastic golden halo and threw it on the ground, stomping it out like it was on fire. "That ruins everything! Every goddamn thing she did or was going to do! All of the *bad things*! It doesn't even fucking count now!"

He yanked off his shimmering white angel gown—revealing an *Alvin and the Chipmunks* T-shirt, Bugle Boy khakis, and a pair of KangaROOS sneakers with his house key and lunch money zipped safely inside.

"It's all just one big fucking joke now!" he grunted, trying to rip the gown in half—until he realized he couldn't and threw it aside. "Just like all those fucking dodgeball games!"

His rosy-red cheeks turned a deep, dark purple. His tightly combed hair was a frazzled, frizzy mess.

"And all those goddamned, stupid-ass, useless fucking warning stickers!" Pastor Peter Pringle raised both fists to the heavens and shouted, "FUUUUUUUUUCK!!!"

Then, for the first time in his ten-year-old life, he finally realized that maybe he was in a little over his head.

And all he wanted to do was to go home and play with his Cabbage Patch Kid.

"What's this we're watching, fellas?" the President asked, shuffling over from his desk with his usual vacant smile. His advisors quickly turned off the TV and exchanged nervous glances. They didn't say a word, but everyone was thinking the same thing.

It was the same thing people all over the world were thinking: the case against heavy metal had just fizzled out more completely and embarrassingly than when Geraldo Rivera jackhammered open Al Capone's secret vault on live TV—only to find a few empty bottles and a dusty pile of nothing.

And now, with the court of public opinion lost, the Freedom through Unconstitutional Containment for Kids (F.U.C.K.) Act—with all its carefully crafted statutory language and twisted canons of construction—would be torn apart by judges everywhere. No amount of contorting from the president's advisors could save it.

They knew they couldn't risk the president siding with the losing team in this culture war now that the tide had suddenly turned. They couldn't risk him looking like a fool. Okay, like a *bigger* fool.

But who would tell him?

An awkward silence fell over the Oval Office.

Finally, the president couldn't resist. "Well… uh… fellas, does this mean I can watch *Muppet Babies* now? You know, the one where the little blue fella loses his library book and tells a bunch of fibs until his nose grows real long?"

One of the many balding white men in the room finally piped up, "Yes, Mr. President—right after you veto this silly legislation that Congress tried to trick you into signing."

"Well, okay, then. Whatever you say, fellas," the president replied, his mouth already watering in anticipation of that big bowl of jelly beans.

Tori pressed her body against Mark and tore the duct tape off her mouth. Radiating an effortless, otherworldly cool, she tilted her head and asked once and for all, "You ready to rock?"

"Whoa..." he started—he didn't think it was possible, but somehow Tori had gotten even hotter with a tan. Then he hesitated. "But... there's something I should, like, tell you, y'know... before..."

Tori's sly grin hardened into her trademark sneer. Her fists clenched and she started wondering where she'd left her studded backpack. Maybe skipping town wasn't such a bad idea after all. "What the fuck is it, Mark Looger?"

He smiled sheepishly—another tooth fell out—then confessed, "Well, actually, this is, like, um... my first time, too."

Tori burst out laughing—big and fucking loud. "No fucking shit."

Chapter 40

BANG YOUR HEAD (METAL HEALTH)

And so, that night, as the world watched the Satanic Panic come to an end live on their "boob tubes," the youth went wild. Record stores were immediately swarmed by long-haired kids eager to trade their measly life savings for the latest, greatest, and most "forbidden" albums. They came in droves, united by their love of the music, knowing that they were part of something powerful and unstoppable.

Just like Monster Mick himself had done so many times before, Satanic Temple Records, Tapes & Tanning clawed its way back from the brink of horrific death, flourishing once again as the kids of Liberty Bend packed the aisles. Heavy metal records and tapes flew off the shelves and the constant sound of the cash register *ka-chinging* drowned out any sounds of a colostomy bag filling at inopportune times.

In arenas around the world, heavy metal rock stars were welcomed like messiahs. The crowds roared, banged their heads, and the unholy communion of distortion and rebellion erupted. It was glorious. And it was loud. Together they celebrated all that heavy metal was about: standing up for yourself and fighting back against the fucking assholes of the world who lock you in a fucking basement, who give you detention for wearing a fucking *shirt* and who make their six-year-old kid feel like it was *his fault* his dumbass dad climbed up on the roof during a lightning storm, and then hold that shit over his head for years.

News magazines like *Time, Newsweek,* and *People* gradually pushed their stories about music corrupting America's youth farther and farther to the back pages until they vanished altogether, finding a new home in the trashy tabloids of *Weekly World News* and *Star Magazine,* where they belonged.

Newscasts and specials that once stoked the flames of the Satanic Panic—Pat Robertson's *The 700 Club, Inside Edition,* Geraldo Rivera's *Devil Worship: Exposing Satan's Underground,* even *Hear No Evil with Pastor Peter Pringle*—quietly changed the subject. Some shows were canceled. Some hosts were never seen again.

As for Pastor Pringle, the FCC fined him an unprecedented six hundred and sixty-six million dollars for airing extreme violence, graphic gore, and using the f-word one too many times during a "family program." His show was swiftly yanked off the air and he was disavowed by the Holy Christ Church of Unwavering Condemnation, which was forced to file for bankruptcy and soon after rebranded itself as the Holy Christ Church of *More-Selective* Condemnation™.

And for his role in failing to stop or even report the attempted murder he broadcast—not to mention staying up way past his bedtime—the perfect little angel was promptly grounded for a week and sent to bed without supper.

In the end, no fanatical crusade, no television show, or even a ten-year-old child, ever stood a chance of bringing down heavy metal. Not when the spirit of rebellion thrives in the heart of every kid around the world who has ever had a shitty parent.

And so, heavy metal lived on, stronger than ever.

…at least until a bunch of sad clowns from Seattle showed up on MTV and heavy metal died a quick and painless death almost overnight. But that's a whole other sick and twisted tale.

And Fox Chastain? The glam rat poser who'd spent his life playing dress-up?

Well, once he finally got inside, Fox was deeply disillusioned by the experience of Mark's party. Maybe it was the dead bodies everywhere. Or the lack of frozen margaritas. Whatever it was, something cracked, and he realized that maybe things aren't always as "glam-bam-thank-you-ma'am" as he thought.

And maybe it was time to take a fucking hint.

His sister wasn't jealous of him. His Aunt Milly wasn't "in awe" of her androgynous nephew. They were just bitches.

And all those metalheads who found his mere presence to be more annoying than mass murder? They weren't "just grumpy." They were right. Fox Chastain *was* a glam rat—shimmering in a satin blouse to distract from the ugly truth.

As he drove home that night, the corporate playlist on Stardust 105 FM—those jaunty blues riffs and power ballads of Malibu Bad Boys, Knights in Shining Glamour, and Kitty Kitty Bang Bang—just wasn't cutting it anymore. So he spun the dial until it landed on AM 666 The Tower of Power, cranked up Midnight Massacre, belted along with Flavor of the Weak until his voice gave out, and banged his head to Big Fat Witch so hard that he ran right through a red light without even realizing it.

He threw his glitter-studded Trapper Keeper planner out the window, drove straight past the rehearsal dinner, went home, and hosed himself down—washing away the Drakkar Noir, the headbanger farts, and his sister's lipstick.

The next morning, he torched his wardrobe in a bonfire of vanity and traded in his nearly brand-new candy-apple-red Pontiac Fiero SE for a beat-up matte black-and-rust 1970 Dodge Challenger. He wasn't Fox Chastain anymore. He was Freddy Chastain. He was real. He was raw. And he was metal.

A few years later, at the ripe age of twenty-two, Mark Looger finally graduated from high school. By then, his and Tori's horny teenage infatuation had blossomed into full-blown love. Built on trust and a shared everlasting devotion to Fätal Fäte, their relationship truly and finally "rocked." A lot. Like, all the time. Because they were, like, always rockin'. I mean, like, you can't expect anyone to track *all* of their rocking when it was happenin', like, constantly. And, like, practice makes perfect. Or at least a lot of babies, because they went on to have five kids: Piper Jr., Edward Jr., Metal T.E.D. Jr., Sir Greg of the Golden Realm Jr., and Fogey Jr. Aside from the terrible names, they did their best not to be shitty parents.

Unlike *someone* we all know…

The justice system dismissed Mother's "but I was hypnotized" defense as "baseless supernatural hogwash." They weren't interested in reopening a can of worms to blame heavy metal, either. Instead, the court focused solely on the overwhelming evidence: it was *her* fingerprints all over everything. The blood and guts of 42 butchered headbangers were on *her* hands. And in *her* digestive tract.

The verdict came down swiftly and decisively.

Beyond the shotgun-wielding guards in the watchtowers, lazily flipping through *Hustlers*, was the Black Rock Falls Women's Penitentiary. A massive, decaying brick fortress wrapped in double layers of chain-link and razor wire, it stood directly across the street from the high school, like a constant, ominous reminder to stay in line.

Inside its fortified walls, the stench of piss, bleach, and cigarettes was strong enough to make even the most depraved criminal gag. And the flickering, sputtering glow of half-dead fluorescent lights would sometimes dim to near black when one of the residents was put out of her misery.

Deep within these grimy, cacophonous corridors echoing with groans, screams, and psychotic giggles—was Mother.

She sat crumpled on the floor of her tiny concrete cell, banging her head against the wall—not in joyous heavy metal catharsis like her many victims, but in hopeless frustration.

Acknowledgments

Headbanger! began as a screenplay for what was meant to be a scrappy, low-budget horror movie. After a few doomed attempts at self-financing and crowdfunding, I realized the only way to ever get it in front of an audience might be to turn it into a novel. As I expanded the scope of the story, the characters, and especially those dangerously suggestive song lyrics, it became clear this was the way the tale was meant to be told all along.

But like a perfect demo tape, that initial screenplay was raw, full of ideas, and absolutely essential. Those first jam sessions took shape with the help of my co-conspirator, Aaron Pfeifer, who co-wrote several drafts—and a few shockingly different versions—with me over the course of a few years. Much of his unique sense of humor, killer instincts, and twisted genius from the script are still splattered throughout these pages. Without him, *Headbanger!* would never have taken shape in the first place, so I throw eternal horns to Mr. Pfeifer.

Epic thanks to my editor, Kevin Shamel, who got exactly what I was trying to do from day one (turns out we'd grown up around the same kinds of weirdos, misfits, and legends that so much of this book is based on). His insightful feedback and infectious enthusiasm for the book and the world of Liberty Bend kept me inspired to make this story as loud, wild, and funny as it could be.

To the sharp eyes of my proofreader, Lillian Boyd, without whom I would have suffered the eternal embarrassment of misspelling

Voorhees—with *two* Os! (throws horns to indicate the Os).

To the cover and interior designer, Matthew Revert, whose brilliant work made *Headbanger!* look like the kind of book your mom would freak out about if she found it under your bed—which, like heavy metal, is exactly the point.

To my high school heavy metal band, Section 8 (as in the military discharge for insanity—*not* the way-less-badass low-income housing term) and everyone who ever banged their heads at our shows… or even just showed up. Thank you and goodnight!

And, of course, to the gods of metal—Sabbath, Priest, Maiden, Megadeth, Metallica, Slayer, Anthrax, and all the rest… for defining an era.

I also want to thank the PMRC and all who tried to bring metal to its knees in the 1980s. Your pearl-clutching panic, your warning labels, and your lies made metal—and all of the edgier music of the time—angrier, scarier, sexier, and far more popular than it ever would have been without you. Actually, forget it. I don't want to thank you. Just wanted to point out the irony.

To my wife and kids, who put up with me banging my head against the wall for over a year (and years before that on the screenplay) as the epic rock 'n' roll splatter-fest that is *Headbanger!* came to be, I thank you from the bottom of my metal heart.

And finally, to completely misquote AC/DC: *for those who read this book… I salute you!*

About the Author

Audie Harrison is a writer, filmmaker, and animator. A graduate of the CalArts Character Animation Program, his writing and directing credits include the punk-rock indie feature *The Last American*, the Cartoon Network series *Uncle Grandpa*, and *Trick or Treat Scooby-Doo!* for Warner Bros. Animation.

Headbanger! is Audie's debut novel, born from a lifelong devotion to heavy metal, horror movies, and Saturday-morning cartoons. He lives in Pasadena, California, with his family and a collection of dusty guitars.